The man wants to see you."

"Who is this man?"

"Don Augustine Cusimano."

"No thanks," I said.

He shrugged his shoulders inside his tailored jacket. "Suit yourself. You come or you don't. Either way, it's no skin off my ass."

He was making it hard on me. If he had threatened me, I would have felt compelled to resist. Maybe he really didn't care, or maybe he was shrewd enough to know that threats wouldn't work. Whatever way he was going, he had found the right button to push.

"All right, take me to him," I said.

Other Gil Disbro Mysteries by
James E. Martin
from Avon Books

AND THEN YOU DIE
THE MERCY TRAP

Avon Books are available at special quantity discounts for bulk purchases for sales promotions, premiums, fund raising or educational use. Special books, or book excerpts, can also be created to fit specific needs.

For details write or telephone the office of the Director of Special Markets, Avon Books, Dept. FP, 1350 Avenue of the Americas, New York, New York 10019, 1-800-238-0658.

A Fine and Private Place

A GIL DISBRO MYSTERY

JAMES E. MARTIN

AVON BOOKS NEW YORK

If you purchased this book without a cover, you should be aware that this book is stolen property. It was reported as "unsold and destroyed" to the publisher, and neither the author nor the publisher has received any payment for this "stripped book."

AVON BOOKS
A division of
The Hearst Corporation
1350 Avenue of the Americas
New York, New York 10019

Copyright © 1994 by James E. Martin
Published by arrangement with the author
Library of Congress Catalog Card Number: 93-41034
ISBN: 0-380-71697-6

All rights reserved, which includes the right to reproduce this book or portions thereof in any form whatsoever except as provided by the U.S. Copyright Law.

Published in hardcover by William Morrow and Company, Inc.; for information address Permissions Department, William Morrow and Company, Inc., 1350 Avenue of the Americas, New York, New York 10019.

First Avon Books Printing: October 1995

AVON TRADEMARK REG. U.S. PAT. OFF. AND IN OTHER COUNTRIES, MARCA REGISTRADA, HECHO EN U.S.A.

Printed in the U.S.A.

RA 10 9 8 7 6 5 4 3 2 1

TO

Bert Kohler

You started it all

The grave's a fine and private place,
But none, I think, do there embrace.

—Andrew Marvell
"To His Coy Mistress"

1

He caught up with me in the hallway outside the Records Room at Central Police Headquarters. I had just left the office where I had been wheedling some information out of a civilian employee when a hand landed on my shoulder and swung me around into the little niche by the water fountain. I looked up into a scary black face made worse by a villainous mustache. And the face was really black, a cannonball with eyes and teeth, five inches higher than my six-one.

"What's up, Wally?" I asked.

"Moe wants you back at the office. Now."

Wally Stamm let go of my shoulder two seconds before my bones were ready to dissolve to powder. I kept from rubbing it, and I didn't complain about it. Wally would not have understood complaints. By his lights, he had simply tapped my shoulder to get my attention. Lord knows I had plenty of reason to appreciate Wally's ability to use that grip on a wanted felon. He and I did that a lot when we were working our jobs as bounty hunters for Moe Glickman.

"What's going down?" Not a half hour ago I had left Moe's office to set out on my day's work.

Wally shifted his shoulders in a shrug. "You know how Moe is. He came rushing out of his office in a panic and said, 'Go find Gil.' So I came."

"Then I'd better go see what's up."

"And I'm going to find an excuse to stay away for a while until things settle down."

We exited the police tower in the Justice Center onto the Ontario Street side of the building, out past the odd piece of abstract sculpture composed of brown pipe twisted in a pretzel shape that one of our local disk jockeys has named "Hard B.M." Wally split from me there, striking out for the bar across the street while I went from the police tower into the main lobby of the Justice Center. I crossed that and exited again on the West Third Street side, crossed the street, and headed for the building where Moe Glickman has his office. It was one in a line of buildings slated for demolition, a threat that never seems to be carried out. The ground floor has a used furniture store with a stairway beside it leading up. I climbed the stairs and came to a door labeled:

MOE GLICKMAN
BAIL BONDS

GILBERT DISBRO
INVESTIGATIONS

When I had been laid off by the police department, I had gone to work for Moe Glickman as a bounty hunter, part-time work to supplement his regular man, Wally Stamm. At the time I had expected it to be temporary until the Cleveland City Council got its finances straightened out and recalled me. By the time it became apparent I wasn't going to be called back, I had applied for my P.I. license, one of the requirements for which being an office address. Moe had a vacant room in his suite which he allowed me to have for a ridiculously low rent. Part of our deal had been my promise to hold myself available to assist Wally when he needed help rounding up Moe's bail jumpers.

I pushed through the door and entered Moe's waiting room,

which never fails to remind me of the anteroom to the principal's office at high school to which I had reported for various misdemeanors. In this case the space between the counter and the ceiling was filled by a steel mesh screen behind which pudgy Gladys Keego presided, connected to the public by a slot like the opening of the window at a theater ticket booth. As if that were not enough protection, she kept an attack-trained German shepherd named Rolf at her side. Another part of my deal with Moe was that I paid a fee for Gladys to take my messages.

I stopped in front of Gladys and struck a brace, raising my right hand in a salute. "Reporting as ordered."

"As you were," she snapped back.

Seeing me, Rolf raised his hundred pounds to the counter and tried to stick his snout through the slot. I laid my hand down where he could lick it.

"What does Moe—"

"Is that Gil out there?" The voice came from the other side of the steel mesh, followed by the sight of Moe Glickman coming out of his office. He looked like his usual harried self, a man gone frontally bald who dressed in a plaid double-knit suit so far out of style I expected it to come back any day. His normal pace was that of a man scurrying to catch the bus before it left his stop, and to no one's surprise he was perpetually rubbing his stomach to massage an incipient ulcer. He saw me and said, "Get in here."

Gladys had already pressed the buzzer to release the door in the steel mesh screen. Moe was waiting for me as I started through. He grabbed my arm and pulled me in. "There's a man here who wants to see you."

Despite what experience should have taught me, I was getting caught up in Moe's sense of urgency. Maybe there was a genuine celebrity waiting in his office. "Clint Eastwood?" I asked.

"Be on your best behavior," Moe warned me. "I told him you were just the person he needs."

Moe dragged me into his cluttered private office, roomy as only an old building can be. The walls and surfaces were covered with memorabilia, principally photos of him taken with politicians dating back to Ralph Perk. It was all as I remembered it except there was no one there.

"Gil, I want you to meet Judge Lowell Amerine," Moe said, pulling me on through the door.

Another step solved the case of the missing jurist. He was there, seated in a wingback chair that had totally concealed him. It had been able to do that because he was a frail, elderly man no bigger than a sixth-grader, with sparse wisps of gray hair on his freckled scalp. He was dressed in a tweed sports coat, flannel trousers, and a flannel shirt buttoned to his throat—all of which hung loose on him as if he were wearing an older brother's hand-me-downs. He pried himself out of the chair on which he had left no impression and advanced toward me with the shuffling steps of a cardiac case, bracing himself with an aluminum cane.

"So you are the young man Moe has been recommending so highly." Frail as he was, his eyes—the color of faded denim—were alert behind his plastic-rimmed glasses. "He says you are a competent and thorough investigator, and Moe's word is worth much—as I have reason to know."

His hand in mine was so small and frail I was afraid to squeeze it. "Moe is my landlord. If he doesn't steer business my way, I might not be able to pay my office rent."

"Personal interest noted." The old man let a smile touch his lips. "I am Lowell Amerine."

Moe explained, "Judge Amerine is retired from the probate bench."

"Not voluntarily. A series of heart attacks forced the choice on me." He backed into his chair as if the effort of rising had exhausted him. "Now I have devoted myself to writing my book."

"You're writing a book?" Moe asked, totally surprised. "What is it? The story of a two-fisted judge who brings criminals to justice?"

"Hardly. It's a very technical tome dealing with a few arcane points of estate-tax law. That was my specialty on the bench, not criminal cases. With any kind of luck it will become a basic text that generations of law students will have to master. Making life difficult for lawyers is one of the advantages of being a judge, who after all is nothing more than a lawyer who gets to grade his own examination papers." He paused after the punch line, displaying an instinct native to comedians and teachers.

"Not bad," I told him, "except that Mencken said it ahead of you."

He raised one of his nearly invisible eyebrows. "H. L. Mencken. My favorite iconoclast."

"I read a book once, if that's what you're trying to find out."

"As a matter of fact, I was." Amerine withdrew a charred briar from his pocket. He blew through it and then, satisfied, began filling it from a leather pouch. "Moe was telling me you have a surprising knowledge of a wide range of subjects, in addition to your integrity and your courage."

I glanced sideways at Moe, who was straightening his photo with Frank Lausche. "Living with an English teacher has improved my reading habits."

"Don't degrade yourself. Moe's recommendations have convinced me you're just the man I need."

"You want to hire me?" The idea was hard for me to grasp. I had been thinking Moe dragged me in here to meet an old friend of his.

"Aren't you in business for that purpose? You see, I have slipped off the reservation today. I'm supposed to stay close to my home in Hunting Valley, but when no one was looking, I called a taxi and came downtown to see my old friend Moe. I suspected he could recommend a private investigator, but I had no idea there was one in his office."

Moe gathered up some papers on his desk. "Why don't you two talk in here? I have some things to look up in my files outside." A second later, he was gone, shutting the door behind him.

Judge Amerine was lighting his pipe, drawing slow puffs as the match flame was sucked into the tobacco in the bowl. I realized I had a new client. I pulled up another wingback chair to face him. "What is your problem?"

"Blackmail."

I laughed.

Amerine smiled. "It does seem unlikely, doesn't it? I would never claim my life has been blameless, yet I have always lived quietly, and the statute of limitations long ago ran out on any youthful peccadilloes. Isn't that the way your reasoning goes?" He puffed contentedly on his pipe.

"Something like that."

"I was fortunate enough to be born into a family that made its money long ago. I never had to struggle for a living, so I was able to devote my life to the pursuit of a career that interests me. In addition, I have been a confirmed bachelor simply because that status avoided complications. Or so I thought."

Amerine relit his pipe and sat back in his chair, collecting his thoughts, or more likely dozing off. "I have a nephew." The voice came so suddenly it nearly startled me. Amerine was more alert than he appeared. "Barry Sprague. He is my sister's son. When he was only seven years old, she and her husband went off to Europe for a vacation. They were killed by a snow slide in the Alps, an untoward accident, and the responsibility for Barry's upbringing devolved upon me. There was simply no one else."

Amerine blew clouds of smoke and looked into them as if they were the mists of time. "I botched it. That is hardly a surprise. I was singularly ill-equipped to raise a small boy. I never even raised a dog. All I could think to do was send him off to a private school. There. I washed my hands of him. Now he is the headmaster's responsibility."

"Barry is going to be the cause for the blackmail you mentioned."

"Of course." Amerine was not willing to go into that without laying more groundwork. "Barry grew into a willful, irresponsible young man. When he asked for money, I gave it to him. It was the only thing I had to offer. There were escapades all through his youth. When he reached his teens, they grew more serious—alcohol, drugs, girls. Fortunately, my money finessed all scandals, and at last I sent him off to college. Finally, I thought, my period of travail was near its end, but the habits he had learned in private school merely continued in college. He has an impressive collection of letterheads from prestigious universities informing him his presence there is no longer welcome. After six years of trying, he managed to graduate from Case Western because I could keep an eye on him while he was that close. Upon graduation he found a position with a bank and, contrary to every expectation, he has distinguished himself."

Like a man dropping into bed after a day of heavy labor, Amerine closed his eyes. He had just relived the anxiety and effort of getting Barry through college. For want of any better ideas, I said, "It sounds as if Barry is well on his way to taking care of himself."

"Alas, no." Once more Amerine pulled himself erect. He was willing his body to keep up with his mind and his eyes. "Barry, I'm afraid, had not changed all that much. It was about a year ago he came to me with a problem. He had been gambling, and losing, and found himself deeply in debt to a man named Gus Cusimano."

That name conjured associations for me. "Cusimano Vending Machines?"

"The same. Although I was never on the criminal bench, I am fully aware of Mr. Cusimano's position in the scheme of things. *Don* and *Godfather* are the titles the newspapers confer on him. He rose rapidly to influence a few years ago after the authorities put the Licavoli family away. It is considered poor form to owe Mr. Cusimano money, for he has unpleasant ways of collecting. Barry owed him twenty thousand dollars, and he was becoming insistent on payment."

"So what did you do?"

"I paid it, of course." Amerine relit his pipe. "I also became quite incensed and chose that moment, twenty years late though it was, to assert my authority. Never again would I help Barry out of such a jam. I insisted, absolutely, that he must never again gamble and extracted a promise from him to that effect. You see, I was particularly worried about his association with a bank. If he found himself in debt again, the temptation to embezzle would be overwhelming." Amerine took his pipe from his teeth and blew out a stream of smoke. "Would that he had stayed with gambling. He found other mischief."

Amerine gave another of his dramatic pauses. "You understand," he continued, "that what I am about to tell you will amount to a confession to a crime. Your hearing it will implicate you."

I shrugged. "It would be hard for anyone to force me to tell what I hear. You should know I could lose my license for divulging information about my client."

"You are referring to Section 4749.13 (B) (3) of the Ohio Revised Code?" Amerine shook his head. "I wouldn't rely on that too fully. It doesn't absolve you from failure to report a crime."

"Suppose I worry about that when the time comes."

Amerine dug in his trouser pocket and found a dollar bill, which he handed me. "Now I am your client. You are free to resign at any time if you don't like what you are hearing."

I put the dollar in my shirt pocket in exchange for my cigarettes. "Tell me." Sometimes I do things on impulse I have cause to regret.

"In February, four months after his escapade with Cusimano, Barry came to my home late one night. In fact, he got me out of bed to tell me about his urgent problem. For a time he had been keeping company with a woman named Megan Latimer, an exotic dancer. Earlier that night she had been in his apartment. They had indulged in illegal substances, and she had a bad reaction. Very bad. She died."

The flame of my lighter stopped below the tip of my cigarette while I stared at the judge. "Barry hadn't reported it to the police."

"Afraid not. His request to me was quite simple. He wanted to bury her body on my property. My house in Hunting Valley sits on four acres of wooded land. No one ever goes into it, not even me any longer. A body buried there would never be found."

"You didn't!" My voice made me sound like a teacher remonstrating with a student.

"Well, I had to weigh various issues. As a former jurist, I certainly understood the legal ramifications. Barry bore a degree of culpability for the young woman's death. A murder charge would be totally inappropriate, although manslaughter or negligent homicide were possibilities. Whatever the charge, the resulting publicity would ruin his career, perhaps his life. Could I permit that? I know, I know. My sworn duty and all that. Yet this was a family affair, my own nephew, my sister's child. Not inconsiderable was my own guilt for botching Barry's character development. By that standard, I was already a henchman in the crime. All these factors weighed in my decision."

Amerine turned to look through Moe's window, where a sheriff's paddy wagon was turning into the garage linked to the county jail.

"And then there was the woman herself. Think of me as a snob if you want, but I had to ask what was her relative value? Megan Latimer was a cipher, a drifter. She had wandered into Cleveland from West Virginia and worked in a massage parlor until she acquired a job in a sleazy bar on Prospect. Those women come and go. No one would miss her. No one would mourn her. Much as we like to think every human life is of equal value, that is not really true when it is a stranger pitted against a family member. Could I allow a woman like that to ruin my nephew's life? I had five minutes to decide, and I chose my nephew over the law. That unfortunate young woman found a burial ground in my woods."

I inhaled a final puff and ground my cigarette out in an ashtray.

"Do you wish to leave now?"

Yeah. But all I said aloud was, "Then the blackmail?"

Beside Amerine in the chair, wedged between the arm and the seat cushion, were two file folders. Amerine picked up one and looked inside. He selected one page and showed it to me. It was a typed letter that read:

Tetlow Building, Room 207
2342 Payne Avenue
Cleveland, OH 44114
February 16

My Dear Judge Amerine:

In suppressing the facts surrounding a recent highly irregular funeral service on your estate, I have incurred undue expenses. (See enclosed statement.) I trust you will remit immediately to ensure the facts remain suppressed. Due to difficulties in getting to the bank, I must insist on cash.

Sincerely yours,
G. K. Hatton

The letter had been typed on plain white paper without a letterhead, maybe a sheet from a copy machine. The typewriter was a manual with a *t* consistently above the line. The name had been typed but never signed by a human hand. End of my brilliant deductions.

When I had finished studying the letter, Amerine showed me the next item. It was a printed form for a bill, the kind that could be bought by the pad in any office supply store. It stated: *February expenses . . . $2000.* It had been typed on the same machine as the letter.

"Who is G. K. Hatton?" I asked.

"You know as much about him as I do," Amerine said.

"Put it another way. Who could have known about your crime? Barry and you."

"I'm afraid the circle was a little wider. At least two people were there with Barry that night."

"Hatton was one of them?"

"So it would seem, though I can't tell you the name of either of them. After I had given Barry permission to use my property, I went upstairs to the guest bedroom and looked out its window. Naturally, my physical condition precluded my taking part in the burial. In the dark, I saw a strange car in my driveway—not Barry's sports car but one much larger, a Lincoln or a Cadillac. Two figures besides Barry were there, males I presume, although they were only shadows in the dark. They opened the trunk and took out that unfortunate girl's body, which was wrapped in a blanket. Barry got a couple spades and a shovel from my tool shed, and they went off into the woods carrying the body between them in the blanket as if it were a hammock. Someone had a flashlight, which I saw bobbing in the woods. After a while I could not see that any longer. . . ."

His voice trailed off. It had been a long speech for him, and he needed a moment to rest.

I asked, "Where did those men come from?"

"If you were to recruit someone to help bury a dead body, where would you look? I imagine the fact that Barry had already established a relationship with Mr. Cusimano is not immaterial."

I wondered while I studied the letter again. "How did you get this?"

"The United States Postal Service delivered it."

I made a face at that. "Someone is willing to risk a federal offense by using the mail?"

"It seems to be working. After all, I've been paying him off each month." Amerine handed me the file folder. "There has been a new bill every month since February. The culprit seems to be under the impression he is protected because he couches his demands in the form of a bill for services rendered."

The rest of the letters were similar to the first one, each accompanied by another form bill for two thousand. The latest one was dated October 6. Nine months, eighteen thousand dollars. "Have you checked this address out?"

"No, I've simply mailed the cash to him as he requested."

"The address should be a lead to something. It's probably only a mail drop, but it's a place to start."

"You don't intend to expose this blackmailer, do you?" There was anxiety in Amerine's voice.

"Isn't that why you're hiring me?"

"Perhaps I haven't made myself clear." Amerine knocked the dottle out of his pipe and ran a cleaner through the stem before he laid it aside. "My principal interest is not in identifying the blackmailer. When I broke the law, it was because I wanted to protect my nephew. Now that I am being blackmailed, I am paying for the same reason I broke the law in the first place. I expect to meet the blackmailer's demands as long as he makes them. They are not so excessive that I would upset the status quo by having you search him out."

"I don't understand. If you don't want the blackmailer stopped, why did you come here?"

"Because," said Amerine, "I have started to receive a second series of demands."

2

Amerine's unhealthy pallor was turning even grayer, and he was breathing rapidly. I got up and gently urged him to sit back in the chair.

"Why don't you rest a few minutes." I groped desperately for an excuse to leave him alone. "I have to make a phone call to another client."

He nodded, accepting his limitations, and closed his eyes. Moe was sitting at Wally Stamm's desk riffling through default papers in the in/out tray. As I came up, Moe waved a report at me. "Look at this. He skipped out. He never showed for trial, and now he's left the state. I can't forfeit bonds like this. I'll go out of business. Did you do the eligibility evaluation on him?"

He was waving the paper so hard I couldn't see the name. "Who is it?"

"Satterlee."

I didn't have to think hard about that name. "Yeah, I did the investigation. I recommended against going his bond."

"Well, why didn't you stop me from doing it?" Moe realized he was being unreasonable and slapped the paper down. He leaned back in the chair, rubbing his stomach, and looked up at me. "Can you help the judge?"

"I'm not sure. He hasn't finished explaining all he needs. I'm letting him rest a few minutes."

"Good idea." Moe got up and headed for the small refrigerator in the corner. He took out a quart of milk in a cardboard container, unfolded the spout, and drank directly from it. The milk soothed him. "I wish you would help the judge with whatever he needs. I owe him a lot."

Rolf was pawing my leg to get my attention. I reached down and scratched between his ears. While one part of me yearned to do what I could for Amerine, another, more cautious part told me I was headed for trouble. Now the conflict resolved itself for me. I owed Moe, and Moe owed Amerine. Sometimes in life difficult decisions are not that difficult to make. "What do you think of Amerine's condition?"

"He's a sick man, all right, but his mind is worth more than yours and mine put together."

"So it looks like I'm going to be working for him the next couple days at least."

"We'll struggle along without you," Moe assured me.

I went down to my office to pick up a standard contract form and returned to Moe's office. Amerine was awake and his color had returned. I laid the contract form aside and said, "So you've started to receive a second series of demands?"

"*Series* may be a little premature. There has been only one demand, which arrived yesterday." Amerine picked up the other file folder, the one I had thought was empty, and handed it to me.

I returned to my chair and opened the file folder to find a single sheet of paper. The printing on this one read:

WANT THE WHOLE WORLD TO KNOW? $1000 SMALL BILLS IN BOX. WRAP IN BROWN PAPER. DELIVER TO BUS STATION BAGGAGE CLAIMS NOON THURS. LEAVE FOR AXEL MCCLUSKY. TAKE RAPID DOWNTOWN. NO TRICKS. NO COPS.

The paper I held was limp, slick, and thin—some kind of inferior photocopy. The quality of the printing was similar to dot matrix, yet more blurry. After more study, I decided the faults in quality could be attributed to the photocopying process. But there was more to be said about the printing. The block capitals had not been pecked out on a typewriter, nor were they hand-printed. They were larger than pica or elite, nearly the size of newspaper headlines, except these were too far unaligned to have been typeset. It came to me the original had been constructed using a kid's printing set with each letter a separate rubber stamp. Hit the ink pad, then hit the paper.

"How did this come?" I asked.

"It arrived yesterday on my fax machine. You would have to ask Elaine about the details."

"Elaine?" The name was one that had not come up before.

"Elaine Knoll, my research assistant."

"You never mentioned a research assistant," I said.

"Elaine's father was an attorney and a close friend of mine. When he died, she was left alone. She went through an unfortunate marriage, during which she lost most of her inheritance. I offered her a job working for me while she returns to college to complete her law degree."

"Did she know about the blackmail demands?"

"It would have been impossible to keep the knowledge from her." Amerine suddenly comprehended the implication of my question, and his pale blue eyes flashed with the most fire I had seen in them. "I trust Elaine completely. In many ways, she is what I wish Barry had been."

"You know her, and I don't." I let that settle the point.

Amerine closed his eyes again and folded his hands on his stomach. "You understand my position, don't you? While I have willingly paid the first blackmailer, I have grave doubts now. My money was supposed to buy silence. That makes sense as long as only one other person knows. If there are three, why not five? A score? Hundreds? Soon, in the words of this note, the whole world knows. If this information is really that widespread, my money is wasted. I simply must learn how extensive the knowledge of my lapse has become."

"So you want to find out who's doing it after all."

"I must know the source or sources. Yet I have no desire to

prosecute or to panic the blackmailer into going public. If these two are the only ones who know, that is one thing. If the truth has become general knowledge, that is something else. Can you determine the two sources of the threats without undue fanfare? Or am I asking too much?"

I pondered the problem while I studied the two demands. "It's a sure thing I can check into this G. K. Hatton character. This new one has a lot less to go on. The only thing to do, if you're willing, is to go along with the payoff tomorrow. I can follow you to the bus station and see who picks the package up."

"That seems to be the wise move. However, I won't be physically up to making the payoff in person. Elaine will probably go in my place."

When I produced my standard contract form, he became alert again for a bit. The legal aspects of the contract focused his attention until he had read through all the clauses. At the end, he rendered his verdict: "Not worth the paper it's written on." But he signed it and also made out a check for my retainer. He tore the check off his book and gave it to me. "Please follow one principle as you go about your duties. If it comes to a choice between pursuing the case at the expense of upsetting the situation or dropping what you are doing, I would prefer you back off."

"Understood." I put the contract and check in my pocket. "I think the next step is for me to give you a ride home. While I'm there, Miss Knoll can explain the mystery of how the second threat arrived."

A wicked smile touched his lips. "My home is probably in turmoil with everyone wondering what has become of me."

I pointed to the phone on Moe's desk. "Do you want to call ahead to let them know where you are?"

Instinctively, Amerine reached for the phone, then halted his hand in midair. "It might be more amusing to see what they're doing. It's time they were reminded I'm not a child who needs a pass to leave my house."

I took Amerine's arm to help him out of the chair, out of the office, and down the back stairs to the parking lot where my gray Chevrolet Caprice sat. I helped him into the passenger seat, where he immediately leaned his head against the headrest. He was ready to drift off to sleep immediately. I quickly asked him for his address and then let him sleep for almost the entire trip.

He lived on Chagrin River Road, out in the affluent eastern suburbs. Getting there took us through some less lovely sections of the city until we hit Shaker Boulevard and cruised out on that until suburbs were ready to give way to country. The sight of autumn colors splashed all over the trees out there surprised me, which only goes to show you how cut off you can get working in the city. I had been thinking of autumn as the season when my sports coat is comfortable before it's cold enough to require a topcoat. Now the foliage reminded me Halloween was only two weeks away.

PRIVATE PROPERTY
KEEP OUT

The sign came up on a pipe gate stretched over a blacktopped driveway between two stone cairns. We had been cruising north with the river on our right and occasional houses glimpsed through woods on our left. Many of the places had white-painted board fences around them, the usual sign of a horse farm. I missed the driveway on first try and had to turn around to come back. When I turned into Amerine's driveway, I came up against the pipe fence. Built into the stone cairn to my left were two mailboxes, one labeled *Mount* and the other *Amerine*. Below each mailbox was a speaker and below that a button like a doorbell. I've seen arrangements like that in the lobbies of apartment buildings. I lowered my window and reached out to press the button for Amerine.

The answer I got was a voice, probably female, that sounded as if she were talking through a mouthful of rock candy. "State your business, please," the voice demanded. She should have been announcing arrivals and departures.

Before I could, Amerine leaned across me and said in his strongest voice, "Cheeseburger, fries, and a Pepsi."

Maybe it was a code. It worked, for the pipe gate in front of us started to move inward. It was hinged to the cairn on the right side of the driveway. When it was open, I drove through. There must have been a trip mechanism under the pavement, for the gate swung shut behind us. I drove a hundred yards into the woods on the driveway until it forked. Following Amerine's directions, I took the right-hand road. It climbed gently, rounded a curve, and came to a turnaround before a set of garage doors.

Two cars were there ahead of me, a gray Delorean sports car and a blue Mercedes. I parked between them and the house. I had been expecting a mansion. Instead, this place was rustic, built of stone and following the contour of the hillside. The garage doors in front of me were built into the ground, but as the land fell away, the main part of the house jutted out over a ravine. It had been designed to create an effect, as if long ago the house had been covered by a landslide, and then more recently an earthquake had caused some of the land to drop away to expose two thirds of the building.

Amerine opened the door on his side. I hurried around the car to take hold of his arm again. Before I could get him to the house, a group of people—two men and a woman—burst out of the front door and came up the steps that led down to it.

"Lowell, where the hell have you been?" said the older of the two men. He was perhaps fifty, with gray in his sideburns, a Walter Pidgeon look-alike.

"Are you trying to kill him?" That was the woman speaking. She had coppery hair and flashing green eyes behind a pair of wide oval glasses.

Before I could take a better look at her, the younger of the two men bounded past her. "Let go of him." The young man grabbed my arm and tried to yank me away from Amerine. The move nearly had a disastrous effect. Because my hand was on Amerine's arm, the guy's pulling also jerked the judge and made him teeter precariously.

I let go of Amerine's arm to keep from pulling him down and spun on the younger man. I grabbed his wrist and twisted his arm up behind his back in a hammerlock. At the same time I caught a fistful of his wavy brown hair and kicked him behind the knee. The young man's leg gave way and he sank to the ground.

"Can anyone call off this pup before I have to hurt him?" I asked.

"Barry, you are making an ass of yourself," Amerine said mildly, balancing on his cane.

Barry! I was about to snap the arm of Amerine's nephew. Knowing what I did of Barry Sprague, I was sorely tempted to do it. Sprague saved himself by going limp.

"What kind of brute are you?" The redhead was addressing me. She was taking an imperious stance, helped by her being tall even in flat-heeled shoes. Over her dress she wore a loose-fitting jumper that concealed her curves. She had a pencil thrust into her hair, which was drawn back to the nape of her neck. She was maybe twenty-five. Despite the anger in her eyes and the sense that she was ready to slap me, I suffered no pain looking at her. "You could have caused his death!"

"Lady, he left home on his own. I'm bringing him back." I let go of Sprague's arm experimentally and stepped back.

"Quite right, Elaine. I left the house to attend to urgent business," Amerine assured her.

Elaine Knoll—no surprise on that identification by this point—was momentarily silenced by the information. When she recovered, she spoke to Amerine. "You might at least have told someone. We were in a panic." Her voice could not muster the vehemence with him it had with me.

I thought these people treated Amerine as if he were a kid late returning from the prom.

"Had I told anyone, you would have tried to stop me. Do you suppose I could sit down inside and have a glass of sherry?"

The distinguished-looking man in the charcoal suit came over to Amerine and took hold of his wrist, resting the tips of his fingers against the flesh. He counted for only a few seconds and shook his head. "You have overdone it, Lowell."

With Elaine's help, the man, who I now realized was a doctor, half-lifted Amerine down the stairs to the front door of the house. I stayed behind, watching Sprague get to his feet, flexing the fingers of his right hand. He was no more than medium height but carried enough extra pounds to create a strange blend of features. By nature he had the thin, sharp nose of an ascetic, but he had the double chin and flabby jowls of a glutton. A thin man's face pasted on a chubby boy's head. He wore a tweed sports coat, a turtleneck sweater, and twill pants. Why did I assume he was the one who had arrived in the sports car?

"Who are you?" Sprague demanded.

"The name is Bond," I said in my best Sean Connery voice. "James Bond."

"Wiseass, hunh?"

"What do you intend to do about it? Your first try wasn't successful."

"Listen, I've got to worry about that old man. People try to take advantage of him."

"And you don't?"

A flush started over Sprague's face. He tried to stare me into fright, but that is a game I've perfected over the years. He turned on his heel and strode over to the back of my Caprice to see the license plate. He took a small notebook and a ballpoint pen out of his pocket and wrote the number down.

"What do you do if someone gets really nasty?" I asked. "Take their Social Security number?"

He waved the notebook at me. "I'll find out who you are. I've got friends." He said that as if he didn't think I would believe him. "You'll be sorry."

"My dreams are troubled already."

He put the notebook away, took out a pair of driving gloves, and slid his hands into them. Opening the gull-wing doors of the Delorean, he got in, ground the gears into reverse, and tromped the pedal, turning the car as its tires screeched on the pavement. The guy had a great future as a parking lot attendant.

When Sprague was gone, I turned to the house and noticed the Mercedes left in the driveway. It had a caduceus attached to the trunk lid. My guess that the Walter Pidgeon look-alike was a doctor seemed better by the moment.

3

In all the excitement, no one had thought to close the door to the house. I entered a living room, which had apparently been converted into an office. A desk sat in the middle of the room and more surfaces curved from the end of it to form a horseshoe shape. On those surfaces was a computer, a printer, a modem, a fax machine, and other equipment I couldn't identify.

I took my eyes away from the desk to look at the rest of the room. Furniture had been pushed back against the walls to allow room for the office setup. All the end tables had pipe racks on them holding briars with well-chewed stems and a pipe cleaner run through them to absorb moisture while they were at rest. A golfer would have displayed his trophies; a fisherman, his stuffed catches; a hunter, animal heads. Amerine displayed his pipes. A staircase by the wall led up to the second floor. At the bottom of the staircase was an elevator chair, ready to run on its track to the top.

Voices were coming from another room. I followed the sound and entered the portion of the house that hung over the ravine.

The room where the talking was in progress was something I would have called a study, although it could as easily have been called a den or a library. Whatever you called it, it was plainly the room where the living was done. Except for the picture window that looked out onto the woods, the walls were filled with bookshelves—lots of legal sets but also modern books in bright dust jackets and a heavy sprinkling of trade paperbacks, the sort that appear on the required reading lists for college courses. It was also the sort of bookshelf you see so often behind the interviewee on *Nightline*. At one end of the room was a writing table on which lay a legal pad, its top sheet nearly filled with writing from a black felt-tip pen. Behind the table was a high-back swivel chair and beside it a stand holding an unabridged dictionary.

"Suicide, that's what it amounts to," the doctor was saying. He was bent over Amerine, who was now sitting in another wingback chair that swallowed him. His coat was off, his sleeve rolled up, the cuff of a blood-pressure gauge around his arm. In his other hand was a glass of sherry. The doctor was not happy with the results he saw on the blood pressure gauge.

"You simply must lie down, Lowell. I say that not only as your physician but as your friend and neighbor."

"Can all that alarmist talk be beneficial? Soon you will worry me into a heart attack." Amerine looked up and spotted me. "There you are. Have you met Miss Knoll? Dr. Richard Mount? He has a house on the yonder side of those woods." Amerine spilled sherry waving his glass at the picture window.

I recalled that Mount had been the name on the other mailbox at the end of the driveway. The doctor grunted something without looking up.

"I left home because I had business with Moe Glickman." Amerine turned to Elaine. "You've heard me mention Moe's name many times. It was a wise move, for it allowed me to meet Gilbert Disbro, a private investigator."

Elaine acknowledged me, brute though I am. Bracing herself, she said, "We appear to owe Mr. Disbro our thanks for bringing Lowell home." Her heart wasn't in her words.

Mount was on a roll with his medical advice now. "You should also forget your pipes."

"That's too much to ask," Amerine said. "My pipe has become as much a part of me as my big toe. Why should I forsake it for the little time you leave me?"

"You might have more time without the pipe."

"Without the pipe, my book would never get written."

"And that is a project you could well postpone."

"As sick as you make me out to be, I'd better not postpone anything."

Their exchange had the ring of old arguments being repeated, in part at least because the participants enjoyed the banter. Mount unwrapped the cuff from Amerine's arm and began packing his equipment in his medical bag. "Will you go along to bed now willingly?"

"In a moment or two. I must talk to these young people."

Mount regarded Elaine and me with stern disapproval. "See to it you don't keep him up." Mount gathered up his medical bag and went out, too familiar with the house to need to be shown to the door.

Amerine waited to speak until the door shut behind Mount. Elaine stood at his side, her hand stroking his thin hair. I realized the affection that flowed between those two was genuine. Looking at me, Elaine asked, "Why on earth did you hire a private detective?"

"I told him about my problem with blackmailers."

A gasp escaped from her as she looked down at Amerine. Seeing in his eyes that he was not joking with her, she turned her eyes to me again but continued to speak of me in the third person. "What is he expected to do about it?"

"Don't you think it would be to our advantage to find out what is behind all this?" Amerine had slipped an arm around her waist. "Now that is my decision. Mr. Disbro will have questions for you. I want you to answer them fully without holding anything back, especially to protect me."

Reluctantly, as if obeying an order were the only reason, she said, "All right."

"Good girl." With Elaine's help, Amerine got out of his chair. Elaine and I each took an arm and guided him out of the study and across the outer office to seat him in his chair and run it up the staircase. Elaine walked along beside him and helped him out at the head of the stairs.

While I waited for her to return, I wandered back into Amerine's study and over to his writing table, where I had noticed a legal pad with his spidery script on it written with a black felt-tip pen. Next to it was a pile of typed pages, obviously what Elaine had transcribed on her computer from his handwritten draft. The prose was laced with lawyerly jargon—"whereas," "inasmuch," "heretofore"—that would soon have numbed my mind.

By the time Elaine returned, I was back at her work station. "Did you have to put him under so much stress?" she asked.

I liked her for her concern. "I tried not to. There was no way to avoid upset considering the subjects we had to discuss."

She nodded when she had had time to consider the fairness of my point. "It's an awful mess, isn't it?" She walked back to her work station and tapped out the code on her keyboard for saving the text on the screen. That accomplished, she dropped into her chair. "How am I supposed to help you?"

"Tell me about the fax you got yesterday."

"I was working here at my desk around ten o'clock when the fax arrived. There isn't much more to tell." She plucked a cigarette from her pack.

"Was it a shock to you?"

"The contents shook me up when I saw them. If you mean is receiving a fax unusual, it isn't. The truth is, I didn't pay it much attention at first."

"Why not?"

Elaine lit her cigarette. "You have to understand the routine here. Judge Amerine has to have access to the law libraries for his book. Since he can't go in person to do his research, I have to call the libraries with requests, and they send me faxes—of an article from a law journal, for instance. Normally, there isn't any urgency about them. When this one came in, I was busy with other things, so I simply ignored it until I had a chance to get to it. Once I did, you bet I rushed it to Judge Amerine. He brooded about it the rest of the day. I had no idea he intended to sneak off and upset everyone. Are you really as good as he says?"

"Even better," I said and showed her the fax. "What can you tell me about this?"

She took the paper and studied it. "Start at the top. See this line?"

The message occupied the center of the page. Across the top of the page was a single line:

```
OCT 13    TUES    10:07    MESSAGE EXPRESS    P.01
```

"That shows the date and time the message came in," Elaine explained. "Message Express is a chain of businesses that specialize in printing forms, selling cardboard boxes, making photocopies—that sort of thing. They have stores all over, like K-Mart."

I nodded. I had patronized them myself when I had to send express packages.

"Among other things, they have a fax machine for public use. Bring in your message, pay two dollars per page, and they will send it for you." She went into an elementary explanation. "They insert the message into the machine, which has a telephone as part of it. They dial up the number of the receiver, and when the receiver is ready, the message is transmitted over phone lines. Don't ask me to tell you how it's done. Somehow the message is broken down to electronic impulses and reassembled on the other end."

"Sending this note from Message Express would be like making a call from a pay phone," I concluded.

"That's a good analogy." Elaine opened a desk drawer and took out the top page from a sheaf of papers. It resembled a phone bill and bore the heading *Journal*. There were two parts, *Transmit Record* and *Receive Record*. The page was dated Tuesday, October 13. "That's a printout of our activity on the machine for yesterday."

She had sent out two messages and received five. Opposite the date and time of each message was a phone number, all of them in the 216 area code for the northeast quadrant of Ohio. I looked for the message that had come in at 10:07 and saw the phone number from which it had originated.

Seeing what I was doing, Elaine opened the Yellow Pages for me and showed me the advertisement for Message Express. It listed half a dozen stores in the Cleveland metropolitan area with their phone and fax numbers. I matched up the fax number on the journal printout with the number of the store at Ridge and Biddulph. That put it on the west side, far from Amerine's home in the east exurbs. It was also far from Hatton's office on Payne.

"I don't think it means much," she said. "Anyone can walk in to one of those places and send the message."

"There wouldn't be any way to trace who sent it?"

"You already know that. His name is Axel McClusky."

"I wouldn't count on that being his real name. Cops and lawyers use Axel McClusky in examples, sort of like John Doe or Mr. X." I borrowed her phone and dialed the number of Message Express on Ridge and Biddulph. I told the clerk I was McClusky and needed a receipt for a fax I had sent from there yesterday, one with my name on it to satisfy the company comptroller.

"Sorry, they don't come that way," the clerk told me. "We can give you a printout, but it won't show your name."

"Well, it was worth a try." I hung up and studied Elaine, who was watching me. I had the better view. "So McClusky managed to send an anonymous message. The next question is how would he know your fax number?"

"That wouldn't be hard," she answered. "Judge Amerine has it printed on his letterhead and business cards."

Technology in the underworld was keeping pace with the honest people, I reflected. No more wrapping a note around a rock and heaving it through a window. Now that could be done electronically. I said, "The best opportunity to learn anything about the blackmailer comes tomorrow when the payoff is made. Are you willing to go through with it?"

"It seems to be part of my job description." She inhaled a puff of smoke and studied me. "Did you seriously believe I would refuse? If this is what Judge Amerine wants, it's what I'll do."

"You never know what might happen, what danger you might be in."

"Danger?" It was a new idea to her. "As long as I'm transporting the money, I have a guarantee no one will interfere with me. It seems to me the blackmailer would have an interest in insuring my good health at least until the point I hand it over."

"I agree, except that you never know what goes on in the mind of someone who would do this kind of thing."

She gave it a brief consideration. "I'm not worried."

"Then the plans are simple. Follow the directions to the letter, and I'll follow you. If you have to take the Shaker Rapid, we'd better allow a half hour for the trip downtown, another half hour to reach the bus station, some time before that to get ready. I'll be here at ten thirty in the morning."

She eyed me suspiciously. "Maybe I should ask what exactly your plans are?"

"Fluid," I told her. "When you leave the package at baggage claims, I'll be watching it. Someone is going to have to pick it up. That's the person I'll follow and see what happens next."

"Isn't that dangerous?"

"I'm licensed to carry a gun."

"That isn't what I meant. The real danger is that you will blunder into something and cause the blackmailer to panic into revealing what he knows."

"That was Amerine's concern, too. I promised him I'd back off before I let that happen."

"Then he must trust your discretion." It was clear to me she was not relieved.

Looking at Elaine now, I decided her glasses enhanced her good looks. They called attention to her eyes, which were her best feature. Because I was thinking such thoughts, I blurted out something that had been lurking in the recesses of my mind. "Judge Amerine told me you were married once."

"It wasn't a happy experience." She turned away to crush her cigarette in an ashtray. "Robert deserted me. I'm divorced now."

"Sorry. I didn't mean to pick at scabs."

"It's a piece of my life that's behind me." The clutch in her voice testified that, if it was behind her, it was not far back.

"Judge Amerine thinks the world of you, the same as you think of him. I'm really here to help him and you at the same time. Can we work together on that basis?"

The curtain of suspicion that had been in front of her lifted a little at that point. "Of course we can."

I took out one of my business cards and turned it over to write my address and home phone on the back. "In case anything comes up before tomorrow morning, you can reach me at one of these places."

She took the card. I went off to check into the first of the blackmailers, G. K. Hatton.

4

My trip from the upscale exurbs to the Tetlow Building covered more than distance. It was a descent through social strata. The building sat east of the Innerbelt ravine in an area where the business district grudgingly gives way to warehouses and factories. Across the freeway to the west was the sooty gray hulk of the Third District police headquarters. I parked in a metered space across the street and paused a moment to study the layout. It was a corner building. The ground floor held a restaurant whose name was spelled out in Chinese characters. Above the restaurant were two floors of walk-up offices with the entrance to the stairwell on the Payne Avenue side of the building. Studying the windows in the top two floors got me nowhere. I locked my car and crossed the street.

At the bottom of the stairs was a bulletin board that listed the businesses above. Dentist, chiropractor, novelties, secretarial help, tailor, tax accountant. Nothing for Room 207. No Hatton. Not even Blackmail, Inc. I climbed the first flight of stairs and went down the hall lit by glass globes suspended from a tall ceiling, reading numbers off the pebbled glass doors. Room 207 was down a quirky short side hall, an afterthought when someone realized a little more rent could be collected by adding an office here. In justice, it should have been a storeroom in a larger suite. The legend on its window read: G. K. HATTON. In a corner of the window was a file card on which was typed CLOSED TODAY. The *T* stood above the line.

The lock on the door didn't look impregnable, but I wanted to try a more legal approach before I resorted to burglary. I stepped out into the main hall in search of someone who could direct me to the right place. Across the hall was an open transom with voices coming from the inside. A woman's voice rose shrill. "Damn it, I need the money. Bills are coming due."

"What the hell am I supposed to do about it?" The man's voice asked in only slightly more reasonable terms.

"Pete was your partner. I deserve half the income."

"What income? Your husband, my partner, ran off with the company account. Think I'm not hurting? Until I promote something, all I've got is pocket change."

I sidled down the hall until I could read the lettering on the door: BOTKIN & ORTEGA, SPORTS PROMOTIONS. This was the door to their private office. The door to the waiting room would be around a curve in the hall.

The woman's voice changed, lowering with a sob in it. "I'm broke. I mean it. I don't know where dinner's coming from tonight."

"Listen, Lynette, the Baxter fight is coming up next week. We get a share of the purse. You're going to have to go to the butcher and explain that. They'll cover you for a few more days. You have trouble, have them call me." The man's voice was soft and persuasive.

"Oh, Damon! It's so damned unfair!" Light threw two silhouettes against the pebbled-glass pane of the door. The two shadows moved closer together and merged. In a few seconds, they broke apart again.

"Here's fifty," the man said. "That'll carry you through the weekend if you don't buy a new set of clothes." He was giving in, eager to get rid of her. He opened the door a crack and held it that way to signal their conversation was over.

A moment later they stepped through the doorway, the man with his arm around the woman's shoulders. She was an ash blonde in an ice-blue dress with matching ice-blue eyes. He patted her one last time, and she started off down the hall, walking in high-heeled shoes that required a sway-hipped pace. I watched her, glad I had not gone knocking on another door. Mindful that half an hour ago I had been appreciating the charms of Elaine Knoll, I felt Elaine's image being erased from my mind the way a whisper is drowned out by loud music. This blonde's sexuality was blatant, compelling attention with its overpowering presence, whereas Elaine's attractiveness had been refined and understated. This blonde announced herself with a blast of trumpets while she surrounded herself with a protective shield that stiff-armed any man without a large enough bank account who might try to approach her. Arresting as her features were, her buxom and voluptuous body also screamed for notice, even though that kind of figure isn't to my taste. She passed me, paying me no more attention than another slat in the wainscoting. The sympathy I had been feeling for her hard-luck plight dissipated somewhat when I noted the silver mink stole around her shoulders. Hocked, it could have kept her in comfort for six months.

The man had been leaning against the jamb in the office doorway, watching me watch her. In shirtsleeves, with gaudy red suspenders over his shoulders, he was a trim man whose black pompadoured hair looked like patent leather. His complexion was dark, his features all planes and angles, with a pencil-line mustache across his upper lip. He struck a match on the door jamb and applied the flame to his cigarette. I guessed he was thirty-five.

"Know anything about your neighbor, Hatton?" I jerked a thumb at the small office.

The man with the patent-leather hair studied me as if something about my appearance might change his answer. "Understand he specialized in short-term investments on blooded mares."

"Bookie?" I was hardly surprised, considering his environment. "Where will I find him?"

"Try Forest Hill Cemetery." My informant wore a blue shirt with white pinstripes, white collar, and white cuffs. His hand-painted necktie showed boxing gloves and punching bags.

"Dead?"

"If he wasn't a couple years ago, he sure is now with all the dirt on his face." The man snorted smoke out his nose. "They never got around to taking his name off the door." He turned and went back into his office.

I stepped into the doorway before the door could close. The office beyond was decorated with photographs of fighters and newspaper clippings related to signing fighters by Botkin & Ortega. Several of the photographs showed two men posed with different boxers. In each picture one of the men was the one with the patent-leather hair. The other had hardly any hair at all, was about a decade older, and fifty pounds heavier. There were two desks in the room, one with a nameplate for Peter Botkin. The man with the patent-leather hair went to the other, Damon Ortega.

"Who is the landlord for these offices?" I asked, supporting the door jamb in Ortega's absence.

"A widow in Miami Beach most of the year. You probably want to see the building super." Ortega pointed at the floor. "He has a place in the boiler room. The name's Rossiter."

"Thanks." I closed the door for him and went down the stairs to the street level. Behind that staircase was another flight to the basement. Down there I came to another door labeled BOILER and when I pushed through that, I found a tangle of pipes like the intestines of a behemoth. I made my way through the pipes, ducking under this one, and climbing over that one, until I reached the furnace in the midst of it all. Beside the furnace was an ancient wooden swivel chair, probably something discarded from one of the upstairs offices, and in the chair was a man. He wore a pair of bib overalls and a T-shirt that might have been white as recently as 1978. At the moment he was occupied with drinking from a pint bottle of whiskey.

"Rossiter?"

He looked around in an effort to locate the source of the voice, without much success. His eyes were recessed under an awning of eyebrows that had fused together. Jug ears stood out from the sides of his head. "What the fuck's it to you?"

I shook my head and smiled. "Something about this building

makes everyone in it a sweetheart." I vaulted the pipe in front of me and walked out into the open where Rossiter could focus on me. "Who's renting Room Two-oh-seven?"

Rossiter fortified himself with another slug from his bottle, causing the Adam's apple in his scrawny neck to bob, and looked me over. "What the fuck's it to you?"

I showed him one of my cards. He looked it over, shrugged, and stuck it in one of the pockets on the chest of his bib overalls. "Goddamn! I'm impressed." His bare arms were thin, decorated with tattoos. His whole frame had the emaciated appearance of a man who ate little and drank a lot.

"So who's renting Two-oh-seven?"

"Nobody. Hatton, the prick, died owing me seventy-five bucks." Rossiter took comfort in another swallow from his pint. "Only time in my life I hit a daily double, and that prick Hatton has to keel over in the North Coast Café from a heart attack, or maybe the blue plate special, before he can pay off."

"That was a couple years ago."

"So what? I can hold a grudge longer than that."

"So who's renting the office now?"

"Office is a dog. Hatton was the onliest one ever wanted to rent it on accounta all he needed was a place to plop his ass while he figured the day's take."

I reached out and plucked the pint from Rossiter's fingers. Holding it up, I tilted it until a little whiskey ran out the neck onto the boiler-room floor.

"Hey!" Rossiter started out of his chair, but I put a foot on his chest to hold him in place. I poured out a few more drops.

"Two ways this can go," I told him. "You can tell me what I want to know, and do yourself some good at the same time, or you can lie to me and end up holding the shitty end of the stick." I smiled what I hoped was a wicked smile. "Up to you."

"Nobody's renting the place."

"Bullshit."

"Look at the books. You'll see it's empty."

"I believe that. Know why? Because whoever rents the office pays off directly to you. The owner is none the wiser, and you pocket the rent."

My guess had come close to home. Rossiter quickly exchanged

his belligerence for whining. "Man's got to play the angles to get by these days."

"Yeah." I took my foot off his chest but held on to the pint. "Who rents the place?"

"A guy. Any name he woulda give me woulda been a phony, so what's the use to ask?"

"What did he look like?"

"I'm not sure."

"Think again, Rossiter. You think I came here for no reason? Do you think a man would rent that office to teach a Sunday School class? These people are waist deep in shit. Someone's going to Lucasville for a good long jolt. You cover up for them, you end up sharing a cell."

"I ain't involved."

"Then you got no reason to hold out."

Rossiter fought a battle with himself that showed in the strained expression on his face. At last good sense wrestled a victory over greed. "The guy who came around was a Dago. Don't know much else about him."

"But you're sure he was Italian? Did he talk with an accent?"

"No, but he looked like a Dago or a Hebe."

"And what is that?"

"Not very tall, dark complexion, dark hair. He was around your age and thin. Dressed real sharp, though."

"Mustache? Scars?" I tried pressing for more details of the man's appearance, but Rossiter had no answers to give. His senses dulled by whiskey, he simply was not observant enough to do better. In an odd way, that added to his veracity. If Rossiter had started recalling too many details, I would have suspected him of lying to please me. He had looked no further than the man's wallet and had found it advantageous in his life to forget much of what he saw.

"How did it work?" I asked.

"The guy asked to rent the bookie's office."

"That's the words he used?"

"Yeah."

"When was this?"

"Back in cold weather. Winter? Early spring? I was working on heating pipes on the third floor when he showed up. Paid me cash on the spot for two months and said he'd leave his rent in the office first of each month. I go in the office and there it is in an envelope on the table."

"How often is he around?"

"Almost never. I might've passed him on the stairs twice in all that time."

I returned the bottle and waited for him to down a swallow. "I'll need to look at the office."

"I can't do that," Rossiter protested. When I dangled a ten-dollar bill in front of him, he said, "I'll have to go along."

We climbed the stairs together to the second floor, where Rossiter brought out a key ring and unlocked the door to 207. I flicked the light switch, illuminating the room from a green-shaded bulb hanging from the ceiling. Set directly under it was a small table and a chair. A typewriter sat on the table. There was nothing else in the room.

"This shouldn't take long," I noted. I went over to the table—two steps from the door—and looked it over. It was carelessly constructed and scarred from years of use, probably something picked up from a junk dealer after passing through many hands. The chair, which showed a similar biography, was a captain's chair. I found a drawer in the table and opened it. Inside was a stack of typing paper, plain envelopes, and a pad of expense statements.

Rossiter hovered by the door. He took his pint out of his hip pocket, treated himself to a snort, and returned it. "Ask me, you should be checking on those people across the hall."

The typewriter was a Remington standard that was older than I am. I took a sheet of paper out of the drawer, inserted it in the carriage, and began pecking out nonsense words and phrases.

"Fight promoters is what they call themselves. Fight fixers is what they are. When Botkin and Ortega arrange it, someone's going for the Olympic diving championship." Rossiter was so pleased with his joke he congratulated himself on his wit by treating himself to another swallow of whiskey. "Got so brazen the boxing commission started to investigate them. They caught one of the partners, Pete Botkin, taking a payoff to fix a fight. The grand jury indicted him."

Rossiter was like a schoolboy caught in some minor infraction attempting to evade punishment by pointing out all the sins of the kid across the aisle. I ignored him and concentrated on typing.

"That put the kibosh on their business. Everyone was watching them too close for them to fix any fights, and honest matches wouldn't have them. Business went down the crapper. Then a few months back, when Botkin was about to come to trial, he took it on the lam. Left the business, left his wife, cleaned out the bank account, and vamoosed. Guess the thought of prison scared him. It would take more than that to get me to leave that wife he had."

I looked at what I had typed. No matter how careful I had been, the *t*'s were consistently above the line. I folded the sheet and put it in my pocket—evidence, if things ever came to that.

"Soon as Botkin was out of the picture, that Spic partner of his put the moves on the wife. Maybe he was dipping his wick before Botkin was out of the picture, for all I know. Bet the Spic framed his partner just to get rid of him. You see the wife, you'd know why a man would take risks."

I took one more look around the office and then was ready to go. "I think I saw her. Blonde named Lynette?"

"That's the one."

When I stepped out into the hall, Rossiter turned out the light and locked the office door behind me.

5

Lacking any further ideas, I drove across downtown Cleveland to my home base on West Third across from the Justice Center. I parked in the rear lot and climbed the stairs to the second floor, where I pushed through the door into Moe Glickman's office. Behind the counter, Rolf reared his hundred pounds and stuck his black snout through the slot in the screen. I laid my hand on the counter so he could lick it and looked over his head to Gladys, who was busy typing. Without turning her thick glasses my way, she said, "A man came by to see you."

"He leave a name?"

"He didn't leave anything. I put him in your office to wait for you." Now Gladys looked up at me and bobbed her head toward the bench. "Waiting out here didn't seem to be a good idea."

"I guess not." The prospect of a stranger waiting in my office didn't alarm me. My business being what it is, people who aren't eager to give their names drop by occasionally. The reason my office is down a hall on the outside of the steel mesh is a sign I don't have anything worth stealing. I walked down that hall and opened my door.

"Come in, sweetheart. Take a load off your dogs and put it on your buns. Then you can tell me what load of grief is weighing you down."

Barry Sprague sat in my swivel chair with his heels on the corner of my desk. I closed the door and came in.

"Told you I had friends," Sprague said. "They checked on your license number and gave me your name. Jesus Christ! A shamus. A peeper. A rent-a-cop. I didn't know there were such things." He looked around my nine-by-fourteen room at the file cabinets, at the map of Cleveland on the wall, at my coffeemaker. "What is this? Some kind of Junior Achievement project?"

I stepped over to my coffeemaker and poured myself a cup, conspicuously not offering him one. "Did you have a reason for coming here?"

He quit inspecting my office long enough to turn his head in my direction. "Sure. I want to know why my uncle had you out to his place."

"He wanted to hire me." I settled into my client's chair and reached for a cigarette.

"To do what?"

"Investigate."

"Investigate what?"

"Personal matters."

Sprague took his feet off the corner of my desk and began rocking back and forth in my swivel chair. It creaked at the rearward tilt. "I asked a civil question. I deserve an answer."

I got up from my seat, took down my framed license, and held it out to him. "See that? *Private* investigations."

He read the license carefully. "Class A. Is that good?"

"It means I can do security work in addition to investigations." I hung the license in place and sat again.

He shrugged. "I don't see why you can't tell me what Uncle Lowell wanted done."

"I could tell you all right, but I won't."

"Why not?"

"You wouldn't understand. It has to do with morality and ethics."

"Aha." Sprague started swiveling my chair back and forth in an arc. "I've heard of ethics. How much do they cost?"

"Twenty dollars an hour, plus expenses."

Sprague stopped the chair. "Let's see. Twenty dollars times two thousand hours. That means you pull down, maximum, forty thousand a year. Do people really live on that kind of money?"

"Some get by on even less."

"Yeah, I've heard that. But you also get expenses. That's a game that can be played for an advantage. Let's say you break even on your car, and maybe you eat half your meals on the account. There's two big items disposed of. Your rent on this dump can't be very much. If you've got any sense, there's a line item in your expense account that covers the office rent. What's left? Clothes?" He examined my sports coat and Dockers with a critical eye. "You don't blow it on fancy duds. That only leaves your housing. Maybe you stretch that forty grand pretty far."

I let him prattle on. The fact that our positions were reversed—that he was in my chair and I was on the wrong side of the desk—was bothering me more than I wanted to let on. No wonder my clients tend to squirm when they sit here.

Sprague reached into his pocket and came out with a clip of bills. He peeled off a ten and laid it on my blotter. "I want to buy a half hour of your time."

"To do what?"

"Search your files and tell me what Lowell Amerine is up to."

"Why don't you just ask him?"

"I'm afraid he wouldn't be honest with me."

I drained my coffee cup and set it down on my desk. "No deal."

Sprague's eyes actually welled up. He wasn't used to not getting his way. "You can't discriminate against me!"

"Sure I can. That's what's so great about being self-employed. I can choose the people I work for. I like your uncle, and I don't like you." I stood up, went to my door, and grasped the door knob. "Hit the pike."

"You can't throw me out!" Sprague stuttered.

"Wanna bet?"

"Look, we can work something out." A hum of pleading was in Sprague's voice. "What the old man wants you to do concerns me, doesn't it?"

I said nothing, but I did not open the door.

"How can we work this out?" Sprague asked. "You know something, and I know something, and neither one of us wants to give it away."

"Why don't you just come out with it?"

"Megan Latimer."

I let go of the doorknob. "What's the connection?"

Having scored a point, Sprague leaned back in the swivel chair and began swinging it back and forth. "Blackmail."

I nodded and sat again. "Keep talking."

"It goes something like this: While I was romancing Megan, I gave her some narcotics to which she had a violent reaction and died. My uncle allowed me to bury her body on his grounds. Now a person is blackmailing him to keep all that quiet." Sprague gave his chair a spin so that he made a complete circle and came back to the desk facing me. "That about cover it?"

"It's interesting that you know about the blackmail," I observed.

"It would be very strange if I didn't know," Sprague said, "considering I'm the one doing it."

If you ask me how I reacted to that, I'd tell you I held myself rigid in magnificent self-control. The truth is I'm not at all sure I carried it off, but I was trying. "You're the blackmailer." Which one? I wondered.

"Can I claim a reward for solving the case?" Sprague beamed.

"I'd rather hear your thinking."

"I suppose it does seem strange on the face of it." Sprague took out a pack of cigarettes and shook one loose. "It probably is not a normal circumstance to find the one responsible for the crime making blackmail demands. Do you mind if I go into a bit of history?"

"Be my guest."

Sprague inserted his cigarette into an ivory holder. "More than a year ago I made a series of unwise decisions betting on games of chance. I kept redoubling my bets in the hope of recouping my losses, but that never works, does it? Before long, I found myself in a great deal of debt to Mr. Cusimano, who began couching his demands for payment in the most unpleasant terms. He let me know that I must either pay or suffer severe physical damage." Sprague lit his cigarette and exhaled a stream of smoke from the side of his mouth. "That left me in a dilemma, for I did not have the resources to meet the demands. In desperation, I turned to Uncle Lowell.

"Actually, he was cooperative up to a point. He agreed to pay off Cusimano, but he had demands of his own. Because I have a job in a bank, Uncle Lowell feared that other gambling debts would tempt me to embezzle money. Therefore, he put a condition on me. I must never again gamble. If I did, if I got myself into a similar situation, he would not rescue me a second time."

Sprague flicked ashes into an ashtray and looked at me to gauge my reaction. "So much for the background. The rest of the story, alas, is dreadfully repetitive. I gambled again. I lost. I redoubled. I lost more. Cusimano made threats. Once more I found myself in a quandary, for my one avenue of salvation was cut off. I could no longer appeal to my uncle. Then, in a flash of brilliant insight, I saw what must be done. I would force Uncle Lowell to pay my debts while deceiving him into thinking the money was for another purpose. It had to be something so serious he would have no choice but to pay. Ergo, the homicide."

I studied Sprague, who was waiting expectantly like a dog looking for a pat on the head after performing some trick. Sprague was actually proud of himself. "Then Megan Latimer died to save your skin."

"Of course not. It was all a trick, don't you see? Simply because I *told* Uncle Lowell a fantastic but plausible tale does not make it true. He knew very well I was seeing Megan, and he looked upon her with disapproval. He would easily believe she was taking narcotics, and he would further believe she had died—if I could stage a little drama properly. I explained what I intended to do to Cusimano, and he assigned one of his minions, Georgie Pockets, to assist me. I went to my uncle's home in the middle of the night—deliberately. I didn't want him to see too clearly what was happening, and I knew he was too ill to leave the house. Pockets, a man he brought along, and I gave a convincing performance of carrying a dead body into the woods to bury it. I don't know what Uncle Lowell might have told you about that night, but whatever he saw was a charade for his benefit, play acting to deceive him. One salient fact you should have spotted: Uncle Lowell never saw the body. Did he tell you otherwise?"

I reviewed what Amerine had seen and conceded a point. It had been a blanket with something heavy in it, what he had believed was a body only because Sprague had told him so. In the dark, from a distance, it could have been anything.

"Obviously that bundle did not contain a body for the simple reason that Megan Latimer did not take narcotics and did not die," Sprague said definitely.

"Some people will tell me that Elvis is alive, but that doesn't make it so. How do I know you're not lying now?"

"You could go out into Uncle Lowell's woods with a spade and dig to your heart's content. You won't find anything." Sprague drew on his cigarette holder. "You could ask Gus Cusimano, though I wouldn't advise it. He would probably be reluctant to confess. Or you could go see Megan. When you observe her breathing and walking about, when you take her pulse, when she answers your questions, that should satisfy you."

"Where would I find her?"

"She is no longer dancing in a topless club. The vice squad took a dim view of that situation and shut it down. Now she teaches aerobic dancing at a reducing studio on Broadway called Inches Off." Sprague looked at his watch. "If you hurry, you should find her there yet this afternoon."

I made no sudden rush for the door, if that was what he expected. "How did your blackmail work?"

"We sent my uncle a letter asking for two thousand dollars each month. He has been mailing the cash to an office on Payne Avenue."

"You set that up?"

"Cusimano made the arrangements, which is to say he probably delegated the work to Georgie Pockets. He relies to a great extent on Pockets for various activities."

"Then it was Pockets who rented the office?"

Sprague shrugged. "Cusimano has any number of men in his employ he could send on such errands. It may have been Pockets, or it may have been someone else. Do you think *henchmen* is too strong a work to describe them?"

"That's all you've done?"

"No point in doing more." A worry caused Sprague to frown. "Say, you're not going to tell my uncle, are you?"

"He's the client. He deserves to know the truth." No sooner were the words out than I had cause to reconsider them. Amerine's doctor and his research assistant, along with the evidence of my own eyes, had testified to his delicate health. All that led me to say, "I'm not sure he could handle the shock. Besides, there's more than you know that needs to be investigated, so it will be a few days until I'm ready to spring it on him. Nothing says you can't tell him."

Sprague shook his head. "Facing the music ain't my style."

"It wouldn't be a bad policy to adopt. There's a lot to be said for making a clean breast of it. It's a sign of growing up."

"What's the big thing about growing up? You have so many responsibilities." Sprague shook his head again and stood up. "I do have to be getting back to my office. My employers are so tiresome on that point. They have the quaint notion that because they pay my salary, I should appear at work. Do consider all that I've told you before you act rashly."

Sprague exited, and I sat in the client's chair mulling over everything he had told me. In the end I had no choice but to follow up on the information Sprague had given me. I picked up my phone and called home. No one would be there that time of day, but I was able to leave a message on the answering machine. I told Helen I would likely be late for dinner because I was going to get a massage from an exotic dancer.

6

I headed down Broadway to find Inches Off. On the way I drove across the Kingsbury Viaduct, a point of absolutely no significance unless you have an interest in bizarre Cleveland history. It was in the area below the viaduct, Kingsbury Run, where the Mad Butcher was leaving body fragments in the 1930s. Eliot Ness, who was then head of the police department, spent three frustrating years tracking down the killer and saw twelve bodies accumulate. He never caught the killer. Or maybe he did. You can get arguments either way. In Cleveland there have been two notorious cases that can start a fistfight any day. The other one is the Dr. Sam Sheppard homicide.

In all candor, headless, armless, and legless bodies were not the kind on my mind as I tooled down Broadway. Below East 55th, I came to a shopping plaza created where an entire block of buildings had been razed to be replaced by a parking lot and a line of one-story buildings. Between a shoe store and a dress boutique was the storefront labeled Inches Off. I found a parking space not far from it and entered the building.

A partition running the length of the main room had been put up six feet from the right wall to create a hallway that led to the back. A series of picture windows in the wall gave a view of the exercise room on the other side where a class was in progress. The instructor had her back to me while she led the pupils in leg kicks. From that perspective, I could see her head of chestnut hair held in place with a headband like an Apache warrior, the graceful curve of her back in a Spandex gym suit, her hips and legs muscular but thick like a true dancer's. Twenty pupils were lined up in three squads with enough excess weight among them to form a fourth rank. Music was playing, but only the instructor was keeping up with it. The pupils were kicking with about twenty percent effort while their flesh jiggled to a different beat. Anyone who tells you watching women exercise is sexy has to be the kind of person who gets his rocks off watching the SS drill team doing the goose step.

I followed the hall until I came to a reception room. It had a desk, which was unoccupied. An open door led into the exercise room and on the other side was a closed door labeled Locker Room. A lone man was there sitting on a couch, a newspaper in front of his face. Below the newspaper crossed legs were encased in blue pinstripe trousers and shoes polished to a liquid gloss. As I came in, he looked around his newspaper, a *Racing Form*, and I saw his face.

My jaw must have dropped open, for a word escaped from my mouth. "Slick!"

Felix Underhill grinned, and his forty-year-old face lit up with boyish innocence I had reason to know was deceptive. "Disbro? I'll be damned."

Neither of us moved for a full ten seconds after that. "What the hell are you doing here?" I asked.

"Waiting for my wife to finish."

"Wife? Mind if I look at your marriage license?"

Underhill smiled tolerantly, willing to go along with a jest. He had the knack, probably a key to his success, to fit himself into any situation. There was a sense about him that he had been sculpted to specs. He was a little taller than average—being too short or too tall would have made him stand out. He was slender—a man with disciplined eating habits was a man who would be prudent in money matters. His light brown hair was long enough to be styled in graceful waves with a blaze of gray at the temples to offset his youthful features. He wore a Savile Row suit, double-breasted this season, invariably with a white shirt that had a starched collar. His tie was flamboyant enough to be hip, subdued enough to suggest generations of Ivy League education. He would have been believable as a televangelist or an anchor man. Slick Underhill happened to be the premier con man in the Midwest.

He pointed toward the exercise room with his cleft chin, letting me see the profile in which his nose had absolutely no bridge at all. "Megan is the instructor in there."

"Megan Latimer is your main squeeze?" Two contradictory ideas were competing for space in my mind. Megan had been seeing Barry Sprague. Megan was married, or something, to Slick Underhill. "Thing I always admired about you was your lack of shame about living off your wife's income."

Underhill took no offense. "Now wouldn't it be a waste of money for me to support a woman? Where is the profit in that?"

I had no doubt that Underhill wouldn't be above pimping his wife, but that was not the major thrust of my thinking at the moment. Call me prejudiced, but the presence of Underhill on the scene in a situation where money was being extorted only convinced me I had solved the identity of the second blackmailer.

"Tell me what brings a private investigator to a place like this. You don't look as if you need to trim down."

There was the Underhill technique, a simple question accompanied by subtle flattery. Could a slender private eye fail to respond? I said, "Megan is the one I came to see."

"Isn't that interesting?" His forehead corrugated and his eyebrows lifted. The invitation was there for me to expand without his pressing hard.

As it turned out, I didn't have to answer because the class broke up and the herd headed through on their way to the locker room. Last to come was the instructor, who was wiping her face with a towel. When she passed through the doorway, she hooked the towel around her neck and climbed onto Underhill's lap to give him a passionate kiss. Underhill responded as if he were having his shoes shined.

"Honey, there's someone to see you," Underhill said when she was done.

Megan squirmed around in his lap to see me for the first time where I was standing in the corner. She was somewhere in her twenties and something of a disappointment, considering what I had been expecting for an exotic dancer. Walk down the center aisle of a shopping mall, and you would pass a hundred like her between Penney's and The Gap, women who are neither ugly nor likely to parade down the runway wearing a crown and holding a bouquet. Her face was elongated and, under her makeup, pitted with pockmarks. Her expression was in neutral waiting for a cue.

Underhill gave it to her. "This is Gil Disbro. He's the private star who nearly queered my deal with the New Woodstock Corporation."

A flash of spite went through her eyes, replaced by an expression of calculation. I had once deprived her of money; maybe now there was a way to make me pay for it. I decided to keep my hand on my wallet.

"Why, what could you want with li'l ole me?" The memory of a West Virginia accent in her voice was exaggerated by her deliberate parody of a Southern belle.

"Barry Sprague sent me here."

"Barry?" She turned her head to look at Underhill. "You remember him, the banker you wanted me to be nice to when we applied for the loan for this place."

"Sure, I remember him," Underhill told her.

I couldn't see what looks, what signals, passed between them. If Underhill was cultivating a banker, it meant he had some scheme percolating away.

Megan stood up, showing me her Spandex leotards were spray-painted on her body. Her mammaries stood out with proud nipples outlined. The body, more naked in the leotards than if she had been nude, was her best advertisement for the salon. You bet my judgment was being eroded. Megan took a step away, then stopped to look back over her shoulder. "Let's go inside and talk about it."

The door she went to was marked Office, and there were a desk and chair inside to make the name official, but that was the least of it. The focus of the room was a couch facing two matched chairs over a coffee table. Megan dropped onto the couch and peeled off the headband, giving her head a toss to let her chestnut hair fall free. Her performance for the exercise class, maybe more than the physical exertion, had taken its toll.

Underhill, who had followed us into the office, headed for a credenza that turned out to be a liquor cabinet. He put ice cubes in a glass and added three fingers of bourbon, then handed the drink to Megan. She downed it with a toss of her head and held out the glass, which Underhill refilled.

"Care for some?" she asked me.

"He doesn't drink," Underhill told her.

"Really?" Megan stared at me as if I were some kind of strange specimen. "You a health freak? Religious nut? Reformed drunk?"

I shook my head at each option. "It never appealed to me. One day I was forcing a beer down my throat and trying not to gag, so I asked myself why I was doing it. The only answer I could give was that I was trying to be one of the boys, to conform. Conformity has never been a big deal for me, so I put the beer aside." Maybe I was trying to justify myself when I pointed out, "One third of the adults in this country don't drink. Another ten percent have quit. That's nearly half."

She gulped half her drink to prove she belonged to the other side.

"Do you do drugs?" I asked.

"Say, what is this? Are you a narc?"

"No way. I'm only asking."

She wiggled her glass, causing the ice cubes to clink. "That's my habit."

"Does Barry do drugs?"

"I've never known him to use anything."

Underhill had been fixing himself a drink, keeping out of the conversation. Now he spoke up. "Maybe if you'd come right out and ask us, we could tell you what you want to know."

My mission here had been to establish that Megan was still alive. I was satisfied that she was still walking and breathing. To that extent my purpose had been accomplished, yet instinct told me I was missing something. "Who was that girl Barry was squiring around a while back? The dancer from the club?"

"That was me," Megan said. "I was a dancer until the vice squad shut the place down. After that, Barry got me the loan to open this place."

"I heard there was someone else."

"You heard wrong. If Barry had me, what else would he need?"

I had to agree with that. She would be a handful by herself. "Sorry I had to bother you. Thanks for your time."

I found my way out the door, checking one more time to make sure my wallet was in place. A few of the overweight customers, now in street clothes, were gathered in the parking lot discussing where they would go for a hot fudge sundae. "All this exercise sure builds up an appetite," one was saying.

I lit a cigarette and made my way to my car, churning everything I had been told today in my mental blender. First Megan Latimer's body was buried in the woods. Then she was alive. The whole thing was screwy, but given Sprague's problem with his uncle, it was a plausible solution. If I could accept all that, I had solved the problem of the first blackmailer. So Megan was still alive, and there was no dead body to contend with. But was the woman inside really Megan Latimer? That would be easy enough to check out. Then what of the second blackmailer?

While my thoughts were occupied, I had reached my car and started to unlock it. A gold and black Chrysler Imperial pulled up behind my Chevrolet and stopped there, blocking my intention to back out. The smoked window on the driver's side slid down of its own volition. The driver was a young man, no more than thirty, with dark, razor-cut hair and sharp, delicate features. He was pretty rather than handsome.

"Let me out and you can have my parking slot," I told him reasonably.

"You're Disbro." The way he said it left no room for denial.

"That's me—gentleman, scholar, raconteur, bon vivant, notary public."

He was unimpressed. "Get in. The man wants to see you."

I looked beyond the driver to the passenger seat. Empty. To the back seat. Also empty. The driver had no Uzi across his lap. "Who is this man?"

"Don Augustine Cusimano."

I checked the car out again and looked at the driver. With him sitting, I had a hard time estimating his size, but he didn't look big enough to make me do anything I didn't want. "No, thanks."

He shrugged his shoulders inside his tailored jacket. "Suit yourself."

I turned away from him and started back to my car. He shifted into reverse and backed the Imperial a car length so I had room to exit. That was too easy. I walked back to his still-open window. "What's the 'or else?' "

"Ain't no 'or else.' You come or you don't. Either way, it's no skin off my ass."

He was making it hard on me. If he had threatened me, I would have felt compelled to resist just to prove I couldn't be pushed. This guy, however, made no threats. Maybe he really didn't care, or maybe he was shrewd enough to know that threats wouldn't work. Whatever way he was going, he had found the right button to push. "All right, take me to him."

I started around the car to the passenger seat, but the driver got out and came after me. "Hold on. We got a formality first. Put your hands on the roof."

I obeyed. Behind me, the driver ran his hands down my ribs and waist, all the way down to my ankles. On the way, he lifted my .45 Officer's Model out of the holster under my left arm. When I turned around, he was tucking the pistol in his waistband.

"If you don't give that back, I'll get down on the floor and kick and scream until you have to."

The driver rolled his eyes. My guess about him had been right. He was less than average height and thin. He meant to dress fit for Wall Street, but he hadn't got it right. The stripe in his suit was too bold, the plaid pattern of his shirt clashed with the stripe, his shoes were too pointed, and the hand-painted pattern of his tie was too garish. Instead of dressing for success, he had gone over the line to sharp. As long as he held my pistol, though, I had no intention of telling him.

"Get in the car." I did. He went back to the driver's side and pressed the button to roll up his window. That done, he shifted into drive and we started out.

"What do they call you?" I asked.

"Pockets."

7

The Midtown Corridor is a name given to the three-mile stretch of Euclid Avenue on the east side from Playhouse Square to University Circle. People who use that name are mainly Chamber of Commerce types who fill up drawing boards with visions of a vibrant upscale shopping mecca attracting free-spending yuppies to its boutiques. Lots of luck. Let's be honest here. The visions stay on the drawing boards, and what remains between downtown and the cultural complex in the Circle is less a glittering strip than a hummock of despair.

Pockets drove me into the Midtown Corridor past storefronts with enough iron grates for a maximum security prison, past once luxurious apartment buildings with vacant windows staring out, past an abandoned movie theater with JESUS SAVES on the marquee. He pulled over to the curb in front of a corner store whose windows were plastered over with signs that proclaimed food stamps and welfare checks cashed. In front of the store lounged half a dozen young black men drinking beer from long-neck bottles, watching the Imperial with studied disinterest. They sported worn blue L.A. Raiders jackets and baseball caps reversed. The last I had heard, those were the colors of the Crips.

Pockets bailed out without bothering to remove the keys or lock the doors. In this neighborhood, that should have been a farewell gesture, but Pockets was not concerned. I stepped out onto the sidewalk and hitched up my pants, favoring the assembled Crips with a stare intended to be defiant.

"This way." Pockets took me two doors down the street past a variety store and a bar to a door onto a stairway. There was nothing to mark whatever lay upstairs.

We went up one flight. The entire second floor had been gutted to create a single large room. Around the perimeter of the room were gym equipment, weight sets, and punching bags. In the center was a prizefight ring built on floor level in which two middleweights in headgear were sparring. Outside the ropes stood a dour-faced man in a ratty cardigan with a stopwatch in his hand. Two other men with buckets stood at diagonally opposite corners. Around the ring folding chairs had been set up to accommodate a small audience. Pockets went to a row in the audience where a man with broad, thick shoulders overflowed his chair between two women. Pockets entered the empty row ahead of these people and put a knee on the chair seat to lean over its back to speak to the thick-shouldered man in low tones.

Above those thick shoulders was a head of gray-tinged dark hair with a thin spot on top. Below his hairline was the collar of his white shirt and then the back of a gray suit with a subdued plaid that disappeared ten feet away. He nodded in reply to Pockets, who offered him a cigarette and then lit it for him.

I turned my attention to the two women. The one on the right had broad, thick shoulders—enough like the man's to suggest a family trait. Her white hair was tinged with blue, and she wore a simple dress with a tight flower pattern that verged on dowdy. The woman on his left was another matter. She was much younger and blond, wearing a knit dress that was very short. Her arm was slipped through the bend of the man's elbow so that her breast pressed against his arm, and her legs were crossed, her knee rubbing against his. He was not pushing her away, but his attention was on the action in the ring.

The middleweights were circling each other. One of them was

a tall black man, the other a short, hairy white with tattoos on his arms. The taller fighter put his energy into movement while the hairy one stayed planted, pivoting to keep the dancer in sight. The black dancer threw an occasional punch that the hairy one took without apparent damage. Then the hairy one saw an opening and lashed out with a sudden left to the chin that staggered the black fighter into the ropes.

"That's right! Flatten the nigger!" the blue-haired woman called out.

The dour-faced man with the stopwatch rang the bell and crawled through the ropes. "Take it easy, Jake. You're only sparring."

The hairy one nodded, beating his gloves together. The dour-faced man turned his attention to the fighter against the ropes. "Baxter, you okay?"

Baxter tried to push his trainer away, but he insisted on placing a palm on either side of Baxter's face to look into his eyes. Satisfied, the trainer turned to Jake. "Watch what you're doing."

The concern for Baxter tipped me that he was supposed to be the star—opposite of the way I had doped things out. I wondered how he was going to sharpen his skills if his sparring partner held back.

The trainer climbed out of the ring and rang the bell again as a signal for them to resume. Before the bell rang, Baxter was already moving in on Jake. He threw three quick punches to Jake's head in revenge for the blow he had taken. Jake drove his fist into Baxter's stomach with a force that left him standing on his toes. It would have been a great opportunity for Jake to drop Baxter. Instead, he backed away.

"Get that nigger!" the older woman shouted. "Don't back off from the bastard!"

The thick-shouldered man laïd a restraining hand on her forearm. "Easy, Mama."

Mama?

The fight lasted less than another minute. When the bell rang again, everyone but the fighters began moving. The man turned to his mother. "Don't insult our own fighter," he said levelly. "It's bad form, and your language does us no honor."

Mama jerked her head toward him, letting me see her face in

profile. She had a prominent nose and a gleam in her eye that edged toward madness. "Don't you talk to your mother like that! Shame on you!"

His jaw muscles moved as he strained to contain himself. "I mean no disrespect. I want to protect you."

"That goddamned jigaboo can't hit, and he can't take a punch. He's useless as tits on a boar." Mama's voice was carrying across the room to the fighter and the trainer.

"That's not important. Please restrain yourself."

For an answer he got a rush of words in Italian—what sounded like Italian to me—in emotional tones that ended in a sob. Then the old woman broke into tears and buried her face in her hands.

Her son threw up his hands and stood up, disentangling himself from the blonde. "Take her away. Take her to the ladies' room."

"Why me?" the blonde asked.

"Because I told you to. Do it."

The blonde looked at the old woman as if touching her would cause pain. "She ain't right, Gus. Whenever she starts talking dirty, that's a sign she's slipping the rails again."

The man turned away from the blonde and jerked his head to Pockets. As the man walked off, Pockets stepped up to the blonde and slapped her, hard. "Get your ass in motion, honey."

She sat, stunned, for a few seconds. When Pockets raised his hand again, she got out of her chair and took hold of Mama's arm. "Let's go somewhere until we both feel better."

The blonde tugged and pled and finally got Mama to her feet. Sobbing and jabbering, Mama was led off, turning as she went to stretch her arm back to her son. He was too busy to look at her, occupied with dropping his cigarette on the floor and stepping on it. Only when the two women were gone did he finally look at me. When he was done, I knew I had been thoroughly noticed.

"I'm Cusimano," he announced.

As often as I had seen his picture in the newspaper or his face on television, this was my first sight of Gus Cusimano in the flesh. He was in his fifties now with a ruddy complexion that was part nature and part the result of time spent at his Florida bungalow. His face was dominated by a prominent nose, his mother's bequest, and his eyes were hooded by lids that wanted to droop shut. That might have been a sensitivity to light, for his glasses were tinted a light shade of brown. If the thick trunk of his body had accumulated any fat over the years, the cut of his suit minimized it.

"I'm Disbro," I said.

He nodded, realizing I was parodying him. "We must talk." He drew me aside, strolling toward a remote corner of the gym. His feet thunked louder than normal on the hardwood floor. The heels of his shoes were built to boost him up a few more centimeters that left him just under average height. Pockets followed us at a distance.

"You have been talking to Barry Sprague, who owes me a debt of honor," Cusimano began in his modulated voice, pitched just low enough to make people strain to hear him. "He described to you a scheme he devised to make sure his debt is paid. Is that a fair statement?"

I nodded. "Barry didn't waste any time reporting to you."

"He is concerned. This whole affair has the sense of a childish prank, which is understandable since Barry is in many ways a child." Cusimano gave me a weary sigh to demonstrate how reluctant he was to be involved. "It was a mistake for me to participate in this affair. I would never have become involved save for my regard for Barry." Cusimano's diction was as much an overlay of respectability as his tailored suit.

"You're going to have to run that one by me again."

"You are a man of the world," Cusimano told me. "You understand how it is with debts of honor. Barry allowed himself to build up a gambling debt, much against my advice to the contrary. He tried to recoup his losses by doubling his bets and succeeded only in landing deeper in debt. You must appreciate my position. A debt of honor must be collected. The money?" He gestured with his fingers opening in a way that suggested discarding a used Kleenex. "It means nothing to me. I put more than that in the poor box. But I dare not let a debt of honor go uncollected, or else I would betray my own honor in these matters. Yet I bear Barry no malice. I have no wish to break his kneecaps. What was I to do?"

"It must have caused you to toss and turn for nights on end."

Behind his shaded glasses, Cusimano's eyes flicked over me like beams from an X-ray machine at an airport. "Your sense of humor is sometimes inappropriate." Cusimano shrugged and went on, "While I was mulling over my dilemma, Barry came to me with a scheme. True, his uncle would no longer cover gambling debts, but he would pay to keep Barry out of serious trouble. Barry outlined his plot to blackmail Judge Amerine. My good sense should have told me to stay away, but my heart was so overwhelmed with relief I agreed to go along."

My sense of restraint kept me from vomiting on his built-up shoes. "If you understand affairs of honor, you understand my position now. Judge Amerine hired me to find out who was blackmailing him. I've done that, and I have to tell him."

Cusimano showed an expression of pain as if his last meal had not agreed with him. "This saddens me. You take such a short view of honor. Think of Judge Amerine's best interests. Do you believe for one minute he wants to see his nephew injured?" He paused to let that idea gestate. "Oh, he made threats in a rash moment a year ago, but he would be the first to repudiate them if he saw Barry in the hospital. In the depths of his soul, Judge Amerine wants to pay Barry's just debts."

"The depths of his soul and the depths of his pocketbook might not be in agreement."

"Then consider the consequences of what might happen if you expose us to Judge Amerine. He is sickly with a weak heart. God forbid that your words to him might shock him to death." Cusimano crossed himself at the thought of death. "Don't you think it is better for him to live in deception than to die for the truth?"

Before I could answer him, Baxter drew up with his trainer. The fighter was now in a robe, still dancing with his footwork. "Did you see me in there? I'm ready for Grogan now."

"Leroy's ready," the trainer agreed. He failed to put enthusiasm in his voice.

"You did well." Cusimano directed his words to the trainer. "You have no need to worry about the outcome, Max." His assurance conveyed more than it said.

Max had a dour face that hadn't smiled since bell-bottom stretch knits were the rage. He massaged his stomach as if he were rubbing a sore spot. "We won't disappoint you."

"I am never disappointed in people I trust," Cusimano told him with an emphasis that weighted his words with more meaning than the dictionary gave them.

I had been watching Baxter's face. He was light-complexioned with freckles spattered across his cheeks and nose. His lips and teeth were set in a vacuous smile, but his eyes smoldered with resentment while he jived for his white masters. Baxter and Max started off, one husky and athletic, the other old and thin. The back of the fighter's robe bore the words *Leroy "Battling" Baxter*.

Cusimano turned his attention back to me. "We were discussing honor."

"We were talking about my duty to a client."

Cusimano ignored me and turned to Pockets, who again handed him a cigarette and lit it for him. Cusimano inhaled and turned back to me. "Have you observed that I carry nothing on my person? My clothes have no pockets in them. See?" He demonstrated to my satisfaction that all his pockets were sewn shut. "A terrible inconvenience but one I find necessary. There is a story that will explain that."

"Should I take notes on it?"

"Best you listen well." Cusimano inhaled and blew out a puff of smoke before he launched into his tale. "In nineteen sixty-eight, before I was as successful as I now am, the fucking cops were trying to pin crimes on me. Once, in a crowd, a pair of detectives tried to plant a gun on me so they could charge me with carrying a concealed weapon. Because I did time for burglary in my youth, it could have been a dreadful mess. Fortunately, my attorney got it quashed, but I learned a lesson. Never again would I give the fucking cops a chance to screw me." Cusimano crossed himself again. "The detectives in question have passed on."

He paused for a few seconds of silence in their honor. "The upshot is that I carry nothing, and the son of Alphonse Pottero is now known as Georgie Pockets because he must carry everything I need." Cusimano laid a hand on Pockets's shoulder. "More than my right arm, he is my money, my keys, my pen, my matches."

Pockets laid a hand atop Cusimano's. "I am honored to serve."

Ass-kissing like that in any other organization would have been merely disgusting. Here it was sinister. I said, "That sure is an interesting story. What am I supposed to learn from it?"

"I will go to any length to avoid trouble. When trouble comes, I am no man to cross." Cusimano's shaded eyes narrowed, nearly closing, as they focused on me. "Drop the Amerine investigation."

I gave it serious consideration, mindful of his take on Amerine's health. That very point had been bothering me. At last I shook my head. "I suppose I should tell you I'll go along. That would get me out of here without those gangbangers downstairs breaking my bones. But if I told you that, I'd be lying."

Cusimano laughed, a forced sound. "I have made no such threats."

"You don't have to, and it wouldn't do you any good. Scared as I am of what you could do to me, there's something I fear even worse—giving in. I'm more scared of that even than of dying. What the hell, if I'm not my own man, I'm already dead."

For an instant, Cusimano's eyes widened, burning with a fire that approached hatred. Then they narrowed again, becoming calculating. He looked over my shoulder to Pockets. "Listen to him. What do you think of that?"

"He's got scruples." Pockets batted eyelashes that might have been painted with mascara.

"The world today is lacking scruples. Such men deserve a reward." Cusimano signaled, and Pockets pulled out a wad of bills and stuffed them in my breast pocket. "Think about what is really in Judge Amerine's best interests. Think hard, while you still have your health."

Without looking at the money, I grasped Cusimano's wrist, feeling strength and resistance, but my grip was stronger, and I managed to turn Cusimano's hand over. From the corner of my eye, I saw Pocket's hand sliding under the front of his jacket. I took the bills from my pocket and slapped them into Cusimano's palm. "I think better on an empty stomach."

Cusimano's eyes flared danger until, realizing I no longer held him, he looked down at the money lying atop his fingers. He pulled a ten out and gave it to me. "Bet that on Grogan. We will talk again when you have had time to think." He returned the rest of the money to Pockets and walked briskly away, out of reach before I could hand the ten back. Across the room, Cusimano again dropped his cigarette on the floor and, watching me, ground it out.

Something was tapping my shoulder. It was Pockets, beckoning me to the door with a jerk of his thumb. I put the ten-dollar bill away and went along. We crossed the gym and went down the stairs to the sidewalk where the Crips were keeping watch on the

Imperial. Keys in the ignition, tape deck, radio, hubcaps. It was a miracle. Giving no indication of how much he appreciated the watchfulness of the guards, Pockets got behind the wheel and drove me back to the strip mall on Broadway.

Pockets pulled up behind my Chevrolet again and shifted into park. He took my .45 out of his waistband and turned it over in his hands, studying it. "Compact, but isn't it awful light for the size of the bullet?"

"It takes some getting used to. I use my Gold Cup in competition, of course, and then I went down in size to the Commander. This Officer's Model is one more step."

"You shoot IPSC?"

"When I can."

Pockets returned my pistol butt first. "Keep it clean and oiled and loaded," he advised.

"I always do."

"Was it up to me, you wouldn't walk away. Gus is getting soft. You queer this deal, you'll find out he ain't so soft after all."

Looking into Pockets' face, I saw he wasn't simply menacing me. He really believed he could do a better job than Cusimano. I got out of his car and back into mine.

Before I called it a day, I had one more stop to make. It was a half hour before rush hour traffic would get under way, so I had an easy drive downtown to St. Clair and the party store on the corner. Mort Koblenz was behind the counter swatting at flies. I walked through the aisles once to make sure we were alone and came back to the counter with a Hershey bar, no almonds. Koblenz wore his glasses on his forehead five inches above his eyes.

"How's it going, Gil?"

"Fair." I paid for the Hershey bar and asked, "What's the skinny on the Baxter fight?"

"Baxter?" Koblenz had to reach under the counter for a schedule even to remember it. "Nothing. It's a grounder at the bottom of the card." Koblenz was a bald, stolid man who obviously found no thrill in gambling. For him it was a calculation on a preordained result.

"What do you know about Baxter?"

"Strong kid that Max Gruen found working on a loading dock

somewhere. He isn't half what he thinks he is when he faces real competition. Can't throw a punch or take one. His record is fourteen K. O.'s, two draws, no losses."

"Pretty good for a fighter who can't punch."

"Cusimano owns a piece of him." Koblenz shrugged, showing that those few words explained everything. "He won't lose."

I understood the signals well enough to figure out that Baxter's opponents had been taking dives. "And Grogan?"

"Kid Grogan, a real roughneck fighter. He's got a manager with a good business sense who will see Grogan does what he's told."

"What are the odds on Grogan winning next week?"

"I dunno. Five to one against, maybe. Doesn't matter if it's a hundred to one. He'll lay down."

I took out the ten Cusimano had given me and laid it on the counter. "On Grogan."

The hint of emotion entered Koblenz's face for the first time. "Ain't my place to judge, but I can't do that. I'm stealing your money."

"It's money I found. I'm trying to get rid of it."

"You say so, you're down." Koblenz studied me a while longer. "What do you know?"

"I was tipped to bet on Grogan by someone who should know. Someone who should favor Baxter."

Koblenz snapped the bill a few times. "It's a nothing fight to begin with. The action is light. Anyone with smarts knows what the outcome will be." *Snap! Snap!* "Betting on Baxter is only a hair better than even money."

I nudged his thought processes along. "Fixing a championship fight is tough. But who's paying attention to Baxter and Grogan? A nothing fight on the bottom of the card."

"Suppose," Koblenz speculated, "Kid Grogan never got the word. Suppose the fix is *not* on like everyone thinks."

Now I tried playing devil's advocate for the other side. "That couldn't happen. Cusimano would never stand for it."

"Don't be so sure." Koblenz tapped the bill against his chin. "Who's promoting this fight? Guy named Ortega, who used to have a partner named Pete Botkin, who pulled off some tricky deals that hurt Cusimano and then hustled himself out of town. Good thing for his health he did. But that leaves Ortega to take the heat. What would happen if Baxter should lose? Ortega goes down the tubes."

I was beginning to see sense out of what had puzzled me. "Would Cusimano sacrifice his own fighter just to get back at Ortega?"

"What's Baxter to Cusimano? He's used up. He's never going to go any further. Sure, Cusimano could want to get rid of him."

"Cusimano would have to have a real hate for Ortega to take a bath on the fight."

"He probably hates Ortega that much. But who says he has to take a bath? He'd put his money down on Baxter locally, but that doesn't mean he couldn't be laying off bets out of town on Grogan. That would show up in the action, if I checked."

"Why don't you ask around? But quietly, so you don't drive down the odds."

"I could lay off some bets on my own." Koblenz came as close as he ever would to smiling. "By God, if this works out, we could clean up betting on Grogan."

"In that case," I said, "put my money on Baxter."

8

My working day was over. Already the evacuation of the downtown had begun as the workers from the office towers headed for the nearest freeway ramp like refugees fleeing a disaster area. As I joined the viscous flow, I allowed myself a moment of self-congratulation for the job done. Before noon I had been given two problems, and now both were cleared in my mind. The identity of G. K. Hatton was firmly established as Pockets, and I was certain that tomorrow would unmask Axel McClusky as Slick Underhill. Not bad for half a day's work.

For all that, smug satisfaction left a hollow feeling. Cusimano had stated my problem better than he could have known. Did I really want to tell Judge Amerine his nephew had betrayed him once again? What did I owe my client? He was a man who had dedicated his life to the law, yet had been willing to cover up a crime to protect his nephew. I couldn't begin to imagine what that had done to his conscience. Now I could tell him the whole thing was a sham. What would that mean to him? Relief? Something worse?

Then there was Sprague. Bad enough for the kind of life he lived, he had been willing to put the old man through hell to weasel out of a bad situation. Worse, the arrogant jerk had been proved right when he calculated Amerine would cast off the meaning of his long life to save Sprague's worthless hide. I didn't know whether I hated Sprague worse for what he had done or for being right in his assessment of Amerine's character.

Last on my hate list came Underhill. Sitting on the sidelines, he had seen the blackmail scheme working. How? I wouldn't put it past Sprague to brag to Underhill's woman. Whatever, Underhill had cut himself in on the blackmail payments with the threatening note set by fax. Proof? None yet, but I expected to find all I needed tomorrow. Underhill would not be as close as he was to money without managing to slip some in his own pocket. I knew him.

Helen's gray and black Honda was already parked in the driveway when I got home. When I had jotted down my ending mileage for the day—necessary to keep the IRS at bay—I crossed the patio and entered by the back door. Helen was a few steps inside the kitchen tending steaming pots and pans on the stove.

"Feel better after your massage?" she asked.

"It loosened me up, took the tension right out of my muscles." I looked at the equipment atop the stove. "Is there going to be enough for me? Or were you figuring to eat alone tonight?"

"Your portion is the one with the rat poison in it."

"Adds flavor." I turned her around and looked into her eyes—dark, almond-shaped, not quite Oriental. Amusement was dancing behind them, no matter how hard she tried to keep it out, and her mouth was going through contortions to keep a smile off her lips. I pulled her to me and kissed her. For a second or two, she tried to remain stiff, but she soon melted against me, and her arms went around my neck.

Why I should have such an effect on her is something I never quite figured out. Helen Scagnetti is a professor of English at Cleveland State University, where I met her when I was her student in a class on writing the argumentative essay. That was a low point in my life, when I had been hit by a double wallop. I had been laid off by the police department in the same month Linda walked out on me. Maybe another man in my position would have taken to hanging out in bars, but that has always bored me, so I had invested some of my savings in getting a few more college credits. Professor

Scagnetti liked my acerbic style but found my handwriting abominable. My typing was based on the obvious proposition that if God didn't mean for us to make mistakes He wouldn't have put *x*'s on typewriters. She decided my only salvation lay in learning to use a word processor and offered to show me on hers. That led me to her house in Ohio City.

Helen, I soon learned, had been married to an orthodontist about the time she finished her master's thesis but had forsaken her teaching career to settle down as a housewife. After a few years, when they learned she would never have any children, she became restless and went back to college to get her doctorate. Her husband had been supportive until she got her degree and started teaching at Cleveland State. Her sudden independence was more than he could handle. He turned into Lord North trying to whip the colonies back into shape. Among the petty tyrannies he visited on her was his demand she quit smoking, made simply to show his authority. Helen quit for exactly one year. Three hundred and sixty-five days later, she bought a pack of cigarettes and filed for divorce.

When she got her settlement, Helen invested part of her money in this house on Bridge Avenue. The section of Cleveland's west side known as Ohio City was undergoing gentrification, snatching it back just as it was about to slide over the cliff into slum status. She had been right in thinking the house she purchased, besides providing shelter for her, would be a wise investment, but the place needed a lot of modernization. While I was there learning Wordstar, I toured the place and pointed out things that should be done. Not accidentally, I dropped strong hints that I could do most of the work. I was still unemployed and getting only occasional bounty-hunting jobs from Moe Glickman. Helen took the hint and offered to pay me for the work. That threw us into an intimate situation and—telescoping things here—we became lovers by the time I was evicted from my apartment on Parkhurst. Moving in with her had seemed so natural, it was unremarkable. We have been together for three years now.

Helen hit me with the wooden spoon in her hand. "Let go, or we'll both starve."

I let go and went into the living room to hang my coat and tie on the newel post at the foot of the stairs and my shoulder holster harness in the downstairs closet. Back in the kitchen, I took out glasses, silverware, and plates and began setting the table in the dinette.

Helen said, "Don't forget that Monday night you'll have to fend for yourself."

"I will?"

"It's pledge week at WVIZ. Monday is the night the faculty from Cleveland State will be manning the phones."

"Shouldn't that be 'personing' the phones?" I asked, just to get her goat. Helen bows to no one in her support of women's issues, but as an English major, she balks at corrupting the language with nonsexist terms. "Grammar before politics" is her motto.

"PBS expects everyone to do his or her duty," she answered.

I leaned against the counter and watched her at work on a domestic chore. When we had started living together, we had agreed to divide the cooking chores. That fell apart like a Middle East peace accord after my first few attempts. In my bachelor days, I had learned the best solution was to eat out. When I couldn't afford to eat out, I found it easier to skip meals than cook for myself, which might explain how I tend to be an ectomorph. Helen is not much more of a chef than I am, but she plunges into it with enthusiasm that keeps us from starving. She had changed out of her teaching clothes into a pair of jeans, sneakers, and a bulky sweater that hung down over her hips. She had the sleeves pushed halfway up her forearms. In that kind of get-up, her figure was concealed, a shame. She is not very tall, and slender, with all the curves in the right place. Her hair is black with red highlights, worn to her shoulders and waved so that it nearly touches the outer corners of her eyes. She's ten years older than I am but passes for much younger. It's hard for me to study her like that without congratulating myself for being so lucky.

Helen began pushing dishes at me for the table setting, and a few minutes later we were sitting down to eat. I began the meal with relish, but after the first few bites, I slowed down to pushing my food around my plate. Maybe Helen was watching me from her side of the table. She suddenly asked, "What, besides the obvious, were you up to today?"

"I ran into Slick Underhill." As soon as I uttered those words, I realized I had been eager to talk. "Remember him from a year ago when I got into the New Woodstock swindle?"

"The confidence man who signed up corporate sponsors for a phony rock concert?"

"Eco-aid, he called it. Corporations are always eager to get on the right side of ecology issues. Slick set himself up in an office as a concert impresario and claimed to have rented a farm to hold the concert. It was supposed to be big, the Woodstock of this generation. Before long, the big corporations were all lined up to invest."

"Hard-headed businessmen, as I recall," she said.

"Easiest marks in the world. Remember the guy a few years ago who got Wall Street to invest in the self-cooling beer can? That wasn't Slick, but it was his style." I pushed my food aside and lit a cigarette. "The way he went about this scheme, he got something on the golf pro at a country club where the CEO types hung out. All the golf pro did was talk up this Eco-aid concert to the CEOs. What do they know about rock stars? Not much, but they know the money is big and they want to be on ecology's side. When the CEO hears all his friends are getting in on the ground floor, the CEO puts a bug in the ear of his PR man.

"Now the PR man goes to Slick and asks how to get in on it. At this point, you'd think Slick would take the man's money, but that's too simple. A good con man plays with the mark until the mark begs him to take the money. So what Slick says to the PR man is, 'Sorry, you're too late. Your competitor has already bought in, and it wouldn't be ethical to take your money, too. We can't have two similar sponsors. Too bad, because it's such a good deal,' and he goes on to talk it up. He even pulls out a file and shows the PR man letters from all kinds of superstars committing to the Eco-aid concert. Bruce Springsteen, Van Halen, Linda Ronstadt, John Cougar Mellencamp, names like that."

"Forgeries," Helen said. She, too, had stopped eating to listen to my retelling of the story.

"Not exactly. What Slick had done was write fan letters to these people. They sent him replies on their stationery with their signature at the bottom. More likely it was a form letter from their publicity person. All it said was 'Thank you for your kind words,' but Slick had what he wanted. He cut off the letterhead down to 'Dear Mr. Underhill.' He also cut off the signature. Then he went out and found a typewriter with the same typeface his reply had used and typed up a new body that said how thrilled the star would be to appear in Eco-aid. Then he put the three parts together and ran them through a copy machine—the letterhead, the body, the signature. Out comes what looks like an authentic letter."

Helen was sitting back in her chair now, her right elbow cupped in her left hand while her right hand held her cigarette. "But all this was a waste of time if Slick wouldn't let the corporation in."

" 'Yeah, too bad,' Slick told him. The PR man is thinking of ways to get his company logo seen at the concert. And on the video, too, because there's going to be a video made. 'But as a matter of fact,' Slick says, 'my phone is going to ring any moment and your competitor will be committed.' 'You mean they aren't committed yet?' the PR man asks. 'Well, as good as,' Slick tells him. 'But not official?' 'Well, no, not yet.'

"Right then Slick's secretary buzzes him on the intercom to tell him the competitor is on the line. The PR man jumps up. 'Don't answer it!' 'Why not?' Slick asks. 'My company will buy the competitor's shares.' 'No,' Slick says, 'I'm morally committed. Besides, the money is the same no matter which one of you buys in.' So the PR man makes a snap decision: 'We'll make it worth your while.' Slick has his secretary tell the competitor he's in conference and will call them back. Then he turns to the PR man and asks, 'How much?' "

Helen was having a fit of giggles. "It's so obvious!"

"To you and me sitting here, it's obvious. To the mark sitting in the office, with only seconds to make a decision, it's convincing. Besides, that's where the con man's personality comes in. He makes it so damned believable. So you see what Slick did in this case. He gets the mark to pay him a bribe to take the mark's money. Slick gets it in small bills that day from the company slush fund. Then a few days later, the company cuts him a check and signs a contract. After Slick has worked half a dozen companies like that, he folds his office and splits. Of course, there was never any concert."

"Still, you caught him."

"I investigated long after the fact when the company lawyers called me in. It ended in a standoff because Slick had videotapes of the corporation's agent bribing him. If he had been prosecuted, Slick would have raised a stink, so the money was written off to experience. That's an important part of the con man's method. He almost never cheats an honest man. Instead, the mark is involved in something dishonest, which makes it hard for him to call in the law, even when he realizes he's been swindled—if he ever does. Slick has a point of pride about that. His marks always thank him for taking their money. Half the time they refuse to believe he did anything wrong. It must have been someone else who double-crossed them both."

Helen studied me across the table. "I think you admire him."

"Me?" I felt suddenly defensive, maybe because I feared she was right. I didn't answer directly. "He's a thief, a liar, probably a pimp, a crook, a—"

"You really do admire him, don't you?"

"Well, it's impossible to *dis*like him," I conceded.

"It's more than that. There's a kinship between you."

"We're on opposite sides of the law."

Helen waved that aside with a gesture of her cigarette. "A minor consideration. The fact is, you're a con man yourself. You're constantly talking to people, convincing them to tell you things they'd rather not. I don't mean to say you're gypping them of their money, but you're getting them to reveal secrets they've kept hidden, sometimes for generations. Criminals confess, not because you threaten them or beat them up, but because you work a con game on them, convincing them they're better off to tell you what they've done wrong."

"That's not being a confidence man."

"It isn't?" Helen shrugged and added in a tone that sounded as if she were conceding a round but really meant she had won. "Then I guess I'm wrong. You never con anyone."

Now she had me wondering. "Maybe I've conned a couple now and then."

"Daily. I remember the time you dressed yourself in a gray suit, a white shirt, and a blue tie and walked into a CPA firm giving the impression that you were an auditor. Before the day was over, you had them assigning you a secretary and running off copies until you got the papers you wanted."

"I was working for the defense lawyer in an embezzling case." Somehow that didn't seem like an answer.

Helen put her cigarette out and went back to eating. I carried my dishes into the kitchen, rinsed them off, and stuck them in the dishwasher. By that time the early news was coming on television. I carried my coffee into the living room and turned on the set, catching the local news. Helen came in when McNeil-Lehrer started and watched with me while I clicked the channel changer, jumping from one network to another. I ended my dinnertime feasting on news shows by watching *Crossfire* on CNN. After that, the sitcoms started, Helen left the room, and I shut off the television. She had gone into her den to read some journal articles and prepare for tomorrow's classes. I spent the next couple of hours with *The National Review* while she studied a few feet away. That might not strike you as a scintillating evening, but I took a lot of satisfaction from it.

I stayed up long enough to check out Ted Koppel, who was back to playing secretary of state that night, so I shut it off early and went to bed, where Helen was waiting for me. As I slid under the covers in the dark, I thought of something.

"I might need to use your car tomorrow. Maybe all that will happen is that I'll leave it in a downtown lot all day."

"All right. You drop me off at the campus."

That settled, I reached for her in the dark.

9

In the morning I followed Helen downtown until she turned her Honda into the parking lot I had chosen. I had a brief conversation with the attendant, during which money leaped from my pocket to his. I prepaid for the whole day and added enough to ensure that the Honda would be parked nearest the exit. Then I drove Helen on to the Cleveland State campus. When I had dropped her at the Rhodes Tower, I crossed town to my office, staying there only long enough to learn nothing awaited me. That left me two free hours before I had to appear in Hunting Valley. I moseyed over to the courthouse, where I sifted through the records for land deeds in connection with a job I had from a law firm. I paid to have the records photocopied and added the results to my file on the subject. With that chore out of the way, I headed for the east side.

This time the gate opened at my ring, and I drove through without any conversation. At the turnaround at the end of the driveway, I parked where I had yesterday. Another car, a blue Taurus, was there ahead of me, already parked facing out. I walked around it to the front door and rang the bell.

Elaine Knoll answered the door. Her hair was down today, and she wore heels with a no-nonsense business suit. When she caught me admiring her, she asked, "Is this outfit appropriate for paying off a blackmailer?"

"He'll probably be too busy counting the money to notice."

Elaine showed me into the study. Amerine had turned his chair away from the table so that he was facing the picture window where he could look out on the autumn foliage. He turned his head when he heard my step.

"You caught me woolgathering," Amerine confessed. He looked rested. It might also have been that turning his problem over to me had relieved his mind. "I was meditating on the change of seasons. Soon those branches, so beautiful now, will be bare. I shan't see them green again."

Much as I recognized the truth of his statement, I felt compelled to lie to him. "You'll probably outlive us all."

"No, I'm at the end of my life." Amerine relit his pipe and tapped his manuscript. "Sometimes I think the only reason I've lived as long as I have is that I'm too ornery to go before this is finished. Soon it will be, and I will no longer have a need to go on living. You young people have a quaint notion that death must be a scary prospect. The truth of the matter is that it can be a welcome relief. Still, a man at my stage feels an urgent need to set things aright. Do you believe in God?"

I had learned long ago how to fend off that question. "For someone who takes His name in vain as often as I do, I'd be foolish to try denying His existence."

Amerine chuckled. "An excellent evasion. Shortly I shall know for sure, and I'll report to you if I can. Meanwhile, in preparation for facing my Maker, I have taken steps to correct my past sins."

"Meaning what?"

"Nothing that need concern you, except that I have provided legal protection."

Before he could say more, Elaine entered the room with supplies. She laid them out on Amerine's writing table—a stack of cash, a box, brown wrapping paper, and package-sealing tape. I counted the money to verify it added up to a thousand dollars and placed it in the box. Half the size of a shoe box, it had once held a thousand blank 3×5 index cards. Elaine closed the lid, wrapped the box in brown paper, and taped it down. When the package had been made up, she wrote *Hold for Axel McClusky—Will Call* on its outside.

"There." Elaine acted as if she had finished lugging a heavy load a long distance. "I can't get rid of this soon enough. Hadn't we better leave?"

"Whenever you're ready." I had deliberately timed my arrival here without much margin for social discourse. If I had been alone with Amerine much longer, the temptation to spill all I knew to him would have been overpowering. I recalled Cusimano's words from yesterday in an effort to convince myself that suppressing the truth was in his best interest.

"Will you let us know what happens?" Amerine asked as Elaine and I started out.

"I'll call as soon as there's anything to report."

Outside, Elaine went directly to the Taurus, confirming my guess that it was her car. She set the package on the seat on the passenger side, a lone object in a car that was pristinely clean, and turned to me. "Isn't it awkward for us to take the Rapid? I could drive to the bus station in half the time."

"We'd better stick to the instructions. This might be a test to see if you will follow orders." I didn't want to tell her I half suspected there would be an attempt to snatch her package along the way. "I'll be watching you the whole time. Ignore me if you can see me at all. If you can't see me, don't worry about it. I'll still be there. After you deliver the package, come back here and wait for word from me."

Elaine took off her glasses and slipped them into a case in her purse. It was the first time I had seen her without them, and the sight only reminded me of how lovely she was.

"I only need them for reading," she noted. "Other times they're a bother."

While I went to my car, she started her Taurus and started down the drive to the road. Somewhere along the way, we tripped the electronic device that opened the gate before we reached it. I followed Elaine to Shaker Boulevard. We passed under the freeway and went on to Green Road, where the Shaker Rapid ends or begins, depending on your perspective. Elaine found a parking space on the lower level of the two-step lot while I crossed the tracks and parked on the upper level on that side, where I could look down on her from a height. Out here the Rapid tracks are in a ravine that runs down the center of the wooded strip separating the eastbound and westbound lanes of Shaker Boulevard.

Elaine walked out onto the concrete platform and took a seat on a bench in one of the two glass-walled shelters. There were other people idling around the platform—a group of three middle-aged women who appeared to be on their way to a downtown shopping spree, mature men in business suits who were high enough in the corporate structure not to have to report for duty at the crack of dawn, younger men in casual clothes in no apparent rush to get anywhere. Seeing no train in sight, Elaine lit a cigarette and sat with the package on her lap.

Ten minutes passed like that. Although there were a dozen people on the platform, they staked out their personal space, as urban dwellers will, and granted one another the same courtesy. Only the three women, chattering among themselves, were within arm's reach. No one came near Elaine at all.

When the train arrived, powered silently on its overhead electric lines, it passed the stop by a few lengths, then backed into place on the westbound tracks. There was no need for a roundhouse or complex maneuvering. The driver simply moved from the cockpit at the east end of the car to the cockpit at the west end. I locked my car, walked down a flight of stairs inside a glass tube, and crossed the tracks to mingle with the passengers. I bought a *USA Today* from the vending rack and, pitching away a half-smoked cigarette, my last for a half hour, I climbed aboard.

Rapid trains divide in half, with the seats in each compartment facing opposite ways. To avoid riding backward, most passengers entered the compartment facing west. Elaine sat in the second seat behind the driver. I took the rear seat in the forward compartment and opened my newspaper. One of the executives across from me was studying *The Wall Street Journal* as if it were holy writ. The three ladies on the shopping spree were chatting about last night's performance at The Front Row. Elaine still held the package on her lap. The train started forward.

After ten stops, we had picked up seven more passengers. At Shaker Square, three young men got on. They were students, or so I deduced from the textbooks and notebooks they carried. When they spotted Elaine, they nudged one another and settled into the seats across the aisle from her. Two of them began whispering things to the third, urging him to strike up a conversation with the chick. Elaine ignored them. I imagined she had experience fending off advances.

After Shaker Square, we passed from the affluent suburbs into some of Cleveland's less lovely parts. At Woodhill we got our first glimpse of the downtown skyline and then slowed for the switchyards beyond East 79th.

The students, who never worked up the nerve to approach Elaine, got off at East 34th for Cuyahoga Community College. The rest of us stayed on to Tower City, the end of the line. When we got off the train, we paid our fare as we passed through the turnstile. Elaine was ahead of me. I tarried to light a cigarette while I watched her ride the escalator up two flights to the Public Square level.

Tower City is what used to be the railroad terminal. Anyone who has ever passed through Grand Central Station in New York will recognize where its inspiration came from. Now it is a shopping mall built on two balcony levels above the RTA station. Elaine lingered there, checking out shop windows on her way to the doors to Public Square. When Elaine passed through them, she went directly to the bus stop. I hung back inside to see what she would do next. It was possible to walk to the bus station from here, but it was not easy. The blackmailer's instructions were not clear on the next step. Elaine looked at her watch, looked at the taxis down by Stouffer's, and then checked the buses lined up. Chester Avenue was among them. She boarded it. I held back as long as I dared before I hopped on.

Elaine was seated midway down the aisle with the package on her lap again. I settled into the rear bench, and we started off. One stop later Danny the Dip Fitzsimmons got on doing his cerebral palsy act. Trembling and staggering in a pigeon-toed walk, he lurched his way down the aisle. He stumbled and landed across a man in a business suit, and immediately mumbled, "Excuse me. I'm sorry."

"It's all right." The passenger helped steady the Dip until he regained his balance and made it to an empty seat. The Dip was good at his work. Close as I was watching him, I barely saw the motion of his hand slipping the passenger's wallet up his sleeve. As he was groping for a seat, the Dip's eyes locked on mine. We stared at each other for a long time until he was satisfied I must be on another assignment that had nothing to do with him. He fell into a seat and trembled. It was not much of a movement, but it was enough for him to slip the money and credit cards out of the wallet and stuff the wallet behind a seat cushion.

I stood up, worked my way forward to the Dip's seat, and dropped down beside him. Grasping the first two fingers of the Dip's right hand, I bent them back. I smiled at him and said softly, "If you're still on the bus after the next stop, I'll break them."

The Dip held his breath in pain, eyes watering, and nodded. The dexterity of his right hand meant more to him than every dollar on the bus. I returned to my seat. The Dip got off. Before he had gone half a block, he was walking normally.

Elaine got off beyond Chester Commons and headed for the bus station. I entered the doors behind her and turned into the cafeteria, where I could find a seat with a view of the terminal floor through the glass doors. Elaine crossed over to Baggage Claims and handed the package to the clerk behind the counter, a husky young man in his mid-thirties. She went away after that, mission completed. 12:02. I stayed in the cafeteria, watching the baggage counter over my copy of *USA Today*.

People came and went, checked bags, bought tickets. An older clerk showed up and relieved the younger man, who came to the cafeteria and ordered lunch. I had a cup of coffee in front of me, but I restrained myself from reaching for it. Whatever happened next, I figured, a full bladder would be a handicap. It can be the ruination of a private eye on a tail job.

At 12:33 a man approached the counter. I saw him only from the rear—a baseball cap, lots of black hair hanging over the collar of his flannel shirt, which hung outside his jeans. He had a brief conversation with the older clerk, who reached under the counter and found the package addressed to Axel McClusky. The man in the baseball cap took it and started back to the door onto Chester.

I was exiting the cafeteria door when the man passed me only an arm's length away. He was Hispanic, with a heavy black mustache, not very tall, probably under thirty. His cap advertised the

Browns, and his flannel shirt was open to expose a Richie Valens T-shirt against which his stomach pressed. He could have been the man with two bandoleers across his chest who rode in the third rank behind Pancho Villa.

Well, let's see where you take me, I thought as he passed out of the bus station onto Chester.

10

Subject exited bus station and turned west on Chester. Subject then proceeded west along the south side of Chester. Already I was thinking in terms of the language of a surveillance report. That's one of the few advantages of tail jobs. It's so mechanical you get a chance to let your mind wander over all sorts of weird territory.

Subject crossed me up before we had reached the end of the block by getting into a car parked illegally at the curb. I understood now why the blackmailer had insisted we take public transportation. By entering the car, he was about to leave me marooned on foot. I took a hard look at his car so I would know it—an aging Ford with lots of rust, but originally green, except for the red driver's door. STP and AHRA stickers were pasted in the right rear window. A yellow BABY ON BOARD sign dangled in the back window over a statue of a dog with a bobbing head, and Garfield was suction-cupped to the left rear window. The license plate came from Texas. I thought I would be able to spot it in traffic.

I dashed across the street to the parking lot where Helen's Honda

Accord sat. The money I had slipped the attendant that morning had bought me a parking space facing out directly in front of the exit, keys in the ignition. I jumped in, kicked the motor over, and pulled out into traffic while Subject was still hung up on a red light at the first intersection.

Helen had left the radio set on some FM station that played music. I switched to AM and punched up Rush Limbaugh pontificating on the latest environmentalist idiocy. Better. I lit a cigarette and wallowed in relief at being released from mass transit. It's not just your car, it's your freedom.

Except I wasn't free. I had to follow Subject, who was now moving west on Chester. He reached East Ninth Street and seemed surprised to discover that Chester ended there. He sat until someone behind him honked, and then he turned right. We went to Superior and made some more awkward turns until we came to the bus station again. Now we turned left and went all the way to St. Clair. We turned right and went east across the Innerbelt. South again. West on Chester. Hello bus station.

Subject was being very clever in trying to throw off pursuit, but he was missing opportunities to ditch me. He drove slowly in obedience to every traffic law on the books. When he approached a traffic light about to change to red, he slowed to a stop for it instead of speeding up to leave his pursuer hung up. He stayed in one lane even when he should have changed lanes, electing to circle the block rather than switch for a left turn. By the time we passed the bus station again, I changed my mind about how clever he was. He was lost.

Tailing a subject who knows where he's going is difficult enough. Tailing a subject who is lost is not only frustrating but also fruitless. Now there were two of us aimlessly wandering the city streets. I tried to hang back and leave a screen of cars between us, but Subject kept turning down side streets where we would be the only two cars on the block. I was afraid he would flag me down to ask directions. Which might not have been a bad development at that. At least I would have known where he was headed.

As it turned out, after twenty minutes of groping around the business district, he took Superior east across the Innerbelt again and found a service station where he stopped to consult with an attendant. While I squatted by my tires to check the air pressure,

I saw the attendant point south and bend his wrist to indicate a right turn. When Subject pulled out of the station, he was headed south. I followed.

Subject found Carnegie Avenue right where the city fathers had put it. He turned west and followed Carnegie with renewed confidence. We entered downtown again, passed the open area where buildings have been razed for the Gateway Stadium project, and crossed the bridge over the Cuyahoga. Now Subject drove as if he were on familiar ground. That figured. The Hispanic community lies out this way.

In the West Fifties, Subject turned up a side street to the intersection with Franklin, where a cantina occupied the ground floor of the frame corner building. Above the cantina were flats. Subject pulled into the alley behind the cantina, where he entered a reserved parking space. I passed the alley and pulled over to the curb ahead of a pickup truck and adjusted Helen's side-view mirror to focus on the mouth of the alley. Subject emerged from the alley above the legend that told me objects in the mirror were closer than they appear. He had the package in his hand.

I got out of the Honda and concealed myself behind the pickup to follow Subject. To my surprise, he did not head for the cantina but for a door at the rear of the building at the head of a stoop on the side street. I hurried after him as Subject entered the door.

It opened onto a stairwell that led to the flats above the cantina. When I entered the door, I could hear Subject's feet on the stairs ahead of me. I climbed the stairs until my eyes were level with the floor of the upper hallway. Subject was standing in front of one of the apartment doors fishing a key out of his pocket.

Things had gone far enough. I drew my .45 from its shoulder holster, stole quietly down the hall behind him, and shoved the muzzle into Subject's back. "Hold it right there."

Subject stiffened visibly. *"Madre de dios!"* He jabbered some more that would have been too fast for me even if I knew Spanish better. It ended with ". . . *no dinero*."

"Never mind that," I said in a hoarse whisper. "Open the door, and we'll see who's inside."

Subject turned the knob, and I gave him a hard shove. He hit the door, knocking it open as he went sprawling. I stayed by the door, training my pistol on what I was sure would be confederates inside.

The noise upset the baby in the playpen, who began crying. The cries of the baby brought a woman running from the kitchen. She stopped when she saw the man on the floor and clapped both palms against her cheeks. Another door opened as a boy of five came running, followed by a girl a couple of years younger, still wearing diapers. They all stared at Subject, then raised their eyes to me, menacing them with a gun.

Maybe there have been times when I have felt more foolish than I did at that moment, but they escape me. I had barged in expecting a den of thieves only to face a domestic scene suddenly disrupted by my entry. The smell of spicy cooking came from the kitchen. I could not explain why that bit seemed so poignant to me.

The woman rushed to Subject and dropped on her knees beside him. "Hector! Hector!"

Subject—Hector—pushed himself to his knees. "All right, Rosalita. I'm all right."

Rosalita looked up at me while the baby wailed. She was a woman not far out of her teens whose life of drudgery had not yet sapped all her dark good looks. "What is the meaning of all this?" she demanded.

"I'm not sure," I admitted. I shut the door behind me, letting my gun hand sag, and picked up the package Hector had dropped. "It all has to do with this."

The baby continued to wail. Rosalita got up from the floor and lifted it out of its playpen, holding it against her shoulder, patting its back, making cooing noises. Its cries subsided. The older children pressed against her from the sides and grasped handfuls of her dress while they looked at me with big black eyes that told me that for only fifty cents a day I could support them. Meanwhile, Hector stood up, brushing off his shabby clothes with great dignity.

"You have no right to break into my home like this, frightening my whole family."

"You're right." I holstered my pistol and looked around the flat. The furniture was old and worn, but the place was kept clean as a barracks awaiting inspection. A crucifix hung on the wall flanked by portraits of Jack and Bobby Kennedy done on carpet material. I set the package on the dining room table.

"Who are you?" Hector asked.

"A detective." I gave him my name and one of my cards.

He studied it carefully, trying to translate. He said in a hushed tone that feared speaking the word would call forth a demon. "Immigration?"

"No. I'm investigating a crime. I don't round up people to throw them out of the country. What's your name?"

The worst possible outcome having been avoided, he relented enough to give me an answer. "Pavia."

"Not Axel McClusky? Then why do you have his mail?"

Rosalita gasped. "Oh, Hector, I told you—"

"Hush!" Hector Pavia turned to his wife and said in a softer tone, "The children do not need to see this."

Carrying the baby, herding the boy and girl ahead of her, Rosalita took them into the room from which they had come and shut the door. When she was gone, Pavia faced me, arms at his side with his fingers curled into fists. His Browns cap had come off in his fall.

"Do you smoke?" I asked.

The question was so far from anything Pavia had expected, it took him aback. "When I can afford it."

I held out my pack of Camels. Pavia stared at it dumbly for a moment, then plucked one out.

"Light up and relax," I invited. "We've both been made fools of. We might as well enjoy it."

Pavia set a cracked saucer on the table for an ashtray. I lit his cigarette and one for myself, and we settled down across from each other to talk. "How did you come to be picking up a package for Axel McClusky?"

"I was hired to do it."

"Hired how?"

He eyed me from across the chasm of a cultural gap. "You know about street-corner hiring halls?"

"I've heard about them."

He explained it to me anyway. "When you have no green card, you can't get a regular job. You go stand on a certain corner and wait for someone to come by. Rich men in big cars. They need some labor for a day or two or three. Maybe to carry heavy stuff at a project. Maybe to work in their yards or serve at a party. That kind of thing."

"Where were you waiting?"

He was still hesitant about giving anything away. "Over on Lorain. Yesterday a man came up to the crowd and asked who owned a car. I did, so he took me down the street and bought breakfast. While I was eating, he made the offer. A hundred dollars! A fortune!"

I smelled the meal cooking in the kitchen and wondered if that was a treat from the hundred dollars. "That was for picking up the package? Nothing else?"

"Nothing else. I swear. All I had to do was go to the counter in the bus station at twelve thirty today and pick up the package being held for Axel McClusky. He made me repeat the name until I knew it."

"What did this man look like?"

"A gringo." Pavia was stumped for a clearer description.

"Wavy light hair? A straight nose? A good suit?" I was still looking for a way to pin this on Slick Underhill.

"Nothing like that. He wore no suit, only a sweater. Maybe thirty years old, as tall as you, heavier but not fat. His hair was light but straight. Blue eyes."

It described no one I had met so far on this case, especially not Slick. I felt my face going into a frown. "What arrangements did he make to pick up the package?"

"None."

Now I was confused. "Did he ever ask your name? Your address?"

Pavia thought it over and shook his head.

I looked at the package and saw Elaine's handwriting: *Hold for Axel McClusky—Will Call.* I tried to make sense of this. The blackmailer had sent Pavia to make the pickup. That would be a precaution against the possibility the drop was being watched. But to leave the money with Pavia with no arrangements for later meant he was not only forfeiting the thousand dollars but also another hundred he had paid for Pavia's errand. All that to test for a dry run? Somehow I couldn't imagine a person greedy enough to commit blackmail being willing to make such a sacrifice.

Suddenly there was an alarm bell clanging. I took out my pocket knife and cut the tape sealing the package. Unwrapped the brown paper. Opened the lid of the index card box.

There was nothing inside but strips of newspaper cut to the shape of dollar bills.

"The hell of it is I know the switch was made under my very eyes, but I'll be goddamned if I know how it was done."

"This is interesting." Helen took her eyes away from her driving long enough to glance at me in the passenger seat. "Sort of like trying to figure out how a magician pulls off one of his tricks."

We were driving toward Shaker Heights after I had swung by the campus to pick up Helen in her car. Now she was driving me back to the end of the Rapid line so I could pick up my Chevrolet. All I could think to say was, "It's embarrassing."

"Did you inform the client?"

"I called him. He laughed a lot when I told him."

"A least he's taking the loss of a thousand dollars well." Helen drove another two blocks while I brooded. "Let's go back to basics, step by step. Who touched the package?"

"Elaine had it all the way to the bus station. She handed it to the baggage clerk, who put it on a shelf behind the counter. The clerk handed it to Pavia."

"That's three people."

"Four. There were actually two baggage clerks. A younger man was on duty when Elaine arrived. Before Pavia came in, he went to lunch, and an older one came on duty."

"Make it four, then. Now let's go back to the very beginning. You say you counted the money and put it in the box yourself and watched Miss Knoll wrap it up. What are the chances the switch was pulled right there?"

"None."

"I'll have to take your word for that. You were there, and you saw it. Or what Miss Knoll wanted you to see."

"Elaine didn't pull any sleight of hand. There was no trick box. I would have seen that."

"Excuse me? Since when has Gil Disbro ever concentrated on a cardboard box when there was a gorgeous redhead in the room."

"For Christ's sake, she wears glasses," I snapped defensively.

"Oh, well, that makes all the difference. Still, you keep referring to Miss Knoll as Elaine." Helen glanced my way again. "You can't eliminate her as a suspect simply because you don't want her to be guilty."

"And you can't make her into one because you're jealous of her."

"Me? Jealous? Do I have cause?" She nearly clipped the rear bumper of the Pontiac ahead of us as she changed lanes.

I gritted my teeth. We were swooping along the stretch of Fairhill between the park and the reservoir. The east side of Cleveland is not an ideal spot for a motorist to engage in a dispute with another driver. "You have no reason."

"Fine." Helen accelerated through an almost-red light.

"But watch the exotic dancer."

Helen laughed then, and I laughed. "All right, my attention could have wandered, but I really was watching. It's just such an improbable thing. Aside from the physical impossibilities, there's a question of character. Elaine is like a daughter to the judge. There's a strong relationship there that would have to be broken."

"She's like a daughter, and Barry is his nephew, and Barry has his own thing going." Helen's voice had a trace of cattiness in it. "Forget that now and look at the facts. Miss Knoll carried the package in her car alone while she drove to the RTA stop. She could have made a switch there."

"There would have had to be a duplicate package in her car. I got a look inside before she drove away. It wasn't there."

"You're sure the package in Pavia's flat was the same one you saw Miss Knoll wrap?"

I reached into the back seat and picked up the box and brown wrapping paper. When Helen stopped for a light south of Kaiser Hospital, I showed the paper to her. "That's Elaine's writing—what I saw her write."

"No handwriting expert has analyzed it."

"Come on. You're stretching. Let's see what else turns up."

"You rode the train with her and had the package in sight at all times?"

"Correct."

"You walked through Tower City, still with her in sight. You boarded a bus. Danny the Dip got on. Talk about sleight of hand! What possibilities must be there!"

"He passed her on his way to his seat. He sure didn't snatch the package out of her hand. When he passed her, his hand was already occupied with the wallet he'd lifted." I reviewed that episode and shook my head. "I don't see it at all."

We had turned onto Shaker Boulevard now, headed for Shaker Square. "Now we're at the bus station. She hands the package over to the young clerk. That removes Miss Knoll from the picture. The young clerk puts it on a shelf. The older clerk comes in and relieves him. The young clerk goes to lunch. Empty-handed?"

"Empty-handed."

"All this time the package is sitting on a shelf, but you're not seeing it. Anyone who had access to the back door of the bus station could have come into the baggage room and snatched it."

"Elaine's handwriting on the package," I reminded her. "We can't get around that."

Helen drove on, turning it over in her mind. I felt some thought nibbling at me and studied the wrapping paper again. *Hold for Axel McClusky—Will Call.* I looked at the box—which had held one thousand lined 3 × 5 index cards. The thought was gone.

As Helen drove through Shaker Square past the Van Aken cutoff, she moved on to the next step. "Pavia comes and picks the package up. You follow him all the way to his flat. Nothing happened on the way?"

"He stopped to ask directions from the gas station attendant. It's conceivable something happened there."

"Aha! We're on to something. What do you think of that?"

"I don't like it. If that should be true, then Pavia would have to be part of the conspiracy." I shook my head. "Whatever happened, he was no more than a dupe." We were now driving down the boulevard with the Rapid tracks down its middle, the same route I had ridden that morning.

"Then we had better start back with Miss Knoll. That means the package. If I take your word that her handwriting on it in Hunting Valley was the same as her handwriting on Franklin Street, then somewhere between those two places it was opened, and the money was exchanged for the cut-up newspapers, and then it was sealed again. Could Miss Knoll have done that while you were watching her? Could Pavia? So what does that leave? The baggage room."

I relived what had occurred in the bus station. Elaine handing the package to the young clerk. The young clerk, out of sight for only seconds, putting it away on a shelf. The older clerk, stoop-shouldered, coming in. The young clerk, tall and husky with light hair, going to lunch. Pavia coming in, speaking to the old clerk. The old clerk going in the back room, emerging seconds later with the package. Pavia getting the package.

Hold for Axel McClusky—Will Call. The words the same in Elaine's handwriting. One thousand lined 3 × 5 index cards, the box the same. I studied the articles in my hand and conjured up a vision of what I had seen in Amerine's study. That was it!

As Helen turned into the parking lot at Green Road, I looked at the digital face of the dashboard clock. "There's time to get to the courthouse before it closes."

"Why do you want to go there?"

"So I can solve this mystery," I said with a smile.

Elaine Knoll came to work Friday morning while an overnight hoarfrost was still on the grass and a chill still in the air. When she turned her Taurus off Chagrin River Road into Amerine's driveway, she nearly clipped my Caprice parked off to the side. I got out of my car and walked up to the side of hers as she rolled her window down.

"Good to see you," she said like a hostess greeting guests. "Sorry about coming so close to your car. I didn't expect it to be there. Or you, for that matter."

"I wanted to see the judge as early as possible. When I got here, I wasn't sure if I should ring the bell this early." She was wearing her hair down again this morning and no glasses.

"He should be up by this time. Let's go in." Elaine brought out a gizmo that looked like a channel changer, pointed it at the gate, and pressed a button. The gate swung open.

I got back in my car and followed her through. We drove up the driveway in tandem and arrived at Amerine's house. Elaine put her car in the garage while I parked on the turnaround and followed her through the garage door. We entered the kitchen, a part of the house I had never seen before, and passed into the front hallway so Elaine could hang up her coat.

"It looks like the judge is still in bed." She was looking at his elevator chair at the top of the stairs. "It's just as well. After the strain of these last few days, it's good for him to sleep late."

"Don't disturb him on my account."

"I was going to fix breakfast first and put the coffee on. Care to join me?"

"I've had breakfast, but I'll take a cup of coffee."

We returned to the kitchen. It was designed to resemble a Colonial hearth with fry pans and skillets hanging from overhead hooks around a central work space, but everything here was modern, including a microwave built into the brick wall. I wondered if Elaine had had a hand in designing it.

She put on an apron and set to work preparing the meal. I laid the box and wrapping paper, which I had carried in from my car, on the counter out of the way to free my hands for starting the automatic coffeemaker, the outer limits of my culinary skills.

Elaine looked at the remains of yesterday's package. "That certainly is a mystery how the money disappeared."

"I thought so at first, too. But then when I figured it out last night, it was really simple."

"You figured it out?" Elaine opened the refrigerator and removed two eggs. She turned back to me, letting the refrigerator door close behind her. She was smiling now without a lot of feeling in it. "That's—wonderful."

"If you really think so, can I use you for a reference?"

"How did you do it? Your sheer mental powers of deduction?"

"My colleague, Hercule Poirot, handles that end. I found the answer in the courthouse."

Elaine, holding the eggs in her hand, stared incredulously at me. "The courthouse?"

"Amazing place. They collect all kinds of records on people—birth, death, marriage, divorce. It's all there for the asking. For instance, you mentioned your ex-husband's name was Robert. I looked up your divorce proceedings and found out his full name was Robert Orton."

"Wouldn't it have been simpler to ask me?" she wondered acidly.

"You told me he deserted you. That's true, as far as it went. He didn't exactly desert you voluntarily. He was sent to Lucasville for armed robbery."

A spasm of Elaine's hand crushed the egg she was holding, oozing yolk out between her fingers. "Oh, shit!" She threw the egg into the sink and ran water to wash her hand, then to send the eggshell down the disposal. When she turned around, wiping her hands on a paper towel, she was composed. "My marriage was a foolish, youthful mistake. I don't like to think about it, much less explain that Robert turned into a criminal. Calling it desertion saves complicated explanations."

"Sure, I can understand that." I sat down the wrong way in a kitchen chair and folded my forearms atop the back. "When I saw Robert Orton had been sent to prison, I checked a little further. He served three years and was paroled in February."

"Oh?"

I waited a few seconds to see if she would add more. When she didn't, I went on, "I hunted up Robert's parole officer to get some more information. Robert is six feet two, weighs two-ten, light brown hair and blue eyes. I saw his mug shot. I also looked up his address, an apartment on Lancashire. Know who else lives at the same address, same apartment? You do."

Elaine drew a deep breath, holding in anger as much as preparing for a statement. "When Robert first got out of prison, he needed a place to stay, to get out of the cold and snow. He was there less than a month before he could afford a rooming house. He appealed to me when he got out of prison, and I couldn't refuse him. But that's all it was. He slept on the couch."

"I wasn't asking," I said. "Another thing the parole officer told me was about Robert's job. He's working for the bus company. I told you I saw his mug shot. What do you know? He was the clerk you handed the package to yesterday. And you didn't even show a flicker of recognition."

Elaine leaned back against the sink, clutching it with both hands as if it were the only support she had. "I was so shocked I didn't know what to do. It wasn't the time or place to confront him."

I ignored her answer. "One more thing. I borrowed the mug shot from the parole officer and took it to Hector Pavia. He identified Robert as the man who gave him a hundred dollars to pick up the package."

The coffeemaker had done its job. I found a shelf where the coffee mugs were kept, took out two, and poured coffee into both. I offered one to Elaine, but she only stared at it as if she expected the coffee to leap out of the cup and splash her. I shrugged, set her cup on the drainboard, carried mine to the table, and sipped some. "Hits the spot."

Elaine still said nothing. Her fingers, gripping the counter, were white.

I picked up the brown wrapping paper and showed it to her so she could read the lettering on it. "Do you need your glasses to see that?"

" 'Hold for Axel McClusky—Will Call,' " she answered as if any easy question gave her confidence.

"You don't deny writing it?"

"Deny it? You saw me do it."

"Did I?" I showed her the index card box and pointed to the lettering on it. "Can you see that?"

"One thousand lined three-by-five index cards. So?"

"This box held *lined* cards," I agreed. "This is the box I opened in Hector Pavia's flat, the dummy box with cut-up newspapers. But the box that you made up here, the one with the money in it, was a box that once held ***blank*** cards. That means there were two entirely different packages, a genuine one and a dummy one, and your writing was on them both. That means you made up both packages, which were supposed to be identical. But you slipped up on that one point about the kind of index cards the boxes had contained. People are always making mistakes like that when they take up a life of crime."

"A life of crime? What are you accusing me of?" Her indignation rang false, but her voice rose high enough I feared it might wake Amerine.

"You know damned well what it is," I said softly to bring the conversation to a quieter level. "Do I have to go through the whole thing?"

She said nothing, but under the unrelenting gaze of my eyes, her chin trembled.

"It went something like this," I told her. "For six months you've been watching Judge Amerine pay blackmail for a body supposed to be buried out there in the woods. You decided if he paid once, he'd pay a second time. You made up the latest blackmail note with stamp pad letters and had your ex-husband fax it here. You needed Robert's help because his job at the bus station made a perfect cover for delivering the blackmail payment."

"You're wrong. It wasn't the way you make it sound." She reached out a hand to me, then dropped it. "Yes, I knew about those other payments. I was worried sick because I was in the middle of something I couldn't handle. I had to talk to someone. I turned to Robert because he'd been to prison, because he might know what to do. I was desperate for any help, don't you see? But Robert was the wrong person. He decided that if the judge paid once, he'd pay a second time. Robert made me help him by threatening to expose Judge Amerine. God, that's the truth."

I thought it over. "Say I believe you. That doesn't change much of what happened. Instead of paying the second demand, Amerine sent for me. You had to start improvising fast. Robert went out and hired Pavia to make the pickup—at twelve-thirty after Robert had gone to lunch so Pavia wouldn't recognize him as the man who hired him. You made up another package with newspaper clippings inside, and Robert took that one to work with him. He put it on the shelf to be picked up. When you arrived with the genuine package, Robert hid it somewhere, maybe in his own locker. When Pavia showed up, the relief clerk handed him the package from the shelf, the dummy package. All this to confuse me."

"I didn't want it to happen that way." Tears rolled down from the corners of her eyes. "Oh, God!" She sagged and started to fall.

I got up and grasped her shoulders before she could hit the floor. Her head hit my shoulder even as her fingers dug into my sleeve. I slid my arms around her and pulled her to me, holding her that way while she shook with sobs. It went on like that for a long time without me voicing objections. I had nothing more important to do that day than stand there and hold her. By slow degrees she brought herself under control.

"I betrayed him," she said to my shoulder. "He's been so kind to me. I didn't want to do it. Robert made me. You've got to understand."

"Amerine will understand."

She took her head off my shoulder and looked at me from inches away, her green eyes wide with fright. "Tell him? No!"

"It's the only way."

She was pushing away from me, squirming to get out of my arms. "I can't do that. It will kill him."

"Not if we go about it the right way. We'll do it together."

She shook her head. "I can't. Let me go away. You can tell him after I'm gone."

"You'll stay here and tell him yourself." Her efforts to escape my grip were causing our bodies to rub together, something that would have been welcome under other circumstances. Despite everything, I felt my erection growing, and my own embarrassment made me desperate to end this. I pushed her away more violently than I intended, and she crashed against the sink.

"You bastard! You're a little boy playing Sherlock Holmes, and you have to have an audience so everyone can see how brilliant you are." At least her dismay was coming out now as anger.

"If you think I've been smart so far, wait until you hear what else I have to tell him." I grabbed a box of Kleenex and threw it at her, not wanting to get close enough for us to touch. "Dry your eyes, or whatever you have to do. Then go wake him."

She blew into a tissue and dabbed at her eyes, sniffling to hide the signs of her tears. Maybe I took some pity on her then. More gently I said, "You'll be glad you did it this way."

"You're a son of a bitch!" But she went off.

I stayed alone in the kitchen a few minutes so Elaine would have time to prepare herself. I poured another cup of coffee and carried it into Amerine's study, where I stood looking out the window into the woods. I wondered where the exact spot was that Barry and his cohorts had faked the burial. Somewhere downstairs Elaine sniffled and blew her nose. A short time later I heard her climbing the staircase.

I wandered over to Amerine's writing table and touched the manuscript that meant so much to him. Beside it was an ashtray that held one of Amerine's pipes and a used pipe cleaner. The bowl had been filled with tobacco but never lit. I was still staring at those objects, trying to make sense of them, when I heard Elaine's voice.

"Gil! Come quick!"

I went up the staircase in three strides and found her standing in the upstairs hall, which was not a long corridor but simply an area onto which four doors faced. Elaine was staring at the only open one, biting her knuckles. Her face had turned white. "I knocked. He didn't answer. I opened the door. He—he—he—" She was trying to say something about Amerine.

"Stay here." I entered the bedroom, where the light was dim due to the closed curtains. At first I thought Amerine was sitting in a chair, but it turned out to be his robe laid out with slippers on the floor below. Amerine was still in bed on his back in pajamas, his fingers bunching the top of the counterpane. His mouth was open, lips blue, his eyes neither open nor closed. I reached out to touch the carotid artery in his neck but stopped trying to find it when I felt how cold the flesh was. I tried moving Amerine's fingers, but they were rigid in their grip. He had been dead for several hours, long before I had entered the house with Elaine.

I remembered then that I had left her standing in the hall. When I went back to her, she was lying on the carpet. She had fainted, sliding down the wall to a sitting position and then falling on her side. The repeated shocks of that morning had been too much for her. I opened doors until I found a guest bedroom. I picked Elaine up, carried her in there, and laid her on the bed, making sure her clothing was loose. Instead of trying to bring her around, I covered her with a blanket and went downstairs.

Amerine's physician, Dr. Mount, lived next door through the woods. Briefly I wondered if it would be simpler to dash over there instead of wasting time looking for his number. The telephone on Elaine's desk solved that problem. It had been programmed for automatic dialing with Mount's name listed. I lifted the receiver and punched his button.

He answered on the second ring. I needed only a few words to explain the situation. Mount hung up as soon as I had them out.

I opened the front door and stepped out onto the stoop to await Mount's arrival. There I lit a cigarette and inhaled deeply. "Shit!" a voice said. It was mine.

Mount crashed through the woods a few minutes later. He wore a white shirt and trousers, a topcoat thrown over that, and carried his medical bag. The slippers he wore over his bare feet had been soaked by dew. I directed him to Amerine's bedroom and stood in the hall while Mount checked to make the obvious official. Elaine appeared in the doorway to the guest room, bracing herself against the frame. "What happened?"

"You fainted. Go back to bed." I took her arm and forced her to lie down again.

By the time I got back to the hall, Mount had emerged from Amerine's bedroom. He was holding himself up by clutching his professionalism the way Elaine had clutched the door frame. "Coronary occlusion," he announced, "sometime during the night." He stood thinking that over a moment. "Well, it wasn't unexpected. You found the body?"

"Elaine did when she went to wake him."

Mount looked around. "Where is she?"

I indicated the guest room.

Mount examined his living patient and came out of that room in short order. "She should rest for a half hour. Then she will have much to do. Knowing what Barry is like, I imagine she will have to arrange the funeral. At least I can help her by calling the funeral home."

"You're going to release the body?" I asked.

"Certainly. I'll fill out the death certificate and call for a hearse. What else?"

"How about an autopsy?"

Mount, unused to having his authority questioned, looked at me in disgust. "This is not the inner city where people are shot down on street corners in broad daylight. Out here people die in their beds at the end of long and productive lives. Lowell has been under my care for many years. He has had two previous heart attacks and has been in failing health. Last night the end simply came, to no one's surprise. It could have happened last week or a month from now. Do you have any information to contradict that diagnosis?"

My mouth open to speak, I changed my mind. "No."

"Then I will proceed," Mount said huffily. "Lowell was not only my patient but my friend, and I'll be damned if I let some butcher hack him up. Now if you'll excuse me, Miss Knoll and I have a great deal to do."

I realized I had been dismissed. I realized also, whatever else had happened today, the Amerine investigation had slammed to a halt.

12

NOTED JURIST
DIES AT 76

That headline was below the fold when I opened the paper Saturday morning, in a box with only sketchy details of Amerine's death at home after a long illness. Continued on Page 8. I carried the paper inside and sat down at the kitchen table with my first coffee and first cigarette of the day to find my way to the inside story.

Lowell Amerine had been sidelined from the bench three years ago after a lifetime in the law. Born of a wealthy family, he nevertheless pursued a career with single-minded devotion. He had been a Harvard graduate who went on the Yale Law School, had returned to Cleveland to practice, and had eventually been persuaded to run for a judgeship. The rest of his life had been spent on the bench, where he distinguished himself for his expertise in tax law. The funeral was set for Monday at the Episcopal church in Pepper Pike with burial at Fairlawn Cemetery. The photo of Amerine, a formal pose in his robes, was at least ten years old.

Reading obituaries was about as productive as my Saturday got. The nature of my calling usually requires weekend work, while leaving me idle on some weekdays. For once, that was not true, and I had two days off to spend with Helen, highly satisfactory to us but hardly significant on the broad scope of this planet's affairs.

On Sunday morning we slept late and went out to take care of Helen's weekly necessity, buying a copy of *The New York Times*. That's a Sunday paper that uses enough wood pulp to deforest a county and weighs as much as a bowling ball and still doesn't have any comics. She has to see it for a few key sections—the book reviews, the news of the week, the arts, and the magazine. Because it was a Sunday when the Browns were playing a home game at the stadium, we avoided downtown traffic to head for Max's Deli in Rocky River. Helen lugged the *Times* inside while I bought a copy of the *Plain Dealer*. She settled for the fruit bar while I gorged myself on the breakfast buffet. Afterward, we sat drinking coffee and reading while a solo guitarist on a podium in the front window strummed soft chords.

In the Perspective section was an article by a local law professor recalling the career of Lowell Amerine. The professor was full of praise for Amerine's oft-stated belief that the law should be the repository of society's moral values. Because Amerine's family had money, he had never approached the law as a money-making proposition. Because he was a bachelor, Amerine had adopted the courts and his colleagues as his family. Later in life, when his sister was killed, he took it upon himself to raise her son. Amerine's decisions were always sound from a scholarly standpoint, but he also administered the law with humor and a regard for humanity. Not only the law but the world at large was less for his passing, better for his having been here.

Later that afternoon, I booted up Helen's word processor and typed out a final report on the Amerine investigation. I had been asked to look into two problems, and within forty-eight hours I had solved both. It looked good on my box score, but it left me feeling empty. I had proved that the two people who meant most to Amerine had both betrayed him. Maybe it was best that he hadn't lived to find that out.

Monday morning the line of people in Glickman's office, waiting to bail their relatives out of jail, stretched out into the hall. I squeezed past them, waved to Gladys and Rolf, and entered my office. I had brought the Amerine report with me, but now I had a new problem. To whom would I submit it? I was still mulling that one over when Gladys buzzed to tell me the police department was calling.

"About time you got in your office." The accent could have convinced me Ricardo Montalban was on the phone, so I knew it was Detective Manuel Agosta.

"Oh, hell. I thought it was someone important."

"Shitcan the jokes. Twenty minutes from now you will be in my office. You don't haul ass over here, your license is confetti." Agosta hung up.

It struck me that it would be a shrewd career move to haul my ass to police headquarters. I left my office and crossed the street to the Justice Center, where I rode three escalators up to the door into the police tower. They were remodeling again in the Homicide office on the sixth floor—another example of the principle that when volume increases, the business must expand. A detective was trying to fill out an evidence log on a sawhorse while a drill whined beside him. I entered the squad room.

Agosta's desk was along the wall by the windows looking down onto Ontario Street under a sign saying NO SMOKING BY ORDER OF THE FIRE DEPARTMENT. The "No" was covered by masking tape, and Agosta was practicing blowing smoke rings at it.

"I thought you quit," I said.

"I did. Then I rose above quitting." He put his cigarette out and looked at his watch. "Sixteen minutes."

"The elevator was slow."

Agosta's features belonged to an Aztec prince. His shirt, invariably white, was so starched and pressed bullets should have ricocheted off it. With the solid-color clip-on tie attached to its collar, the shirt gave the impression of being part of a uniform. He had dark hair arranged in blow-dried waves and dark eyes that were regarding me without special fondness. He pointed a blunt finger at me. "You're getting a break because of your friendship with me. Without that, you'd be sitting upstairs in a cell. Never forget that."

"I appreciate that, Manny. I really do. Now what the hell am I supposed to have done?"

"Let's find out." He stood up from his desk, not much taller standing than when he had been sitting. Agosta had a wedge-shaped torso that necked down to a waistline that hadn't expanded since he was seventeen. His belt supported a badge in front, a snub-nose on his right side, a pair of handcuffs, and cartridge dumps.

He led the way out of the squad room into a hall going down to the Homicide commander's office. Short of that sanctuary was the office for the sergeants, where Agosta turned in. Only one of the three desks inside was occupied, though not by a Homicide sergeant. I would have recognized him if that's what he had been. The guy sitting with his chair backed against a mustard-colored file cabinet didn't look like a cop of any kind. He was a young man in a gray pinstriped suit with a vest and a watch chain across it. He was toying with a Phi Beta Kappa key on the chain, balancing an attaché case on his lap. He looked as if he would be more at ease in a frat house on an Ivy League campus than in a police station.

"Sit!" Agosta pointed me to a chair facing a sergeant's desk. When he had shut the hall door, muffling the sound of the carpenter's drill, he went around behind the desk to sit facing me. Mr. Ivy League was behind me to my right.

"If at any time you feel the need to relieve your conscience," Agosta invited, "just let it flow. Tell us all about your crimes."

"I really can't recall killing anyone lately," I said. "It's not something I usually develop amnesia over."

"Who said anything about a killing?"

"Come on, Manny. This is Homicide. Whatever you've got the bug up your ass about, it's not writing bad checks."

"So you think there's been a murder?"

"In a city this size after a weekend? If there hadn't been a murder somewhere, it would be a news flash." I dug my Camels out of my pocket. "Are we going to waltz around like this, or do you want to tell me what it's all about."

Agosta looked over my shoulder to the man behind me. "I told you he was too wise to admit anything."

"So it would seem," the man behind me said.

Agosta ran his fingertips over the fake wood grain in the plastic desktop. "This man is Leslie N. Ramford, assistant prosecutor."

"How are you?" I asked over my shoulder and turned back to Agosta. "Is he the one who's going to prosecute me for murder?"

"Forget that crap. We don't think you killed anyone. Just because you're a pain in the ass doesn't make you a killer."

In an awed voice, I said, "God, Manny, I never knew I stood so high in your estimation."

"What you did is almost as bad as murder."

I lit my cigarette. "And what was that?"

Agosta looked at Leslie N. Ramford once more. *Pop! Pop!* That was the locks on Ramford's attaché case opening. He said, "Over the weekend the prosecutor's office came into possession of a significant document."

"The Bill of Rights?" I asked. "Gettysburg Address?"

Ramford ignored me. "The prosecutor was at home Sunday afternoon when an attorney called on him. This attorney—never mind who it was—had an obligation to fulfill as executor of an estate. The deceased had directed his executor to personally deliver this document to the prosecutor following the deceased's death."

"Maybe you had better run that by me again to make sure I have all the pronouns associated with the right antecedents. Who was doing what for who?"

Ramford got up and came to stand in front of me by the corner of the desk. He could not have been more than a few years out of law school, yet he was beginning to have the look of a middle-aged man. He wore glasses with clear plastic rims at least a generation out of date. His short, thin physique was beginning to stoop. His clipped hair was already beginning to thin out. "Lowell Amerine said, 'Deliver this to the prosecutor after I die.'" He held out a sheet of paper filled with a spidery scrawl I recognized.

I took it and read.

Hunting Valley, Ohio
Thurs., Oct. 14

Prosecuting Attorney
Cuyahoga County, Ohio

Gentlemen:

This letter will reach your office only when I am dead. Consider it my attempt to square accounts from the grave. On February 10 of this year I participated in a dreadful crime.

My nephew, Barry Sprague, had an affair with a woman named Megan Latimer. They ingested narcotics together on the night in question, and as a result, Megan Latimer had a violent reaction and died.

My nephew prevailed upon me in the middle of the night to allow him to bury her body on my property. I made a hasty decision, in full knowledge of all legal ramifications, to allow that. I consciously chose my only living relative over the law, a decision I neither regret nor repent.

Since that night, circumstances have altered my perception of things. Now in failing health, I find I cannot face my end without an attempt to set matters right. While this course may put a burden on my nephew, I simply must make some provision to correct my past crimes. I find I cannot endure the thought of joining Miss Latimer in the cold ground without taking steps to see that she has a chance to find a well-marked grave. If I am to have an elaborate tombstone, why not she as well?

I am enclosing a diagram that should lead you to that unfortunate girl's final resting place. All this information has been communicated to an excellent investigator named Gilbert Disbro, who is at this writing investigating all circumstances emanating from the affair. Although he has been sworn to secrecy, I hereby release him from all claims to confidentiality so that he may cooperate with the authorities in seeing Miss Latimer's remains are treated with respect.

Lowell Amerine

When I finished reading the letter, I laid it on the desk. Agosta was leaning back in the swivel chair, rocking. Ramford was holding his glasses up to the light, checking for smears. All of us kept quiet until Ramford put his glasses back on his face and asked, "What do you have to say now?"

"Amerine's style was a trifle stilted, but I sort of like it."

Ramford didn't like that answer. He tapped the letter sternly and showed me the face of a Puritan about to pass judgment on a witch. "This document accuses you of a crime. Now, you can deny it if you wish. Failing that is a tacit admission of guilt. Do I need to explain your Miranda rights?"

Agosta said helpfully, "It looks like you have concealed knowledge of a felony."

"Murder, no less," Ramford added.

I put my cigarette out, taking time to mash it properly. "There's another way of looking at it. I have an obligation to my client not to tell the world what I find out. I could lose my license for blabbing."

"Are you invoking a claim to privileged communication for a private investigator?" Ramford shook his head. "That is highly dubious. The law would support that only in the event that you were working for an attorney. In that case you would be an extension of his person and thus fall under the umbrella of his privileged communications."

"Amerine," I pointed out, "was a lawyer."

Ramford opened his mouth, then closed it. He raised a finger to shake at me, then dropped his hand. He took off his glasses again and pinched the bridge of his nose.

"Hey, that's a good point," Agosta said, innocently. "Is there anything to it?"

"I would have to research the law," Ramford admitted feebly. He sat down on the corner of the desk and placed his hands on his knees, staring down at the floor.

We were silent for a few seconds while we all considered the problem I had presented them. If Ramford had been a more experienced lawyer, he might have disputed me. For the moment he was stunned into silence, preferring caution to reckless statements.

"Oh, hell," I said in disgust. "It doesn't matter. There's no body."

"No body?"

"There never was." I told them about Sprague's scheme to bilk his uncle to cover a gambling debt. I told them about G. K. Hatton's office, about Cusimano's involvement, and about all else I knew. I decided not to mention the second blackmail attempt.

"Without any doubt," Agosta said at the end, "this is the biggest carload of bullshit I ever heard in my life."

"The truth sometimes sounds like that," I conceded. "Anyway, I'm not the one who dreamed this up. It's the people involved who are playing with forty-eight cards in their deck."

"Did you relay this information to Judge Amerine?" Ramford asked.

"I would have, except he died too soon."

"And you can verify that Megan Latimer is alive?"

"She was breathing, belching, and farting on Wednesday afternoon when I talked to her."

"Well, we can hardly take your unsupported word for that."

"I never thought you would. Go see her for yourself and find out she's still alive."

"We will do exactly that." Ramford looked at Agosta. "We must clear this up."

"So where do we find her?" Agosta asked.

"She runs a reducing salon on Broadway called Inches Off, and she lives with Slick Underhill."

"Now isn't that interesting?" He picked up the phone to dial Records and ask for the last known address on Underhill, Felix, with a record of bunco games.

I stood up. "I've already told all I know. I'll be running along."

"Not so fast," Ramford snapped. "You're not getting out of our sight until this story is verified."

I shrugged and sat down.

"Right. Thanks." Agosta hung up the phone and looked at his notes on a pad. "No answer at Inches Off. Slick Underhill is living on Edgewater Drive in Lakewood.

"We'll go there and confront him and his wife," Ramford decided. "You," he added "will come with us."

13

Agosta checked an unmarked beige Celebrity out of the garage under police headquarters, and we wooshed up the ramp onto St. Clair. Ramford sat in the front passenger seat, the seat belt across his chest like a Miss America sash. That left the back seat to me, not a disadvantage since I could sit with my legs stretched out to the side in the tiny car.

We worked over to the Shoreway and headed west. Long before we reached Lakewood, we could see the glass high rises thrusting up along the lake shore. One of them was Underhill's apartment house. Agosta parked in the horseshoe drive out front, and the three of us passed by the doorman on our way inside. The lobby would have done a luxury hotel proud. I waited with Ramford in a corner while Agosta held a conversation with the desk clerk across the lobby.

"You know, this is the first investigation I've ever been on," Ramford remarked.

I wasn't surprised. I figured his time in the prosecutor's office had been short, stuck behind a desk in a remote corner. Today's assignment had probably been palmed off on him because no one with more seniority wanted to trifle with the saintly Judge Amerine. Right now, Ramford still clutched his attaché case.

"There is something about detective work that draws one. It's difficult to describe, but I can feel it even now. Perhaps it's a thrill of anticipation over what might turn up next. Is that the feeling you have?"

What I was feeling was anxiety, but I understood Ramford's enthusiasm. "It's always there, a high that keeps you going."

"Oh, yes. I can see that."

Agosta came back from the desk, casting his eye around the lobby. "Here's a thought: Crime does not pay." He turned to Ramford. "The desk man says Underhill and his wife are still here. At least he hasn't seen either of them go out since he came on duty this morning." He showed a passkey in his hand. "Amazing what a badge and a few threatening words will buy you."

"Why do we need that?" Ramford asked.

"One way or another, we get into Underhill's apartment. No telling what criminal evidence might be there."

"Evidence will not stand up in court unless we are on the premises legally," Ramford stated.

"Oh, right." Agosta gave me a look: Is this guy for real?

We rode an elevator that lifted us silently through layers of credit ratings. Somewhere short of the ionosphere we got off and made our way down the hall to Underhill's apartment. Agosta took up a position on the hinge side of the door and rang the bell. For my part I hung back and let these guys make their play.

Ringing and knocking some more earned Agosta zip. The problem was plain on his face. No one had seen the occupants leave this morning, yet there was no answer. Slick Underhill would not have been out of character if he had skipped out last night. These considerations floated across Agosta's face, and he brought the passkey out of his pocket and inserted it in the lock.

"I don't think we have reason to enter the apartment," Ramford said.

"I thought I heard someone yell 'Help.' It seemed to come from this apartment." Agosta appealed to me. "You hear it?"

"Plain as day."

"There's your probable cause." Agosta turned the key in the lock.

I grasped Ramford's elbow and urged him out of a direct line with the door, over by me on the knob side. Agosta pushed the door open until it hit the wall and only then exposed one eye around the edge of the door frame. Whatever he saw gave him no cause for alarm. With his .38 in his hand at his side, he entered the apartment. I stayed in the hall with Ramford, waiting for word from Agosta that it was safe to enter.

"Jesus fucking Christ!"

That outburst from Agosta was all Ramford could take. He shook free of my restraining hand and dashed inside. I waited. No more sounds came from the other side of the wall. As I made up my mind that there was no reason to wait longer, Ramford came rushing out. One hand held his attaché case in front of him like a shield to clear the way. His other hand was clapped over his mouth, and his color was not robust. He dashed down the hall toward the elevators.

I hesitated, wondering if I should follow Ramford or see what Agosta had found. It occurred to me that Ramford might prefer not to have witnesses when he upchucked, whereas Agosta might need help. On that basis I entered the apartment. It was a spacious living room with furniture that was expensive and tasteful. Its picture window provided a seascape of Lake Erie looking toward Canada and, with a little craning, the skyline of Cleveland to the right. Crime, I reminded myself, does not pay. Then I took two more steps inside so I could see around a chair that had been blocking my view of the salient feature and realized that the old saying, after all, was true.

The late Felix "Slick" Underhill had come to a final resting place on an Oriental rug flat on his back, arms thrust out at his shoulders. He had been wearing a kimono—period. In the center of his forehead, like a Cyclops eye, was the hole made by the bullet that had punched through his scheming brain and forever blew out the lights.

I looked around for Agosta. He was nowhere in sight, but in another room doors were being opened and shut. Careful not to disturb anything, I stooped down to examine the corpse and the area around the rug. Blood and other matter had leaked out of a hole in the back of his head to form an inconsistent halo. It had already congealed to a black crust that, on one edge, showed a strange, U-shaped indentation. The toe of a man's shoe would have fit it.

Agosta came out of the hall to the bedroom, tucking his revolver away on his hip under his sports coat. "No one else here," he reported. "There's women's clothes in the closet and a woman's stuff in the medicine cabinet. If she's run out, it couldn't be with more than one suitcase would hold."

"She's had a few hours to get away." I stood up.

"Condition of the body, I'd say it probably happened last night. He's got beard shadow, and from the way he's dressed, it looks like he was getting ready for bed. Maybe someone who heard the shot can pin it down closer."

"Not likely. That's a contact wound." There was powder tattooing around the entry wound, and the skull had cracked just below the surface. Those cracks showed up on the flesh as tears radiating from the hole, almost like knife slashes. "On top of everything else, it was a small caliber, maybe a .32, and these walls are soundproofed. All anyone might have heard would have sounded like a door slamming."

Agosta was still pondering the time element. "If I can believe the desk clerk, she didn't go out this morning. That also would jibe with leaving late last night."

"You're sure the wife killed him?"

"When a man is killed in his own house, you arrest the wife. Homicide isn't complicated." Agosta preferred simple solutions, which made him right most of the time.

"That's a man's footprint in the blood."

Agosta studied it without being convinced. "Or an elbow, or a knee. If it is a toe print, there's no blood spots going away. Whoever stepped in it did it after the blood had started to dry."

"He was facing the door when he died," I pointed out. "It would figure he opened the door, and there was the killer pointing the gun at him. He backed up three or four steps, and then the killer shot him."

"Or the wife shot him on her way out." Agosta shrugged. "Anyway, it's not my problem. This investigation belongs to the Lakewood police. I'm sure they'll appreciate your input."

He found the telephone and called it in. When he came back, he looked down at Underhill's body. "Gonna be a different world without Slick. Legends are made by guys like that."

"He always claimed marks thanked him for taking their money. Maybe he was wrong once."

"You hear about what he did in Topeka? I heard it was Topeka. Maybe it was somewhere else."

"Is this a new one?"

"It was a few years back. Slick blew into town and started calling all the grifters he knew around the Midwest. Come to Topeka, he told them, I've got the fix in. So con men from all around—K. C., St. Louis, Minneapolis, wherever—drift into town. Slick calls them together at a meeting in City Hall. It was an office of someone on vacation or sick leave or something, but it looks authentic. When they're going in, Slick stops a guy passing down the hall and tells the con men this is the mayor of Topeka. It wasn't. It was some down-and-out actor who looked distinguished. The so-called mayor was in the room a few minutes, just long enough to tell the assembled grifters to listen to what Slick has to say, and then he goes off to a meeting.

"Slick lays it on the line. The fix is in, but to operate here you've got to have a license. Naturally you can't have a license signed by the mayor. What Slick shows them is a playing card. It's not a regular card. This one is filled with weird signs and symbols. You get arrested, Slick tells them, you show this to the cop, and you're home free. Price per card is ten grand cash, payable to Slick.

"So help me, a roomful of con men who should recognize a scam, and they fall for it. Every one of them pays off Slick and gets their card.

"Well, Slick's gone from Topeka, and the grifters start operating. Sure enough, one of them gets pinched. 'Not to worry,' the grifter tells the cop, 'look at this.' He shows the cop his license, and the cop says, 'What the fuck's this?' 'My license.' 'Fuck that. You're going to the slam.' First few times this happens, they think it's a dumb flatfoot who hasn't wised up. When it keeps happening, it dawns on them they've been taken. Con men turned into marks by another con man." Agosta's tribute was a shake of his head. "No wonder Slick was so good."

I reflected that, if we were standing over his body rehashing his triumphs, he probably would turn into a legend. "Where'd Ramford get to?" I wondered.

Agosta was obliged to stay with the body, so I went out in the hall to find our assistant prosecutor. He was down by the elevators sitting on a padded bench with his head between his legs. For him the thrill of investigation was beginning to pall a little. I lit a cigarette and stood watching him until he noticed me.

"I've never seen anything like that before," he said. "There was cottage cheese on the rug, only it wasn't cottage cheese."

Probably it was a good idea for him not to dwell on the sight. I tried another subject. "This screws up the proof I needed that Megan Latimer is still alive. I can't produce her if she's on the run."

"If she's not alive, she won't make a good suspect in this murder." Ramford sat back and rested his head against the wall. "I wouldn't worry on that account. I'm sure we'll find adequate corroboration she was alive as recently as last night. After this, the Amerine affair is going on the back burner."

"That's fine, but it doesn't clear me."

"As far as I'm concerned, you're free to go." Ramford laid an affectionate arm on his briefcase. "Still, the best move might be to apply for a court order and dig up Amerine's property. That would settle this issue for all time."

"Sure, be my guest."

The elevator opened to deliver the Lakewood police to our floor. I directed them to Underhill's apartment and waited with Ramford another fifteen minutes while Agosta passed the torch. It would have been interesting to hear how he explained his presence on the scene.

14

Agosta made me walk from the police garage back to my office—around the corner and across the street. It seemed impossible that it should be barely ten o'clock in the morning. I felt as if I had already put in a twenty-hour day.

The crowd of Monday morning losers had already cleared out of Glickman's office. Wally Stamm and Gladys were working the phones trying to verify the credit references listed on the applications. Swamped with work as she was, Gladys had a tendency to turn surly. "We could have used your help earlier," she said pointedly.

"Sorry. I barely managed to stay out of jail myself."

"It's where you belong." On that happy note, I started for my office, but Gladys called after me, "Wait!" She pawed through the papers on her desk until she found the slip she wanted. "There's a guy been calling you all morning. He won't leave his name, but here's his number. From his tone of voice you'll call him back if you know what's good for you."

The number written on the slip of notepaper meant nothing to me. I unlocked my office door, laid the message slip on my blotter, and studied the number further. It failed to jog anything in my memory. There was only one way to find out. I dialed it.

"Cusimano Vending Machines."

Why is it I could never learn to leave well enough alone? "My name is Disbro. Someone has been calling my office."

Montovani strings played for me. Then the line was picked up. Gus Cusimano said, "You are a hard man to reach."

"The police had me. It took me a while to crawl out through the ventilation pipes." Let him know we were on the same side. That's the ticket.

"You will please come to my office instantly."

The words were framed in a polite form, but they left me no choice. "Sounds important."

"It does not get more important than this." He hung up.

Close up to the front of my mind was the knowledge I had told the police about Cusimano's plot with Barry Sprague to bilk Amerine. He would not be pleased to learn I had done that, but what would it mean at this time? Now that Amerine was dead, Sprague was sure to inherit a large chunk of his estate. That would allow Sprague to pay off his debt with ease. Besides, with Amerine dead, there was no one to complain about the blackmail. I didn't see a way my spilling the beans would hurt Cusimano. So this had to be something new.

Where Mayfield Road turns off Euclid Avenue, it begins an incline up to high ground called Murray Hill. There you enter Little Italy. Don't take my word for it. The city has erected a sign that tells you this is Little Italy. Cusimano Vending Machines has an office halfway up the hillside in a building that is mostly warehouse. Two workmen had a pickup truck backed to the loading dock and were manhandling an electronic poker machine onto the truck bed. The man watching them and telling them to be careful wore a George Raft suit and had delicate features.

"About time you got here," Pockets said as I climbed onto the loading dock.

"I came out of curiosity."

"Right." A jerk of his head indicated I was to follow him inside. The warehouse was filled with vending machines of all kinds, lined up on the floor like platoons of infantry. Off in a corner were slot machines. Pockets led me down the aisles to a staircase at the rear. The stairs were wooden, bowed in the center, worn black by generations of feet. At the top of the stairs were the offices of Cusimano Vending Machines. There was no hallway. We simply emerged from the staircase into the anteroom.

It was a hub from which side halls went off in two directions. The floor was bare wood from the same generation as the stairwell. Across the center was a picket fence with a swinging gate and behind the fence, a door with a pebbled-glass pane on which the word PRIVATE had been painted ages ago in fat black letters by someone whose next assignment had been to paint GENTS. Once again I was reminded that Hollywood has deceived us all about organized crime by portraying the gangster's nerve center as a sumptuous suite comparable to luxurious corporate headquarters. The truth is that the Mafia, reflecting the banality of their lives, operates out of offices that are almost invariably downscale.

At a desk behind the picket fence sat a blonde, someone I recognized. Last week, when I met Cusimano, she had been forced into the role of caregiver to his mother.

The blonde didn't seem to be worked to the point of exhaustion. She was sitting with her elbows on the desk, her fingers interlaced, her chin on her fingers. She smiled at me and batted her lashes in a way that told me I was the single bright spot in a dreary day. I smiled back. She ran her eyes over me and lost interest. She looked down at an appointment book on her blotter.

"Small automatic in an upside-down shoulder holster under his left arm," she said as if she were reporting the temperature.

"What kind of automatic?" Pockets asked.

"Colt, it looks like, but it seems small for a .45."

"It's the Officer's Model." Pockets' hand searched where she had indicated and lifted out my piece, holding it up where she could see it.

"So that's what confused me. I thought he had .45 magazines on his right side, but the gun didn't seem big enough."

"Isn't Jarman something?" Pockets beamed, proud of her. "Who needs a metal detector with her sitting out here?"

Pockets laid my pistol on Jarman's desk. "Careful. He carries it cocked and locked." He led me across the room to the PRIVATE door, knocked, and pushed it open. The door was so loose in its frame he barely had to turn the knob.

The office was a continuation of the anteroom—hardwood floors that, with dark-stained wainscoting on the walls, appeared to flow halfway up to the ceiling. Above that the walls were plaster painted in a beige that had been absorbing stains so long they had darkened to only a few shades lighter than the wainscoting. Opposite the door was a fanlight window, and before the window was a desk and a high-backed swivel chair. Backlighting from the window made it difficult for me to tell if the chair was occupied. After studying it for several seconds, I made out the silhouettes of elbows on the chair arms. I shuffled sideways to give myself an angle out of the way of the direct light. The swivel chair turned a few degrees to face me.

Gus Cusimano sat in the chair, his profile now half lit, half silhouetted by the window light. Cosimo di Medici as painted by Raphael. For all that, his desk was bare and scarred, looking as if it might have been picked up in a secondhand store. In one corner of the room, a chunk of plaster had fallen out to expose the lathe beneath. Opulence was not the hallmark of Cusimano's throne room. Although he could have afforded the fanciest suite in the most modern office tower, he had confidence enough not to need to impress visitors with his furnishings. I stood there not quite sure how I should respond to him, whether I should drop to my knee or genuflect.

"Thank you for coming." The voice was simply in the room, not specifically connected to the man behind the desk. "I regret the way I had to summon you. My only defense is that I had no choice. The time element is that short."

The apologetic tone threw me off balance. "What do you want with me?"

"I have many interests. I deal with many people from all walks of life." The only objects on his desk were an ashtray, a pack of cigarettes, and a lighter. In here he was not dependent on Pockets for all his supplies. "In the course of business, I build up many debts, many obligations, many favors owed. Honor requires me to respond when someone appeals to me to fulfill obligations."

I waited, not sure where these generalities were leading.

"Many times I find myself in conflict with the law. My relationships with the police are complex enough without taking on further troubles, yet when one of my obligations appeals to me, I cannot ignore it. I pay my debts as best I can, but no more."

Cusimano took a cigarette from the pack on his desk and lit it for himself. "Last night someone appealed to me for help, and I responded. At that point my obligation was discharged. To go beyond that point would mean entering an area above and beyond the call of duty. Still, the person who appealed to me needs more help than I have given. Therefore, I am doing what doctors and lawyers often do. I am referring the person to you."

"You haven't said anything yet," I told him.

"My words have been deliberately chosen so as not to give anything away. I am asking you to listen to the problem. After that, you may decide what comes next. Whatever that is will have no bearing on me."

There were so many traps involved in that proposition, I had no idea how I should answer. "You'll have to give me a little more before I commit myself."

Cusimano thought it over and parceled out a little more information. "A man died last night, violently. The man had done me some favors. His widow appealed to me for help, and I granted her a refuge where the police could not reach her to ask difficult questions."

"Slick Underhill."

Cusimano hooked an eyebrow. "You are surprisingly well informed."

"I happened to be with the police when they found his body a couple of hours ago."

"Already?" Cusimano's face showed regret. "We were hoping more time would pass before the discovery. You understand that I cannot afford to be involved in a murder case. The federal Strike Force is hounding me, state authorities, local investigators. The situation is much too delicate for me to involve myself."

"But not me."

"That's up to you. The widow requested I appeal to you when I explained I had gone as far as I could go. Are you willing to listen to her?"

Choice was not involved. I was being sucked into a situation where I had better know what was going on around me for my own protection. For all that, I kept my answer to Cusimano casual. "It can't hurt to listen."

"Very well." Cusimano turned his head to Pockets. "Show him."

Pockets went over to a door at the side of the office, opened it, and waved me through. I crossed the threshold, and Pockets shut the door behind me.

It was a conference room dominated by a library table and chairs. Along the walls was more furniture, padded chairs and couches with aluminum arms and legs. At first I thought no one was there until her head came over the edge of the table and disappeared again. The head rose, sank, and rose again. She saw me then and stopped what she had been doing—knee bends. She stood erect so I had a good look at her.

"So you came," Megan Latimer said. "Slick said you would. He said you were a stand-up guy who could be trusted." The inflections of her West Virginia origins were in her voice, stronger now in tense circumstances than they had been last week in a more relaxed mood. She came around the table and stood a yard away from me, leaning against it. "Slick is dead."

I nodded. "The police found his body this morning."

Megan had outfitted herself at the Banana Republic. She wore a safari suit in an olive shade, a tan blouse, and running shoes. Because her body was concealed by the loose-fitting clothes, my attention went to her plain face. With her brown hair drawn back in a ponytail, her face was more exposed than ever, and without makeup, her pock marks stood out boldly. That wasn't her only mark. On her left cheek, between the corner of her eye and her ear, was a bruise. "I found him first."

"When was that?"

"I dunno. Around eleven o'clock or midnight. I came in the door and there he was."

"How long before that since you saw him?"

"A couple hours." Megan picked an empty glass off the table and carried it over to a corner cabinet, where she took out a bottle of bourbon already half gone. She poured a couple of fingers into the glass. She drank some of it, poured more, and carried both bottle and glass to the table. "We'd been at home earlier in the evening, after we got back from supper. Then I left." She touched the bruise on her cheek.

"An argument?"

"Slick was pissed off." She took another pull on the glass. "It was Sunday and, yeah, I'd been doing some drinking. We went out for supper. Slick said that I was loud, embarrassed him. He started slapping me around when we got back to the apartment, and I left. That's the only way to handle him when he's in one of those moods."

"Doesn't sound like Slick."

"Shows you how little you know about him." Megan took another snort. "Slick spent his whole life sucking up to people. That was too much being nice for him to take. When he got home, it had to come out." She touched the bruise on the side of her face. "Me, I'm what it came out on."

I thought the situation over and nodded. "It might work, the battered woman defense. Juries are buying it these days. There are some lawyers who would be glad to present it."

"Fuck that! I ain't looking for defense. I already toldt you he was dead when I got home."

"Where had you been?"

"Coupla bars. I got out of the apartment and drove around until I saw a bar and went in. I stayed there a little while, but it was dead, so I went to another one."

"Names?"

She shrugged. "Who cares?"

"You should. I'll need the names of places and people who saw you there, if you want me to establish your alibi."

"What alibi? I got no intention of hanging around to be arrested or go to trial."

"Then what do you want?"

"I want outa here. I wanna go somewheres I won't see snow in winter."

"Planes take off every hour. What's stopping you?"

"Money."

I shook my head. "You picked the wrong guy. I have trouble coming up with bus fare across town."

"I've got the money. I can't lay my hands on it is all. Not with the cops looking for me. It ain't safe out on the street." She poured more liquor into her glass. "When all this happened, I appealed to Cusimano. Slick did him a favor onct. Cusimano sent Pockets over to my place to help me out. He brought me back here and gave me a place to stay. That's as far as they go. So I turned to you."

"You could have called the cops when you found the body."

She showed me an expression as uncomprehending as if I had asked her to walk across Lake Erie.

"How am I supposed to help?"

"Slick had this money put away, his fall money in case he ever had to run or bail himself out or bribe a judge. Whatever he made, he put some aside for that fund. Tithing, he called it. He couldn't keep it in the apartment, on accounta if the cops searched they'd find it, and he didn't wanna stick it in a bank. It wouldn't do for me to hold it 'cause I lived with him. What he did, he gave it to a friend to hold."

"How much?"

"Upwards of fifty thousand," she said, merely reciting numbers. "You go to this friend, pick up the money, and bring it back to me. That's all there is to it."

"Right. I walk up to this guy and say, 'Give me Slick's fifty grand,' and he hands it over. Then I bring it back to you."

"You'll have to prove you're who you say you are."

"Show my driver's license and two major credit cards?"

"Something else." She stood up and went over to her purse sitting in a chair in the corner. She rummaged around inside and came up with something she brought back to me. It was a piece of pasteboard. "Show him that."

The back of the pasteboard looked like an ordinary Bicycle playing card. I turned it over to discover the face was something else. Instead of one of the usual cards, there was only a random collection of symbols—an astrological sign, #, @, a shamrock, &, *, and many more. If they made any pattern or sense, I'd never know, for the card had been cut in two. Not torn but carefully cut with a pair of scissors in a deliberately jagged pattern. I knew I was holding one of the "licenses" for graft that Slick had sold to unwary con men in Topeka.

"Take that to the man. He'll have the other half. The two pieces will fit like a jigsaw puzzle, and then he'll know you're from me." Megan picked up her glass. "Your cut is whatever you think is fair."

"Half."

"I'm in no position to bargain. I need enough money to get away and set myself up in the Sunbelt. I can't do that on half of fifty grand. Slick told me you'd be fair."

I relented. "A fourth."

"We're talking an hour's work. Go to the guy, get the money, bring it back."

"A fourth," I repeated.

She stared at me as if she wanted to bargain further. At last she shrugged. "You've got me over a barrel."

The deal was settled. "All right, who's the guy I have to see to get the cash?"

"His name is Peter Botkin."

My face must have showed the surprise, for I saw it reflected in her loss of confidence. "The sports promoter?"

"Yeah!"

"Maybe you haven't heard. He double-crossed his partner, cleaned out their bank account, and lit out. For all I know he had Slick's fifty grand with him."

"When was this?"

"Six months ago, maybe more."

"Shitfuck!" She sat down at her place and wrapped her hands around her glass as if it would give her warmth. She drank and then put her face in her free hand. "What shitty luck!"

I toyed with the card in my hand, studying the collection of symbols as if they held a meaning. Megan continued to moan over her bad luck.

"There's got to be some way around this." She struggled to find one. "Botkin's partner, Damon Ortega. Maybe Botkin didn't take Slick's money. Maybe Ortega knows where it is."

"Why would Botkin swindle his partner but be righteous with Slick?"

"They knew each other from years ago, before I met Slick. Him and Botkin was teamed up on some deals. They had respect and trust for each other."

Mutual regard between confidence men was not something I

wanted to bank on. "It won't hurt to try. How do I bring you the money?"

"Call here. Pockets will get a message to me."

I put the pasteboard away and stood up. "Maybe I'll have something for you this afternoon."

"Hurry it up," she said. "Somewhere in this burg a killer's on the loose. I didn't see anything last night, but he don't know that. If the cops don't get me, the killer might. That's another reason for getting outa here."

15

Four more days of depreciation had not improved the looks of the Tetlow Building when I parked across from it on Payne, probably in the exact same space I had used last Wednesday. I walked down to the corner of East Twenty-third to wait for the light before I crossed over. Parked around the corner on Twenty-third, facing the Tetlow Building, was a beige Yugo hatchback with gray duct tape wrapped around its left headlight. Behind the wheel sat the driver, his face obscured by the map he held before his face. It was no wonder he was having trouble finding his way. The map was upside down.

When the light changed, I crossed the street and climbed the stairs to the second floor. My eyes couldn't keep from wandering to the door to Hatton's office, noting that nothing there had changed since my last visit. Not so with the office of Botkin & Ortega. This time the private door was closed, and I moved on to the main entrance. It was a waiting room without customers, a linoleum floor, and a door into the private office. The secretary's desk was bare—no flowers, no photos, no cute signs about tidiness being the sign of a sick mind—and the Selectric sat under a plastic shroud like a piece of cloth-covered furniture in a vacant house. She had not simply gone down the hall to the powder room. She was gone for good.

My stepping across the threshold had tripped a buzzer in the private office. Lights were on in there, but no one came to tend to my business. I stood there, studying the prints on the wall. They showed fighters from other eras—John L. Sullivan, Gentleman Jim Fitzgerald, Gene Tunney, Jack Dempsy, Joe Louis, Rocky Marciano. I figured those were meant as generic fight pictures. Botkin & Ortega would not have gone back that far or represented anyone so prominent.

The door to the inner office opened at last, and Damon Ortega stood looking at me. Same dark complexion, same pencil mustache, same patent-leather hair. Today he wore a shirt with only a few bold stripes that supported a solid-color tie. His suspenders were yellow, and his pants were navy. He stared at me a moment. "I know you."

"We met last week, right here."

"Yeah. You were looking for the late Mr. Hatton." Ortega's eyes dropped off mine and flitted around his waiting room, as if he were checking to see if I had pocketed anything. "I don't have a secretary anymore. I had to let her go when we suffered some reverses."

"I heard about that."

"So you understand we're not in a position to do much at the moment."

"If I wanted to promote a fight, I'd run out to Ashtabula and see Don King. I have personal business with Pete Botkin."

"Lots of luck finding him. Wish to hell I knew where he was."

"Maybe you can still help me. We could go inside to discuss it if you can clear a few minutes in your schedule."

He shrugged. "It could probably be arranged, Mr.—" His voice left a blank for me to fill in.

"Smith will do. Who I represent is more important than who I am."

"Come in, Mr. Smithwilldo."

Ortega turned and led me into his office. The thought struck me that this place would have been a perfect Hollywood set for the office of a run-down private eye. Ortega went behind his desk and motioned me into a chair across from him. That put my back to the desk Pete Botkin had used. A radio atop a file cabinet was playing music so softly it hadn't been audible until we were near it. Ortega flipped the radio off and dropped into his own swivel chair.

"Let's hear it."

I took out the card Megan had given me and laid it on his desk blotter.

Ortega stared at it, at me, back at the card. He really didn't want to touch it without surgical gloves, but he fought down his better judgment and reached for it, turning it over to look at the meaningless collection of symbols.

"It's not your usual card," I observed.

He dropped it. "I thought it was a license to steal."

"Only in Topeka."

Ortega stood up and walked around his desk, past me, and out into the waiting room. There he threw a bolt on the hall door, flipped off the light switch, and entered his office. He closed the door to his waiting room, threw the bolt on that, and went behind his desk again. There was an ancient Diebold safe back there, something Jesse James could have blown apart. Ortega spun the dial and opened the door so that it blocked my view of what he was doing. He searched through some crannies inside until he found what he wanted.

He stood up at last and came back to his desk, holding another playing card. This one also was cut in two with jagged edges. He put it on his blotter six inches from its mate. The fingertips of a hand on either card half, he pushed them toward one another. His hands were so deeply tanned the fingernails looked pink. As the two halves came together, their jagged edges interlocked like gears meshing. When they were joined, the fit was so perfect the crack disappeared.

Ortega let go and stepped back, proving that his touch had nothing to do with it. I looked at the now complete card. I turned it over and joined the halves again. There was still no sense to the pattern of symbols unless random is considered a pattern. When I looked up, I was staring down the barrel of a Browning automatic.

"Put your hands flat on the desk, Mr. Smithwilldo," Ortega ordered.

I obeyed, sure I was leaving moist palm prints.

"Now tell me why I shouldn't turn you over to the police," Ortega said, the muzzle of the sleek automatic on me.

"Why should you?"

Ortega inclined his head to the file cabinet where the radio sat. "Last news break they had, they reported Slick Underhill's body had been found in his suburban luxury apartment. Now you show up with that card. A narrow-minded man might think you killed him for it."

The muzzle of Ortega's pistol looked to me the size of a ten-gauge. I forced myself to see it with a more objective eye. "Underhill was killed with a .32. That's a .32 you're holding. A narrow-minded man could think you killed Underhill. If you really want to make an official case out of it, ask for Detective Manuel Agosta when you call Homicide. He's the one who found Underhill's body."

That bluff had an effect on him, but not enough that the muzzle moved off me. "Maybe you've got another story about how you got the card."

"Megan Latimer sent me."

"That's not much better. Radio says she's wanted by the police."

"She says she didn't do it." I tried to shrug without taking my palms off the desk. "I tend to believe her, for what that's worth. It doesn't change anything about picking up Underhill's fall money. Her claim to it is legit. She had the card. You live up to your end, or you welch."

Putting it in those terms had the effect on him I had intended. Still keeping the gun on me, Ortega eased down into his chair. "We can talk it over."

"I'm craving a smoke."

Ortega looked at my palms on his desk and nodded. I picked them up and carefully took my cigarettes out of my shirt pocket, then my Zippo out of my pants.

Before I could light the cigarette, the hall door swung open. I tensed, for that was exactly the kind of sudden noise to make Ortega jerk the trigger of his .32. He didn't, though. He kept both eyes and the automatic's muzzle on me. I sent up a prayer of thanks for his self-control. My heels touched the floor again, and I swiveled my head to the hall door.

My first instinct was that an animal had escaped from the zoo and barged in. My second glance corrected that impression. It was a woman in a fur coat, a stunning blonde for all the show-girl hardness in her face. I recognized her a moment later as Mrs. Botkin, the wife of Ortega's absconding partner.

"Damon, honey—"

Seeing me, she hesitated. The sight of Damon honey holding a gun on me didn't seem to faze her.

"Not now, Lynette," Ortega told her, still watching me.

She looked at me with a withering expression, but she was speaking to Ortega. "I've got to talk to you about something."

"In a few minutes."

Lynette looked petulantly at him as if she wanted to say, Can't you shoot this guy later? Instead, she gave me one more disdainful glance and backed out, shutting the door after her.

Ortega sat staring at me impassively. At last I got my cigarette lit and blew smoke at him. "Does Megan get the money or not?"

Ortega considered it. "It don't seem right, handing the money over to the one who mighta done Slick."

"Your deal was to hold the money until the person with this card showed up. Nobody said that the person has to pass a character test. Either Megan gets the money, or you're a welcher."

Real emotion flickered in Ortega's eyes. He could have tolerated many insults except the accusation of welching. It struck too close to the core of his being. "I don't welch."

"Fine." I waited, but he made no move. "Well?"

"It's not something that can happen in two seconds. It's put away where it's going to take some time to lay my hands on it."

"How long?"

"Noon tomorrow."

I weighed my choices. Being put off twenty-four hours had the earmarks of a stall. Yet he wasn't claiming Botkin had run off with it, which would have been his easy out if he didn't mean to fork over. Maybe the fact it that had been put away securely was the thing that had kept Botkin from taking it. If so, that could lend credence to Ortega's story. Besides, what choice did I have? Megan was going to have to wait a day.

"I'll be back then."

"Not here. Someplace public." Ortega sorted through landmarks. "Tower City. On the balcony above the RTA station."

"See you there." I stood up, and for the first time Ortega allowed the automatic to sag.

It was all the invitation I needed to leave. Following Ortega's nod, I left by the private door into the hall. Lynette Botkin was leaning against the wainscoting near G. K. Hatton's office, tapping her toe impatiently and looking at the expensive gold watch on her wrist. As I passed her, she kept her lashes—long and dark in contrast to her silver blond hair—cast downward.

"Isn't it a little warm for that mink?" I asked.

The lashes lifted slowly, allowing her eyes to work up from my knees until they met mine. I thought nature might have been augmented to make those lashes as long as they were. Puzzlement came into her eyes. "I don't getcha."

"It's almost sixty degrees out there."

"If you're one of those TV weathermen, I don't recognize you," she said, confusion adding to her puzzlement.

She really didn't see what connection there might be between the weather and the coat she wore. When I had seen her last week, she had been wearing a stole, and now it was a full coat. She didn't wear them to keep warm. They were badges of status which she would continue to wear if a mob of animal rights loonies were lined up outside with buckets of red paint. "Never mind. Damon honey is free to see you now."

Outside, I jaywalked to my car and started the motor. When I pulled away from the curb and headed west on Payne, the beige Yugo swung into line behind me and stayed there like a bumper sticker. When I turned a corner, he turned with me as if a chain connected us.

Lunchtime was aproaching, all the excuse I needed to smoke out my shadow. The place I had in mind was a narrow restaurant convenient to Third District headquarters and the *Plain Dealer* building over on Superior. A black-and-white zone car from the Third District—its three hundred number was the giveaway—was parked outside the place while the two uniforms ate lunch at a table inside. Also there was an infobabe from WKKC, where my ex-wife is associate news producer, and her cameraman. I nodded to them all and went to a booth where I had a view of the street through the side windows. The Yugo, after circling the block, had come back to park behind me.

Noreen came to my booth to tell me I hadn't been around for a while, and I told her I had been busy defending Truth, Justice, and the American Way of Life. When she had taken my order for soup and coffee, I stepped back into the kitchen, where there was a pay phone on the wall. I dialed the number for Cusimano Vending Machines and left a message for Megan that I wouldn't be able to get back to her until tomorrow afternoon. Instead of going back to my seat after the call, I exited by the back door and crossed the street, approaching the Yugo from its blind corner. Before the driver knew I was there, I was leaning in his open window saying, "It would be simpler all around if you joined me for lunch."

The driver jerked spasmodically and slowly turned his head my way. The face was dour, sagging under half a century of worry. Max Gruen, Battling Baxter's trainer.

"When you want somebody followed, it's best to hire a professional," I told him, and handed him one of my business cards. "Here's a guy I'd recommend."

I didn't give him time for a reply. I walked back to the restaurant and resumed my seat in the booth, where a cup of coffee and a bowl of vegetable soup were now cooling. Two minutes later Max Gruen walked through the door and headed my way. He still wore his ratty cardigan sweater but now with a sports coat over it and a clip-on tie on his collar. The sports coat had lapels wide enough to flop like wings. I'd say his expression was sheepish except that with Gruen's face, it was hard to tell. He slid into the seat opposite me.

He still held my business card. He looked at it as if he were discovering it in his hand, then looked up at me. "You really a private detective?"

"Really." I picked up my cellophane-wrapped crackers and began crunching them. "Of course you could ask me about whatever you hoped to learn. I might be able to tell you."

He waved my card as if he were trying to fan himself with it. "I didn't know what I might learn. I saw you go into the building, and I recognized you. A few days ago you was talking to Cusimano.

Now it was Ortega you went to see. I thought I better see where you went next. It was as good as anything else."

I tore the end off the cracker package and crumbled the contents into my soup. Helen thinks that's a crude habit, which only goes to show how far a professor can get from the real world. "Why were you watching Ortega's office?"

"You working for the Boxing Commission?"

"No."

Gruen was not sure he should believe me. I met his searching eyes, for whatever that was worth. At last he put it to me. "Something ain't right about tomorrow's fight."

"Such as?"

"You seen my boy sparring. What do you think of him?"

Noreen came with my corned beef sandwich and took Gruen's order for a cup of tea. When she was gone, I said, "He can't take a punch or throw one. His footwork is fancy, though."

"You got the book on him. In spite of all that, there's his record. What do you think?"

"The opponents have been laying down for him."

Gruen's thumb touched his own chest. "I set it up that way for him. Years ago Leroy come to me, strong kid who looked like he had what it takes. Wanted me to teach him, which I did. Gave him all the fundamentals. Only thing he lacks is talent. Sure, he's the schoolyard bully. Golden Gloves, he's okay. But with the pros?" Gruen shook his head. "All he's gonna do is get hurt."

"Thing to do," I said, "was tell him. Lay it on the line. Sorry, kid."

"I know." Gruen was consumed with guilt. "I couldn't do that. Leroy came from the ghetto. School dropout. IQ, nothing. What's he got in life? A dream. Who's gonna spoil that? Not me. I see a way. I go to Pete Botkin, accounta I know fights he promotes are questionable. What I also know is he gets his backing from Cusimano. I think, make a deal, see if they can use Leroy. They can. They set up some fights. Leroy wins. He don't know no better, he's happy, thinking he's a real fighter. Also, Cusimano gives him some jobs that need muscle. On top of everything else, Leroy is getting to screw white girls. There's nothing more he could want."

I put my sandwich aside and lit a cigarette. "What happened to end it?"

"Everything starts coming apart. Botkin pulls one deal too many. Cusimano's after him, law wants to see him, he splits. At the same time, Leroy's usefulness comes to an end. No one wants to bet on his fights anymore. They know it's a fix. The odds are nothing and the action dies."

Noreen returned with Gruen's tea. He dunked his bag as if he were trying to drown it. "Now something else comes up. See, I've been putting money on these fights for Leroy. It's something I can do for him, build up a nest egg, you might say. Yeah, I get my own down, too, and I make some, laying it off with bookies outa town. So I'm calling my man in another city and what do I find out? There's heavy action on this fight, really heavy action from a man who should know. There shouldn't be heavy action at all. It's a nothing fight in a tank town. Who's watching? But it's action like a championship fight, and it's all on Grogan. The odds against Leroy are seven to one a couple days ago and getting longer. Why all this betting on Grogan?"

"Isn't he taking a dive?"

"I thought so. Now I ain't so sure. The heavy betting is coming from Cusimano and his friends. Why would they be putting their money on Grogan, less they knew something?"

"Could they have fixed it in his favor without your knowing?"

"Easiest thing in the world. All they gotta do is nothing at all. *Don't* tell Grogan to lay down, and he goes into the ring fighting. Leroy could never stand up to that kind of thing."

I reminded myself I had ten dollars riding on Baxter. My wish had been to blow it, and it looked as if I would have my way.

Gruen was more concerned than ever. "Kid Grogan is *mean*. He likes to hurt people, that's how he gets his thrills. I'd never have let Leroy go inta the ring with him without believing he had the word. If Grogan never got the word, it's murder—plain and simple. I can't allow that to happen to my boy. I love that nigger." Gruen's expression defied me to make a comment.

"Don't show up," I suggested.

"I thought of that. In a way it's even worse. If we did something like that, Cusimano would kill us." Gruen played with my card. "I'm gonna tell Leroy to fall down as soon as he gets hurt. That's the only safe way. It might look bad, but Cusimano will still be satisfied and Leroy will live. If I can make him understand."

Over at the table where the two cops were eating, their portable radio began crackling. They dropped their utensils and dashed for the door. Seconds later their zone car, red and blue lights flashing, pulled away from the curb. The infobabe and her cameraman watched them go, wondering if they should follow. They decided to finish lunch before they chased after the zone car.

"One thing wrong with your thinking," I told Gruen. "Baxter is still Cusimano's boy. Is he going to throw away all his investment?"

"Why not? He'll make up for it with his bets on Grogan. Anyway, Leroy is used up. And don't forget Botkin. After the double-cross he pulled, Cusimano would do it just to ruin Ortega. Plain old revenge with a profit." Gruen shook his head as if he were trying to recover from a series of blows. "It all adds up, and Leroy's total is pain."

I was convinced without blowing a lot of sympathy on the handlers. Baxter was the one I felt sorry for, a man turned into a commodity to be sold and exchanged, and then discarded like a junk car when his usefulness ended. Worse than that, he might be sacrificed simply to spite a man Cusimano couldn't reach.

Gruen finished his tea and stood up. "Tomorrow night is going to decide it. Thanks for listening to me." He turned and walked out of the restaurant.

When he had gone, I sat staring at the door. Sometime later, I put out my cigarette and finished my sandwich. I still had a long day to go.

16

A message from Helen was waiting for me when I got back to my office: She wanted me to meet her for dinner at a restaurant named the 100th Bomb Group. Tonight, I recalled, she was scheduled to field phone calls for PBS.

Gladys was still sorting through all the applications for bail from the weekend arrests. I grabbed a stack from her desk and took them into my office to help her out. From my own phone, I began verifying the credit information the applications contained. Did Evester Williams work at this factory? Does Ramon Guevara have an account at this bank? It was routine stuff that demanded little mental activity but a stout forefinger to punch out the numbers on the phone. Halfway through the applications, I looked at my watch and realized Amerine's funeral was in progress. I felt a twinge of guilt for not being there, for letting the time slip by me. Then I rationalized that I had no business going there, except that it would have given me an opportunity to see Elaine again.

I put that thought aside and forged on through my batch of applications. By the time I had resolved the cases, I had found only two that contained complete fabrications. I wrote brief comments across the bottom of each one and took them back to Gladys to redeem myself in her eyes. She may have been dubious, but Rolf was ecstatic to see me. I scratched him between the ears, and he slobbered on my knee.

Quitting time had come. I beat the vanguard of rush-hour traffic onto the freeways and headed toward the airport. On Brookpark Road, under the descent path of airplanes, is the 100th Bomb Group in a damaged chateau, its yard littered with a wreck of an ambulance and an antiaircraft gun. I passed through the sandbagged entrance and found Helen waiting for me, already being served. We ate in all that atmosphere, watching planes take off and land, until she had to run off to the WVIZ studios down the road. I paid for our meals with plastic, confident that tomorrow my share of Underhill's money would provide enough to cover it.

From the restaurant I drove home and turned the television to Channel 25, where they were repeating *I, Claudius* during the fund drive. When the machinations of Roman emperors were interrupted for a pledge break, the camera scanned the tables where members of the Cleveland State faculty sat waiting for the phones to ring. Helen was there, a pinup among professors. I fantasized about ways I could make obscene calls to her.

Back we went to first-century Rome, and I went to the kitchen to pour a cup of coffee and await the next premium offer. Should I opt for the tote bag, the mug, or the coffee-table book? I was still watching for the next pledge break when the doorbell rang.

A taxi sat at the curb, which in Ohio City meant that it was only fifteen feet from the front stoop. The driver, a man with a beard and a ponytail, was the one who had rung the bell. "Is this you?" he asked and handed me a business card.

It was one of mine. I looked on the back and found my home address and phone number written in my handwriting. The last one like that I had handed out I had given to Elaine Knoll. "That's me."

"My fare says you'd be good for what's on the meter. She says she forgot her money."

I went out to the taxi with him. The sun was down, and in shirtsleeves I felt the chill of the evening air as it made my breath vapor visible. When the cab driver opened the rear door, the dome light showed a woman sitting there in a tweed coat with a hood. I thought of Red Riding Hood, except this cloak was gray. She turned her head toward me, and the light showed me Elaine Knoll's face in a double frame—the hood and her own coppery hair.

"Sorry. I had to see you. Forgot my purse." Her voice was thick, as if her tongue kept getting in her way, and her green eyes had a glaze that might have been feverish.

"No problem." I offered my hand to help her out. She gripped it with real force and relied heavily on me to get her onto the sidewalk. There she had a bad moment when her knees nearly gave out, but she got her balance against the taxi.

"I'll be all right." She took a few tentative steps and found she could maneuver the way to my front door, which I had left standing open.

The cabbie watched me watching her. "Man, you really a private eye?"

"Yeah."

"And chicks keep showing up on your doorstep like this?"

"All the time." I looked at his meter and fished out my wallet. "Where did you pick this one up?"

"In the Coventry Mall in front of the Arabica Coffee House. She must have called from there."

Not far from her apartment on Lancashire. I gave him a twenty, letting him keep the excess for a tip. One thing being a private detective has taught me is that it's best to keep sizable amounts of cash in my pocket at all times, even if that means draining my bank account.

He winked at me. "Whatever she's been using, it's none of my business. Have a good night's sleep."

When the taxi had pulled away from the curb, I went up the front walk, stepped inside, and shut the door behind me. Elaine was in the entrance alcove, leaning against the wardrobe there, her right hand against her left side under her cloak as if she were having stomach cramps.

"Are you all right?" I asked.

She stood erect, the feverish look of her eyes glowing brighter than ever. "I think—I killed—him." She brought her hand out from her cloak and showed it to me. Blood was running between her fingers. "See?" Her eyes rolled up behind her lids, and she pitched forward onto her face.

I caught her before she hit the floor, got my arms behind her shoulders and knees, and carried her to the couch in the living room. I moved a floor lamp closer to direct its light where it would be the most help. On one knee beside the couch, I opened her coat, spreading it out to protect the fabric of the couch. I sensed that Helen was on the screen behind me, watching over my shoulder, so I was particularly cautious about protecting the couch. Around Elaine's waist was a scarf tied to hold a hand towel against her left side near the hipbone. The towel was saturated with blood.

I untied the scarf and lifted the soaked towel from her side, wrapping it in the scarf. She had been wearing a black dress—black because she would have been attending Amerine's funeral earlier, I thought.

There was a hole in the dress at her side near the front, but most of the bleeding was coming from her side. Only a little blood was around the hole, too small to insert my finger, and I could see scorch marks in her dress at that point. I ripped the dress open to see where the blood was coming from.

The wound was a gouge in her side, front to rear, made by a bullet fired at close range. Although the bleeding was profuse, the wound was not as severe as it could have been.

Elaine was stirring, in a semi-conscious twilight state. I went to the kitchen, where we kept the dish towels. The oldest were near the bottom of the pile. I picked a few ragged ones and brought them to her. I folded a towel and pressed her hand against it over her wound. "Hold that."

Upstairs I went to the guest bedroom and ripped the covers off the bed. From the linen closet I got towels to spread over the sheet. Satisfied I was ready, I went downstairs again and made ready to carry Elaine up. John Wayne picking up Maureen O'Hara. Somehow, by the time I puffed my way to the head of the stairs, I felt as if I was failing to meet the standards. I laid her on the bed. Next chore: Get her dress off. That was only slightly more difficult than carrying her up the staircase and even less erotic.

At last her wound was fully exposed. Blood was oozing from it. I went to the bathroom for alcohol, gauze pads, and a roll of gauze bandage, and swabbed her wound out with alcohol, which caused her to stir. I used another pad for a compress and tied it tightly in place with the bandage roll. I waited a while to see if that had stopped the bleeding. A moment later, a dime-sized spot of blood had soaked through. She needed more medical help than I could give her.

Elaine was trembling now, not surprising with her lying half naked atop the bed. I brought the covers up over her. Her eyes fluttered open as I sat on the bed beside her.

"You've been shot. Who did it?"

"He came to my place." That short a phrase was too long for her. "Tried to get in. I got gun. Fought. Went off."

I nodded to let her know I was piecing together an outline from her disjointed statements.

"I killed him," she said.

"You shot him, too?"

She shook her head. "Pushed him. Downstairs. Back stairs. Lying still."

"Who are we talking about?"

"Robert."

"Your ex-husband."

She managed a nod with her eyes closed. The brief conversation had exhausted her, and she was already slipping into unconsciousness again. That was probably the best thing she could do for the time being, but I needed one more thing before she slipped away. I asked her for Dr. Mount's phone number.

She was drifting off as I left her and went downstairs to call Mount. An older woman's voice answered. When I told her it was an emergency, she called Mount to the phone. He was not pleased. I identified myself and told him, "Elaine Knoll has been shot. I got the bleeding nearly stopped for the time being, but she's going to need stitches."

The grumpiness went out of Mount's voice. "I'll be right over."

"She's not next door. She's in a house on Bridge Avenue." I gave him my address.

"That's in Cleveland!" He made it sound as if it were as dangerous as Beirut. "Lutheran Medical Center is only a few blocks away. Can't you take her there?"

"That isn't feasible. You'll understand when you get here."

Mount was still not convinced it was the right move. I had to argue with him some more until I said, "If Amerine were alive, he'd insist you come here."

"There's something you're not telling me."

"I can't, not over a telephone."

"It will take me some time to get there."

When Mount hung up, I turned to the cleanup job. Elaine's hooded coat was still spread over the couch. I picked it up to examine it, seeing that blood had stained the lining but not soaked through. Something heavy was in the pocket, her key case. I stuck that in my own pocket and hung the coat in the alcove wardrobe. Back in the living room, I picked up her scarf, which was wrapped around the bloody hand towel. That went in the garbage. Done with the downstairs, I went up to the guest room to check on the patient. She was sleeping. Her dress and slip were beyond salvaging. I made a bundle of them, along with the kitchen towel I had used, and discarded them.

Between then and the time Mount arrived, I divided my time between checking on Elaine and watching for Helen on the TV. The pledge drive was falling short of its goal, and Elaine was resting. It was nearly ten o'clock when Mount parked his Mercedes at the curb and bustled up to the house. He was dressed in a suit and topcoat. "Where is she?"

I showed him. Mount pulled back the covers and removed the bandage to inspect the wound. He made a sound of disgust.

"Anything you need?" I asked.

"Not at the moment."

"Then I have to leave awhile."

"See here!"

"It's for her sake. I'll be back before you're finished."

Downstairs I put on my shoulder-holster rig and my sports coat, pausing a moment before I added my topcoat, the reversible one with tweed on one side and a raincoat on the other. I got my car out and, running the defrosters to dispel the light frost on the windshield, drove across town on streets that were deserted this time of night.

The streets on the Cleveland Heights border are a mess. They curve and loop and turn back on themselves in a tangle that's hard enough to separate in daylight, let alone night. Worse yet, they are lined with so many apartment houses that every inch of parking space is filled. On Lancashire I located Elaine's building in one pass. There was no ambulance, no police cars outside. Elaine had not been specific about the time frame, but I doubted that a homicide investigation would have packed up this soon.

Two blocks later, I spotted a car pulling out of a parking space. The instant he was gone, I whipped into the vacant spot and walked back, approaching Elaine's building from the alley. Each floor had a balcony with a flight of stairs zig-zagging up the back. I never see a setup like that without thinking of W. C. Fields having his sleep disrupted by a stranger asking for Carl LaFong. I searched carefully in the shadows around the bottom of the staircase without finding a body there. I climbed to the second floor, where Elaine lived, and located the back door to her apartment. One of the keys from her case opened it.

The light was on in her kitchen, which prevented me from stepping into a puddle of blood the size of a saucer. I avoided that spot and entered the kitchen to turn and look back at the scene, weighing it in light of what Elaine had told me. After some time, I could see how it might have happened. Orton would have come to her back door, and she would have answered it cautiously, gun in hand. He tried to force his way in. Argument. Struggle. Gun went off at the same instant she pushed. While Elaine fell, Orton tumbled backward down the stairs. She lay for a while just inside the threshold—accounting for the blood on the floor—and finally got up to staunch the flow. She went out on the balcony, looked down, and saw Orton at the bottom of the stairs.

So where was Orton's body? I couldn't imagine that the police had already carried it away, so I had to presume there was no dead body to investigate. Could Orton have been alive but unconscious? Could he have come to later and walked—more likely, dragged himself—away?

I looked around the kitchen to see what could be found to substantiate the story. In the door to the cabinet under the sink, I found a hole where a bullet had entered at a downward angle, only large enough to insert the sharpened point of a pencil. Under the kitchen table I found the weapon—a .32 revolver, nickel-plated with an ebony grip. It was a Colt Police Positive, a model that had been popular about the time Prohibition wasn't. Just the kind of gun to lie in a drawer for a generation without use. I dropped out the cylinder and looked at the cartridge heads. One of the six had a dented primer.

I dropped the .32 in my topcoat pocket and, turning on more lights, I went through the rest of the apartment. The furniture was better than the place deserved, looking as if it had been salvaged from a period of her life when her fortunes had been better. That was about as much inspection as I had time for. No searching of drawers or papers. In her bedroom, I checked out her closet and selected a sweater and skirt. Helen could probably have been convinced to loan her some clothes, but Elaine was too tall for a close fit. I wadded the skirt and sweater up so they would fit in my topcoat pockets. I gave the apartment a final check and exited by the rear door.

A flight below, on the ground floor, a tenant came out to deposit a contribution into his garbage can. Through his open door came the sound of a television set blaring a commercial, proof he was not tuned to PBS. I stomped loudly on the wooden steps so that the tenant would hear me approaching. He was middle-aged and bald. I flashed my ID case quickly in the dark. "Detective Agosta," I announced.

"Yeah?" He was hesitant but curious.

"I'm investigating a disturbance here earlier. Did you hear anything tonight?"

"Sure did. Lots of crashing down the stairs."

"Then you're the one who complained."

"Not me."

"You must have checked it out."

"Naw. This time of year? When it gets this close to Halloween, them damned kids start playing pranks. Gets worse every year."

"You weren't even curious enough to look out?"

"That's what they want you to do, so one of them can stand up there on the balcony and pour a bucket of water over your head. Or something even worse. Best you ignore them." He turned to go back into his apartment but decided he had more to say. "What's wrong with this generation? My day, there'd been some asses whupped."

"No respect anymore," I agreed.

"Parents don't have no control, that's the problem." Having identified the source of trouble for the universe, the tenant went back inside.

I returned to my car.

17

Dr. Mount's Mercedes was still parked in front of the house when I pulled into the driveway and around to the back of the house. I entered through the kitchen and hung up my topcoat, first taking the Colt .32 out of the pocket. When I had remodeled this place for Helen, I had arranged for a few concealment places against the time when I would have papers or other valuables to put away. One of these is in the living room in the baseboard behind the couch. A foot-long section is hinged to swing up, leaving a hollow space behind it. I put the revolver there and went upstairs to see how Mount was coming along.

He was still with the patient, his suit jacket off and shirtsleeves rolled up, returning his equipment to his medical bag. Elaine lay in the bed, now wearing the top to a pair of my pajamas, the covers pulled up to her chin. She was asleep.

"How is she?" I whispered.

"You can talk. I gave her a sedative," Mount explained. "She will sleep the rest of the night. Tomorrow she should stay in bed. Ideally, she should have a transfusion to replace the blood she's lost. I suppose you would interfere if I tried admitting her to a hospital."

"I'd have to. And you wouldn't want her in danger worse than a scratch on her side."

Mount eyed me suspiciously. "You have never given me a good reason for treating her here. I stitched the wound, the best I could do in these primitive circumstances, but there is much more that should be done."

"We can talk about it downstairs." I turned off the light in the guest room and left her there. Downstairs in the living room, Mount dropped wearily into a chair. The television was still on, tuned to Channel 25, but the fund drive was over for the night. I clicked it off.

Mount took a bottle of pills out of his bag and set them on the coffee table. "For Elaine, for her pain, as needed," he instructed. "I could use a drink."

"Sorry. There's nothing in the house. Coffee?"

"Decaffeinated?"

"No."

He compromised his principles enough to accept the regular coffee. I poured two mugs and brought them into the living room. When he asked for cream and sugar, I was able to offer him milk. He looked at me as if I were a strange specimen. No liquor. Regular coffee only. Nothing to put in it. He sipped his coffee and set it aside.

"Out of respect for Elaine, I have honored your requests," he told me. "I have been assuming you are doing what she wanted. However, there are limits to how far I can go."

"What limits?" I asked, although I had a good idea what he was driving at.

Mount rubbed his eyes wearily. "That's a gunshot wound. You realize I am obligated to report it to the police."

"I don't think so."

He raised an eyebrow. "That is one area where there can be no compromise. The report must be made."

"Do that," I said, "and I'll have to tell the authorities how you signed Judge Amerine's death certificate."

Mount stared at me in what appeared to be genuine confusion.

"You say that as if it were a threat. I assure you there was nothing irregular in what I did. Thus your threat is meaningless."

I let that go. "You don't smoke a pipe, do you?"

"I don't smoke anything. Lowell would be alive today if he never had."

I pointed to my rack of pipes on an end table. "I smoke a pipe now and then. I'm not dedicated to it the way Amerine was, but even I have half a dozen. A pipe smoker never has just one. People who know such things will tell you the minimum number to have is seven, one for every day of the week."

"I assure you this information is meaningless to me."

"Stay with me a little longer. You'll see the connection."

"To what?"

"Murder." I let that hang a moment and went on. "The secret to smoking a pipe is rotation. You want to let your pipes rest between uses. When you finish smoking a pipe for the day, you clean it and put it away with a pipe cleaner through the stem. That's so the pipe cleaner will absorb moisture. Now Amerine had a lot of pipes, over a hundred, and he treated them all with care. When he put them away, he left the bowl empty and a pipe cleaner run through the stem."

Mount closed his eyes, visualizing what Amerine's house had looked like. "Very well. I concede your point. What of it?"

"The morning we found Amerine's body, I was downstairs in his study. There was a pipe on his desk. The cleaner had been removed, and the bowl was filled with tobacco but never lit. Amerine wouldn't have left it that way before he went to bed for the night. Taking the pipe cleaner out of the stem and filling the bowl is something he would have done shortly after he got out of bed."

Mount shook his head. "That's not possible. Lowell died during the night. He never survived to get up in the morning. When I examined him, he had been dead for several hours. He could not have been alive much after midnight."

"Exactly. You have two contradictory facts. He died around midnight, yet his pipe was ready to be lit downstairs. What's the answer? He got out of bed in the middle of the night, went downstairs, filled his pipe, and dropped dead before he could light it."

"But he died upstairs in bed."

"Did he?" I lit a cigarette. "Suppose it happened like this. Amerine retired for the night after he had put his pipe to bed for that day. Then a visitor came ringing the buzzer at the gate. Amerine got out of bed and spoke to the visitor on the speaker. Whatever was said convinced Amerine to release the gate so the visitor could come up to the house. Amerine rode downstairs on his chair-elevator, opened the door, took his visitor into the study. They talked. Amerine was sitting in his chair. He took down a fresh pipe. Removed the pipe cleaner and laid it in his ashtray. Filled the pipe bowl. Then, before he could light his pipe, the heart attack struck, and he died."

Mount rubbed his eyes and pinched his nose again. "You posit a visitor without a bit of proof there was another person in the house."

"The proof is Amerine's body upstairs in bed. How did it get there from the study if no one was there to move it?"

Mount was refusing to accept the notion. "You think his body was moved from the study?"

"We know he died there. We know his body was found in the bedroom. Sure, someone moved the body. It wouldn't be hard. Amerine was small and frail, not much over a hundred pounds. The visitor could have carried him from the study to the staircase, probably not more than a dozen steps. Put him in the chair. Run the chair to the head of the stairs. From there, another short jaunt to the bedroom. Take off his robe and slippers. Tuck him back in bed and leave. Any reasonably fit man could have done it." I could not keep my eyes from flicking toward the ceiling. "Even a woman."

"Why would anyone want to move the body?"

"What would you have thought if you found Amerine's body in the study wearing pajamas, a robe, and slippers?"

"I would have wondered why Lowell had got out of bed," Mount said simply.

"Which would have led you to speculate about a visitor, and then to question the circumstances of Amerine's death. The visitor was trying to conceal any evidence that he, or she, had been there."

Mount sat still a moment absorbing it all. In the end, he shook his head. "Suppose what you say is one hundred percent correct. Suppose Lowell died in his study instead of his bed. The fact remains that he died of heart failure."

"Brought on by what?" I asked. "When a visitor comes calling late at night, it's hard to imagine it was good news. Amerine had a bad heart, capable of being tripped off by any upsetting news. Isn't that right?"

"Yes, I can imagine the visitor failing to break the news gently enough. I can visualize what panic he felt when Lowell had his seizure. Mind you, he may not even have known Lowell was dead. Lowell might even still have been alive when he was moved from the study. The visitor might even have put him to bed and left, thinking Lowell would recover after sleeping a few hours."

I scratched my jaw, drawing a sharp rasp from my late-night beard. "You're being generous, Doctor."

"How else would you describe it?" Mount asked the question as if he were touching something contaminated.

"Suppose the visitor *chose* to come in the middle of the night. Suppose the visitor *deliberately* got Amerine out of a sound sleep. Suppose the visitor *purposely* phrased his bad news for maximum shock value. Everyone knew about Amerine's heart condition. Everyone has warned me to be gentle telling him the truth. The visitor might have known exactly what he was doing."

"You're describing premeditated murder."

"It wouldn't have been as sure as a gun or poison, but it also doesn't leave any traces." I shrugged. "Of course, it could have been something else, all the way down to accident."

"How would you ever prove it?"

I put out my cigarette. "We never will, since you signed the death certificate in such a hurry."

Mount felt the sting of guilt. He leaned against the back of the couch and closed his eyes. "But who would do it?"

"Start with Barry Sprague. He certainly would profit by inheriting Amerine's money, and I happen to know he had a piece of shocking news he could have told. There's Miss Knoll, whose motive I don't see, but who also could have confessed something drastic. Beyond that are several criminal types who might have wanted to see Amerine dead so Sprague would be sure to inherit. That would guarantee their money would come in."

"Richard Mount," the doctor said.

I stared at him. "You have a motive?"

"Hardly. Lowell was my best friend."

"Well, you certainly live close enough, and you could have got him to open the door late at night." I shook my head. "Tell you what. Forget about reporting Elaine to the police, and I'll drop you from my suspect list."

"I'm too tired tonight to report anything." Mount pried himself off the couch and put on his suit jacket and topcoat.

I went with him to the door, saying, "I'll see what I can do about charging your bill to an expense account."

"I wouldn't worry about that. I'm sure Miss Knoll can handle it now."

"Why now?"

"Lowell once told me he was leaving her a sizable block of stock. She must be a wealthy young lady."

When Mount had left, I took Elaine's skirt and sweater out of my topcoat pocket and went upstairs to check on her. Making my rounds, I thought. She was still in a deep sleep that, as Mount had predicted, looked as if it would last until morning. Watching her, I recalled that only a few minutes ago I had said I didn't know of a motive for her to kill Amerine. Now I knew she would inherit from him.

Back downstairs with a channel changer in my hand, I flipped around the dial, hitting commercials more often than programs. I checked out CNN to see if I had missed any major world developments, and when I was satisfied I hadn't, I inserted my copy of *The Wind and the Lion* in the VCR and settled down to watch. It's a movie I never tire of seeing but now I was only killing time until Helen got home.

She pulled in while Teddy Roosevelt was just learning of the kidnapping and flopped on my lap to give me a hello kiss that promised much more.

"How did it go?" I asked.

"You weren't watching?"

"I had a couple interruptions. I missed the end."

"We made our goal, the first night anyone has this week."

"No wonder. They had the sexiest professor in town working for them."

"You say some of the nicest things."

We cuddled awhile in the chair, half watching Candice Bergen taking charge of her kidnappers. Helen began to nod off on my shoulder. She yawned. "I'm tired. I'm going to call it a night."

Helen went upstairs. Three minutes later she came back down and said, "There's a strange woman in the guest room."

"You noticed that? I can't put anything over on you."

Helen picked up the channel changer and touched the off button. The screen contracted to a dot of light and went dark. "Do you want to explain anything?" she asked in a tone of voice that made it a demand.

"Now or in the morning?"

"Definitely now."

So I explained what had been going on in her absence.

18

The ringing of the telephone barely intruded on my dreamless sleep. I burrowed deeper in my covers and folded the pillow over my ears to muffle the noise until the answering machine could take over. No such luck. The phone was on Helen's side of the bed, and she snatched it up. A moment later she was prodding my ribs with the receiver.

"It's the police."

Even with my eyes open the bedroom was dark. Across the room, the blue numerals on the digital alarm floated in the air. A.M. 4:26. Somehow getting the earpiece and the mouthpiece up to the proper orifices was a complex operation involving trial and error. "What?"

"I'm coming by your house to pick you up," Detective Manny Agosta's voice told me. "Twenty minutes. Be ready." He hung up.

For a time I lay there with the phone humming in my ear. At last I gave the receiver back to Helen and swung my legs over the side of the bed.

"That was Manny Agosta," she said. "From Homicide."

"Yeah." I groped my way in the dark, looking for the clothes I had stripped off a few hours ago.

"What could he want this time of the morning?"

It was a question I had been mulling with only one sensible answer coming to me. "They must have found Robert Orton's body."

I dressed as far as my shirt, Dockers, and a sweater. On the way to the staircase, I looked in on the patient. Elaine was sleeping soundly. Downstairs I made a pot of coffee and was sipping the first cup when Agosta pounded on the kitchen door.

He looked the way you would expect someone to look at four thirty in the morning. A sooty beard stubble smeared his face, and his eyes were bloodshot and puffy from the lack of sleep. He wore a trench coat cinched tight around his waist over the sport coat and slacks from yesterday.

"Jesus! It's cold out here." Agosta longingly eyed the mug of coffee in my hand.

"Would you like some?" I asked.

Agosta battled temptation, as if he were wondering whether it might constitute a bribe. That was not his real concern. "Pour it in a travel cup. We can drink it on the way."

I turned to get two of the plastic containers out of the cupboard, and Agosta stayed by the door, reluctant to enter. His shoes and the cuffs of his trousers were caked with mud. "Don't be bashful," I told him, and he entered. I filled the two travel mugs.

"You'll want to wear hiking boots," Agosta said.

I got them out of my closet along with a parka. When I had the boots and coat on, I picked up my travel mug and made ready to leave. "Manny, you'd tell me if I was under arrest."

"Sure would." He jerked his head toward the door.

The same unmarked detective-bureau car in which I'd ridden yesterday was parked at the curb where the taxi and then Dr. Mount's Mercedes had sat last night. Agosta had gone to the back door, I figured, because his feet were so muddy. He got behind the wheel while I climbed into the passenger seat. Before I was settled in, the car was in motion. Agosta drove over the Lorain-Carnegie Bridge toward downtown, but he fooled me by veering away from police headquarters, going instead down Woodland to Kinsman.

These were the dead hours between the last bar closing and the first factory opening, leaving the streets as deserted as they get. Agosta zipped through them as easily as if he had been on the freeway, showing concern for neither traffic lights nor speed laws. By the time Kinsman turned into Chagrin Boulevard, I was confused. Not only had we passed up police headquarters, we had also missed Cleveland Heights. Where had Orton dragged himself before he expired? I decided that would reveal itself in due time and leaned my skull against the headrest.

"You snore," Agosta said as he made a sharp left turn that brought me awake. "How can you sleep at a time like this?"

"Clean conscience." I squinted at what was revealed by Agosta's headlights. While I dozed, we had left the city lights for the genuine dark of night in the country. Now we were on a lane with trees hemming us in on both sides of the narrow blacktop, climbing a steady incline. Though I could see only vague shapes, there was something familiar about the place. Before I could recognize any landmarks, we reached the end of the lane where it butted into a pair of garage doors in a parking area already crowded with cars that had the dowdy look of official vehicles. Agosta cut his headlights as he shut off the motor. In that second before the lights went out, I recognized Judge Amerine's house.

Taking a flashlight with him, Agosta got out of the car and guided me around the side of the house to the back, where the land dropped away to a wooded ravine. Only my memory of the sight through Amerine's window was left to guide me in the darkness as we started toward a woods that seemed to be a solid black mass. But that was not so. As we came around the house, I saw that down in the ravine one spot was brightly lit by floodlights. It looked as if a carnival had set up business there. Poking the flashlight beam ahead of him, Agosta pointed the way to a path that followed a gentle slope into the woods, circling around toward the lights.

When we arrived at the spot, I saw that the lights had been strung across branches to illuminate a clearing. Parked nearby was a county pickup truck with a generator humming in its bed. In the clearing sat a backhoe. A series of shallow trenches had been dug, each a couple of feet deep, spaced about a yard apart. Workers from the county highway department, dressed in insulated Carhartt coveralls and orange reflector vests, stood idle outside the range of the lights. One of them was taking a leak, creating a cloud of steam in the cold air where his urine hit the ground. Others were visible only as the tips of their cigarettes glowed in the dark.

Agosta led me to a hollow tree on the edge of the clearing where Assistant Prosecutor Ramford stood. He wore his suit with a Harris tweed topcoat over it, a wool scarf at his throat, and a wool stocking cap on his head pulled down over his ears. He was still suffering in the cold, his red nose and cheeks vivid testimony. Approaching him, Agosta flicked his flashlight carelessly over his shoulder at me. "Here he is."

Lightbulbs reflected in Ramford's glasses as he raised his head to look at me. "Well, Disbro, what do you think of all this?"

"Interesting." I flapped my arms to stir up some warmth. "You really didn't have to pull me out of bed to see it. I would have believed you if you had just shown me the slides later."

"I apologize for the hour. Believe me, we had no intention of working until this time of morning." Ramford's breath left a vapor on the cold air, a mild surprise. I hadn't thought there was enough warmth in him to do that. "I told you yesterday I was going to apply for a court order to dig up these grounds. It took me until late afternoon to get a judge's signature on the order. Once I had that in hand, I had to negotiate with the county highway department for the backhoe and the crew. By the time we got started, it was dark, so we had to call on the power company to string these lights. I never dreamed how many governmental fiefdoms I would have to deal with."

I glanced around at the holes they had dug. "All for nothing when you get down to it."

"But necessary to confirm your claim that no body is here."

I didn't like the way this was going. They had not brought me out here this time of night to tell me I had been right. They had me here to gloat over me.

"Then there was the sketch Amerine gave us," Ramford went on, "not at all clear in marking the spot. We dug for a while, then moved our lights to another location and tried again. Mind you, we had to go about it very carefully so as not to disturb any evidence if we unearthed anything."

"You didn't find a body?" In my own ears, my voice rang with hope.

"As a matter of fact," Agosta said, "we did."

If you think "weak in the knees" is only an expression, you should have been standing on my foam rubber legs at that moment. "That's impossible. Megan Latimer is alive."

"The Lakewood police haven't been able to find her," Ramford observed pointedly. "Do you know something?"

"She was alive last week. If Barry Sprague is to be believed, the body should have been in the ground eight months."

Agosta said, "That much time in the ground didn't do the body any good. Les didn't stand up too well at first sight. Coughed up his cookies."

Ramford was getting a crash course in dead bodies, two within twenty-four hours after a lifetime of none at all. He bobbed his head to confirm what Agosta had told me. "The body is badly decomposed, an awful sight."

"One thing we could tell about it, though," Agosta added, "it has a pecker."

"The body is male?" I wanted to sit down. I had earned a rest. I had earned a vacation in Bermuda. My confused thoughts had run into a roadblock on the subject of Robert Orton, who I had figured must have crawled here to die. My mind wouldn't tolerate any possibility but him. Yet if the body had been in the ground long enough for it to decompose, it couldn't possibly be Orton.

"Hell of a note, isn't it?" Agosta said.

"Who is the dead man?"

"Let's go see what we can find out." Agosta led me over to the backhoe and around to its far side. There, where I had not been able to see them when I approached, two men were working over one of the shallow holes. I recognized Alec Gottlieb and Bill Fritz from the Scientific Investigation Unit, the crime lab of the Cleveland Police Department.

Agosta stopped at the end of the hole and pointed with his flashlight beam. The grave had been barely deep enough to cover the body, which lay on its back. Agosta's flashlight beam touched a pair of black shoes, moved up to gray trousers and a gray suit jacket, a blue necktie, and finally the face. Ramford had no need to explain why he had thrown up. The flesh was not all gone, but it had melted away to leave only an obscene leer as its most prominent feature. Agosta moved the flashlight beam over the brow to the forehead. In the center was a round, black hole.

"Does that look like a .32 to you?" Agosta asked. "Reminiscent of Slick Underhill, don't you think?"

I was too busy lighting a cigarette to answer.

Gottlieb looked up at the sound of Agosta's voice. "We found a wallet on him. No cash but plenty of identification." He produced a plastic bag with a billfold inside. "You can touch. It's already been dusted for prints."

Agosta located the driver's license and looked at the photo of a frontally bald man in his forties. Comparing it to the corpse's face was a waste of time, but the face in the photo was one I had seen before. It had been in the photos on the walls of Ortega's office—where Ortega, a fighter, and the frontally bald man had posed together.

"Peter Botkin." Agosta read the name aloud off the driver's license. "Mean anything to you?"

"Fight promoter. He had an office in the Tetlow Building across the hall from the one used by G. K. Hatton."

"No shit?"

I added the rest of it. "Last winter he double-crossed his partner and absconded with the company funds."

"About the time the body was buried here?"

"Just about."

"So maybe he didn't abscond very far."

Gottlieb spoke up and produced another plastic evidence bag. "This was in his pocket."

Agosta was able to see what the plastic held by shining his flashlight beam on it without removing the object. Over his shoulder I saw an airline ticket, Cleveland to Chicago, issued last February but never used. The name on the ticket was Peter Botkin again.

Ramford had left the shelter of his hollow tree to join us in time to hear the tag end of our conversation. Patting his mittened hands together, he took up a position with his back to the grave and asked, "How can you be so positive Botkin ran off with the money?"

"I can't. It was never more than a side issue in what I was asking about." I thought carefully about what I knew and had been told. "The man and the money disappeared at the same time. Botkin's wife and his partner are hurting, that's for sure. My informants think Botkin was running off because he'd offended Gus Cusimano."

"Oh?" Ramford loaded that simple syllable with a lot of meaning.

"Cusimano would have had reason to put a contract out on Botkin?"

"That's my understanding."

Ramford was thinking hard about the possibilities in that line of inquiry. Yesterday he had been a junior staff member saddled with an unpleasant inquiry. Tomorrow he could be spearheading a prosecution against organized crime.

"Before we jump to too many conclusions," Agosta pointed out, "we should make sure the stiff really is Botkin. Disbro's record hasn't been too good when it comes to telling us if anybody's buried here and who it might be."

"Of course." Ramford refused to look over his shoulder at the body. "The coroner will have to verify the identity. It would be a good idea to check with missing persons reports to see what information there is on Botkin. I suppose it will take dental charts for positive identification."

"We're going to be here a long time before they're ready to move the body. They've got to sift through all this dirt for clues." Agosta nodded to me. "What about him?"

Reluctantly, Ramford said, "He has served his purpose. We'll have to let him go."

Which could have left me on foot twenty miles from home, except that Agosta offered to return me. When we had trudged back up to his detective-bureau car, he got on the radio and started a search for a missing person report on Botkin. The Cleveland records came up dry, so Agosta sent them after suburban communities. By the time he learned the report had been filed in Botkin's home suburb, Euclid, we were back in the city and crossing the bridge to my neighborhood. The parking space in front of my house had been taken. Agosta stopped in the middle of the street to let me out, greatly inconveniencing the morning joggers. I picked up my two travel mugs and started to get out.

While I was opening the door of the car, Agosta had a parting piece of advice for me: "Protect yourself on this one."

I shut his car door and went up to the house. When I let myself into the kitchen, Helen was finishing breakfast, dressed in one of my old blue button-down shirts that fit her like a pair of shortie pajamas, exposing a tantalizing amount of thigh at the V in the shirttails. She wore it as a smock in the mornings until she had her makeup on. "What the hell is going on?" she asked.

"The usual. The police were stumped by a difficult case and needed my superior analytical powers. How's the patient?"

"She was having a few lucid moments."

I climbed the stairs to the second floor, where I pushed open the door to the guest bedroom to look in on her. Making my rounds, I told myself. Elaine's coppery hair was spread over the pillow. Her eyes fluttered at the sound of the door opening. "How are you feeling?" I asked.

"Dopey. I should hurt, but I don't."

"You will. If it gets too bad, there's some medicine Dr. Mount left for you."

"He was really here? I couldn't be sure if I was dreaming when I thought I saw him."

I sat down on the edge of her bed and touched the back of my hand to her forehead. Warm but not burning. I said, "Robert is alive."

She closed her eyes, then opened them again. "So I didn't kill him after all?"

"You probably knocked him out, but it looks like he walked away."

Elaine thought that over. "Should I say I'm glad? I want him out of my life. He made me deceive a man I loved."

"What was the argument about last night?"

"Money. He came around demanding some. He thought I should have it because I'll inherit some from Judge Amerine, but it will be months before it clears probate and I see any of it. Robert wouldn't believe that."

"Where did the gun come from?"

"Robert had it when we were married. After he was sent to prison, it was around in a drawer. I forgot about it until he came back into my life. Then I held on to it for protection."

Her eyes were starting to close. Before she could drift off to sleep, I got addresses from her for Robert and for Barry Sprague. As I started for the door, Elaine forced herself awake to ask a question.

"Was I dreaming? Was there a woman in here?"

"That was Helen."

Elaine frowned. "Who is she?"

"She owns this house."

"Oh." Elaine was drifting off again. "Very pretty."

"We live together."

"Sort of—old." And she was asleep.

In the bathroom, I stripped off my clothes and climbed into the shower, running the water extra hot until the ice that had formed in my bone marrow had been thawed. When I came out, I wiped the steam off the bathroom mirror and lathered up my brush to spread soapsuds over my beard stubble. I had just finished lathering when Helen came into the bathroom. That was no surprise. Because her husband had used an electric razor, she had not been used to seeing anyone shave with a blade. It still fascinates her to watch me do it. That morning she had other things on her mind.

"What really happened?" she asked as she settled onto the laundry hamper, still wearing only my old shirt.

I told her then what had transpired during the last two hours while trying not to sever any major arteries in the process. Helen appeared to have trouble following it all.

"So there really was a body buried in the woods? A man instead of a woman? What does it all mean?"

"A mob hit. It's as simple as that. Cusimano had Botkin clipped, and then he came up with a unique way of disposing of the body while he squared Barry's debt at the same time."

Helen left me alone in the bathroom to finish shaving and brushing my teeth. By the time I had dressed and gone downstairs again, Helen was in the study, dressed for class now, going over her lecture notes for the day's classes. She keeps her notes on a disk and prints them out on three-hole paper, which she inserts in a ring binder as they are needed. It's so organized, it hurts me to see it.

"Someone should be with Elaine today," I pointed out.

Helen looked up briefly, blissfully unconcerned. "Aren't you staying here to hold her hand? Caress her fevered brow?" There was enough venom in her voice to poison the entire city water system.

"I explained everything last night."

"You explained. You didn't allay my suspicions. It's an audacious move to bring another woman into the house." Flustered, Helen riffled through her notes. "Don't you ever meet ugly women?"

"After you, all women are ugly."

Helen rolled her eyes and groaned.

"I can't stay," I said. "Among other things, I have to meet a man at noon. It means a lot of money."

"You could probably leave her for an hour without having to worry."

"It's not just the noon meeting. I have other things to do. If I don't get them done, I could lose my license, maybe end up in jail."

Helen leaned back in her chair. "Are you trying to lay a guilt trip on me?"

"Wouldn't dream of it."

"Then hire a nurse." Helen returned to her lecture notes.

"That wouldn't be a good idea. We don't want to involve anyone we don't have to."

Helen closed her notes and reached for a cigarette. "I have a life, too. I have responsibilities. You can't expect me to drop everything to babysit for you."

"Of course not. I'll think of something." I turned and started to walk off.

Helen said, "I can call a grad student to cover my classes. Will that satisfy you?"

I paused in the doorway to smile back at her. "You're a treasure."

"About time you appreciated that. Any last instructions?"

"Don't scratch her eyes out."

19

Barry Sprague, it turned out, as it sometimes will in a big city, was practically my neighbor. He lived in Tremont, which is adjacent to Ohio City like two squares on a checkerboard that touch corners. He lived in a line of yellow-brick row houses facing Lincoln Park, in the shadow of the onion-dome spires of Holy Ghost Church, the domes you pass on the Innerbelt, not the church where the wedding scenes of *The Deerhunter* were filmed. That was St. Theodosis, which is farther down the valley at the end of Starkweather.

You can never tell about places like Sprague's in Tremont. They might be on the verge of collapse, or if a stockbroker type has laid hands on them, they could be fixed up fit for a Sunday brunch with brie and wine. I took a turn through the alley behind it, where a row of garages matched the row of housing units. The one behind Sprague's address held his DeLorean—so I saw when I peered through the diamond-shaped window in the door. I got back in my car but had to wait while a woman in a babushka pushed her grocery cart down the uneven bricks in the alley on her way to one of the markets. Tremont is the kind of neighborhood where women in babushkas push grocery carts to the market on daily shopping trips.

Around in front of the building, I parked at the curb, walked up onto Sprague's stoop, and rang the bell. While I waited for results, I turned to look across the street to the park. The band gazebo and the swimming pool were both empty now. The swimming pool, in fact, had not been filled all summer because city finances were at low ebb. Against the wall of the bathhouse, a homeless man was urinating. Across the park, painters were at work on two different houses, readying them for upscale occupants. Paradoxes like that are the reason it's called a neighborhood in transition.

The door opened behind me, and I turned to see Barry Sprague standing there in a tank top and shorts, a pair of oversized Bullwinkle slippers on his feet. The shirt advertised B.U.M., stretched over his ample stomach. Once more I was struck by his ascetic features embedded in flab.

"Now isn't this a surprise!" he said.

"I'm glad I caught you at home. I was afraid you might have gone to work."

"Can't you see that I'm too devastated by grief to think of working? Besides, if the reading of the will goes the way I suspect, I may never work again." He flung the door open and allowed me to enter.

The entrance foyer was two square feet of space at the bottom of the stairs, with an arch leading into the living room on the right. Each unit in these row houses consisted of two rooms downstairs, one behind the other, with a Pullman kitchen at the back. Upstairs would be two bedrooms and a bath. As Sprague led me through his living room, feet flapping in his slippers, I saw that he had taken over two units by knocking out a common wall behind the staircase. That second room was a sitting room with a fireplace, the furniture arranged to focus on a television set. The room behind that had been converted to expand the Pullman kitchen, and beyond that, the two back stoops had been turned into a redwood deck. Bob Vila would have been glad to feature the work.

Following Sprague was an object lesson in why fat men should not wear shorts. He sat on the couch before a glass-topped cocktail table on which sections of the morning paper were mingled with his breakfast dishes. Two versions of Bullwinkle looked up at me cross-eyed through the cocktail-table glass. The television set was on with the sound turned down, tuned to a Tom and Jerry cartoon. Seeing that reminded me that Cusimano had called Sprague a child. His choice of morning television seemed to confirm it, though that might have been bias on my part. I prefer the Roadrunner and the Coyote.

"You know, I was really pissed off at you yesterday," Sprague said.

"How's that?"

He sat on the couch and began fitting a cigarette into his holder. "The police came by yesterday afternoon. Really! As if the trauma of attending Uncle Lowell's funeral hadn't been enough, I had to face the gendarmes. Fortunately one of them turned out to be Leslie Ramford. Knew him, or rather the family. Good people. Leslie graduated from one of those prestigious colleges where I sojourned briefly."

I sat down across from him, letting him ramble to see what turned up.

"Leslie is slumming by doing a turn in the prosecutor's office. A little like going down to serve meals in a homeless shelter, I suppose, public service that will look good on his resume. He brought along a genuine policeman, a Homicide detective, who lacked social graces. When they accused me of blackmailing my uncle, I was sure you had spilled the beans." Sprague got around to lighting his cigarette. "Turns out it was not you but Uncle Lowell who was responsible. He tried to expiate his sins by writing a posthumous letter."

"I saw it when Ramford and Agosta confronted me with it. After that I had to tell them about your scheme to get you off the hook for a possible murder."

"So I figured after a while. I was less pissed off at that point. It's probably for the best to have all this out in the open where the authorities can see it was an essentially harmless plot." He blew smoke toward the ceiling. "Leslie seemed satisfied that it was all settled."

"Maybe," I said. "If they decide it's politically worthwhile, they could make a stink by trying to press charges."

"For what?"

"Extortion."

"A little late, don't you think? With Uncle Lowell gone, there won't be any pressure for them to prosecute. Should they still choose to try, their best witness will be unavailable. The whole sorry thing is best forgotten. Leslie will see that."

Was he being naive, or was it all wishful thinking? It was possible he had convinced himself he had done nothing worthy of punishment.

"Once I get my share of Uncle Lowell's estate, it will be a moot point anyway. I will pay off Cusimano, and we'll be back to square one."

"Not quite. There was a startling development overnight that might change things."

"And what was that?"

I shook my head. "The police will reveal it in their own good time. I wouldn't want to spoil your surprise."

"Oh, you tease!"

"You never told me how you and Cusimano cooked up the blackmail scheme."

Sprague waved his cigarette holder. "I thought I did."

"Not in detail."

"How far should I go?" Sprague crushed out his cigarette and ejected it from his holder. "Cusimano invited me to dinner at one of those Italian restaurants on Murray Hill. Pockets was there with him. He wanted to have a heart-to-heart talk about my debt."

"When was this?"

"In February. God, you don't expect me to remember the exact date, do you?"

"How long before you went to Amerine with your story?"

"Actually, it was earlier the same night."

"Cusimano threatened you then?"

"He impressed me with the seriousness of my problem. He told me he was confident I could come up with the money through Uncle Lowell, and he was willing to explore ways to convince him to pay. I told him Uncle Lowell was adamant about not paying my gambling debts. Cusimano then asked me if he would pay to keep me out of some other kind of trouble, and I said he probably would. Cusimano said that our problem had been simplified: We must devise another area of trouble for me to get into. And we arrived at the blackmail scheme."

"Just like that?"

"Scarcely. This came out after a long discussion that lasted through dinner and drinks. I tossed out many ideas—drinking, drugs, but nothing quite fit the bill. Pockets said it had to be something so serious Uncle Lowell could not refuse me. It would have to involve a death. Perhaps a hit-skip accident? And so it went."

I wasn't about to let him off that easy. "Tell me more."

"My God, haven't you ever been in a conference where you kicked ideas around? I can't give you specifics at this late date. We didn't have a recording secretary taking notes."

"You had decided on a death."

Sprague threw up his hands. "Yes, a death. Not a hit-skip accident. Someone asked who could it have been that died. I suggested Megan Latimer. Cause of death? Botched abortion? No, drug overdose. Gradually the ideas emerged. How do I know who suggested what? The scenario simply developed."

He may not have been sure, but I was certain by this time that Sprague's contribution had been the least of all. Cusimano and Pockets had led him toward a goal they had in mind from the start, feeding him suggestions and complimenting him into believing the latest twist they supplied had been his own idea. For another ten minutes I kept at him, trying to pin him down to naming the exact elements he had originated. Every time he cited something, the next question revealed it had actually come from either Pockets or Cusimano. Even as he told me about it and revealed the truth, Sprague remained more convinced than ever it had all been his idea.

In the end, I eased off the questioning and lit a cigarette of my own. If Sprague wanted to think that the tough questioning was over, let him. "What was actually in the blanket you buried that night?"

"A mannequin, I suppose, and maybe some scrap iron to give it weight."

"Suppose? Didn't you see it?"

"Only imperfectly in the dark."

"Before you went to your uncle's house?"

"No, only after we were there. I went inside to tell my tale of woe to Uncle Lowell while the others waited outside. After I had secured his permission, I went out again. We opened the trunk of the car and lifted the blanket out. That is, I held the flashlight while the others did the work."

"How did the dummy, or whatever it was, get in the trunk?"

"I can't say. I wasn't there." Sprague smiled with an expression that suggested the village idiot.

"You're going to have to explain that."

"Remember that I was sitting in the restaurant with Pockets and Cusimano. We finalized our plans for the scheme, and Cusimano spoke to Pockets, who went out to make a phone call. I presume that Pockets arranged the details at that point. He came back to our table, and we talked a while longer over another glass of wine. Then one of Cusimano's minions came in to tell Pockets everything was ready. At that point Pockets and I left to go to my uncle's house. Pockets drove, and I rode beside him. I never had any occasion to look in the trunk until the time arrived to remove the so-called body."

"There were more than the two of you."

"Two more men were along with us to do the heavy work. They rode in the back seat."

"Who were they?"

"One was a prizefighter named Leroy Baxter. Cusimano owns an interest in him. That means Cusimano also avails himself of Baxter's services when a strong back is needed. I was particularly grateful he was along that night. It was cold, and the ground was frozen solid. Digging the grave was only a charade, of course. I was willing to forego it. Uncle Lowell had seen us carrying the presumed body into the woods, which was all that was necessary. But Baxter insisted on actually digging the grave. The work would keep him warm, he claimed. All this time Pockets stayed in the car with the heater running."

I did some higher math. "You said there were two men in the back seat. Who was the other one?"

"Baxter's manager."

"Max Gruen?" It was hard to think of him doing the heavy work.

"No, the man who promotes Baxter's fights," Sprague said. "Damon Ortega."

20

When I left Sprague, I still had time to spare before my noon meeting with Ortega, more significant than ever now that I knew he had been one of the pallbearers. I expected to include that on our agenda when we met. First, however, I wanted to establish what had happened to Robert Orton. Last night I had assumed he managed to survive his tumble down a flight of stairs. Recent history had taught me to be wary of such assumptions until a full head count had been taken.

The address Elaine had given me for her ex-husband put him in a rooming house off Detroit almost out to the Cudell Tower. There is a pattern to most neighborhoods on the west side where side streets cross the main thoroughfares. The corner building is a store on its ground floor with flats above. Around the corner on the side street, the first building is a brick apartment house with three or four stories. The next building is a rooming house, either frame or brick, followed by a two-decker four-plex, followed in turn by private homes. The variations to the pattern are small enough to add interest without changing the main design. Sometimes there are two apartment buildings, sometimes the frame two-deckers fill the block.

In this case the brick rooming house was the third building from the corner. Its front window supported a ROOMS FOR MEN sign but gave no clue about how to contact someone there. Before I knocked, I tried the door. Unlocked. I stepped over the threshold and came into a hallway with a staircase leading up. There was a door on my left that seemed to lead to the whole downstairs living quarters. LANDLORD on a metal sign, available in any hardware store, was screwed into the door. Hanging from a nail on the frame was a small clipboard with a notepad and the stub of a pencil wired to the clipboard. No one had left a note lately. I knocked on the landlord's door but got no answer. There was no roster of tenants anywhere I could find.

I climbed the stairs to the second floor, a narrow hallway with doors on either side. The hallway bent in a *Z*-shape. At the double curve was a pay phone and a door labeled BATHROOM, the only door with an identification on it except for numbers. I was wondering how I should go about locating my man when a door to the rear section opened, and a woman backed out with a tray of soiled dishes in her hands. She was a stout, middle-aged woman who could have carved out a career in television commercials posing as a gray-haired mother with apple cheeks. As she turned, she saw me coming toward her.

"Help you?" she asked as if her heart were really dedicated to my assistance.

"Robert Orton?"

She indicated the open door from which she had just come. "Go right in. He will be glad for your company."

When anything that easy happens, I become suspicious. I squeezed past the landlady with her tray and stepped into the open doorway. The room beyond was large enough for a daybed, a dresser, a closet, and one easy chair with an end table beside it. Robert Orton sat in the easy chair facing me, his left leg propped on a footstool.

I shut the door behind me and leaned against it, looking down at him. I had seen him twice before, once from a distance at the package check and once in a photograph. This was my first good look at him. There had been changes. His forehead showed a bump turning shades of yellow and purple. His left ankle on the footstool was bound in an elastic bandage. He wore the bottoms to a pair of pajamas and nothing on top except a robe, which was draped over his right shoulder because that arm was in a sling with a cast up to his elbow.

"Do I know you?" Orton asked. For all his injuries, Orton was a handsome young man who looked romantically dashing so trussed up. No wonder the landlady was willing to wait on him. An unwanted thought crossed my mind: This man had slept with Elaine. I felt an unreasonable resentment at those images.

"Take a tumble down a flight of stairs last night?" I asked.

Orton examined me. "Let's say gravity was working against me."

The contest of mutually suspicious stares went on between us. I said, "Stay away from Elaine."

"Or?"

"I'll break your other arm."

Orton raised his good hand to test the light beard stubble on his face. He had missed his morning shave. "Well, well. Chalk up another one. She's got you dancing now."

I felt an impulse to deny that, then thought better of it.

"That bitch has something all right. She's a good-looking woman, but it's more than sex. It's a quality she has that makes you want to put your arms around her and tell her nothing in the world can touch her."

Orton's assessment was coming painfully close.

He laughed at me with more bitterness than humor. "Don't take it so hard. Hell, I've been to the end of the same line you're riding. See my scars?" Orton examined me again. "I've got it now. You must be the private dick, the one Amerine hired."

"The one who broke up your scheme to cut in on the blackmail game," I told him.

Orton looked at the table on which lay a pack of cigarettes and a lighter. He tried to reach across his body with his left hand, but they were two inches beyond his grasp. He looked at me. "As a good Christian gentleman, could you hand me my smokes?"

I shrugged and stepped over to the table to push them closer. "It was your idea to start blackmailing Amerine. You used your job at the baggage counter to set it up. When I was called in, you hired that illegal—Pavia—to pick up the phony package."

"My idea?" Orton lunged out again and speared his cigarettes. "I worked out the details, but ask yourself, how did I know what was going on without Elaine telling me?"

"She says you forced it out of her."

"Right." Orton plucked a cigarette out of the pack with his lips and snicked his lighter to set it afire. He adopted a falsely casual voice. "By the way, has your employer buried anyone on his property in the last few months? He has? Do you suppose we could find a profit in that?" He snorted out smoke. "I sure must have been asleep not to ask obvious questions like that."

He was saying things I didn't want to hear. "Then whose idea was it?"

"Here's the way it went," Orton explained. "She came looking for me. She told me what Amerine had done. She told me he was already being blackmailed for it. Then she put it to me: Come up with a way to cut ourselves in. That's when I worked it out. We figured he was already paying a big bite, so he wouldn't object to a smaller one. He fooled us by going to you before he made his first payment, so I had to arrange for the switch with Pavia to sucker you off."

I said, "You're pretty free about confessing to a crime."

"Oh, hell. Amerine is dead. What difference does it make now?"

"That's convenient for you."

Orton frowned. "You say that like it's supposed to mean something."

"You could have gone to Amerine and told him what Elaine had been up to. News like that could have worked him into his fatal heart attack."

"I could have, but I didn't. Is that how it happened?"

"Could be."

"Then you better look at another possibility. Elaine could have confessed she betrayed him. Hearing that from her would have upset him more than anything I know. I mean, she was like family, like a daughter to him." Orton tilted his head to study me from a new angle. "Don't you like hearing that? Tell me you haven't considered it."

"I've considered it."

"Then maybe there's hope for you." Orton took a drag on his cigarette. "Slept with her yet?"

I stared at him and said nothing.

He laughed, a sound without enjoyment in it. "Take my advice, you'll not pass up the chance. It will be the most expensive pussy you've ever had, but you'll at least have that to remember."

When I could trust my voice, I said, "You're bitter."

"You bet. Not because she divorced me while I was in prison. Hell, I could understand that. What galls me is that she was the one who was responsible for me going there."

I stared at him, confused. "Now you're going to tell me she was in on the robberies?"

Orton allowed a smile to play at the corners of his mouth. "Find that hard to believe?"

"Only when I'm sober."

Orton shifted in his chair to move his broken arm to a more comfortable position. "Someday you should look into the details of my arrest, how I pulled off those robberies, and you might wonder how I handled it all alone."

My mind had created a censor that kept me from believing him. "You had a chance at your trial to lay some of it on an accomplice."

"One thing I learned in prison, you don't snitch on your partner." Orton started a shrug that caused him pain. "So don't believe me. Maybe Elaine was nowhere around. But if that's what you choose to believe, you've got to explain me. I was no criminal, just an average guy who clerked in a men's store, not making a fortune but getting a living out of it. How did I go from that to being an armed robber?"

I lit a cigarette of my own. "You'll tell me."

"I met Elaine, and we got married. Her parents had died not long before that and left her some money. Right away she starts living high. Also, it isn't enough that I'm a store clerk. She wants me to open a place of my own, so I did and went bust, and then I was back to being a clerk part time."

"It was her inheritance that financed you?"

"Yeah, and it was gone. All she had left was papers from her father's law practice. Among them was some stuff he'd taken down about how some armed robbers he'd defended pulled their jobs. I guess he collected it for his information so he could defend them. Anyway, it amounted to a handbook of how it's done. Elaine showed it to me and dropped hints that if I had any gumption I'd put it to use. Well, I studied it and pulled some jobs—markets, gas stations, bars. One of the best techniques was hitting the manager after closing time when he was taking money to the night depository. Lots of these guys were married men, so they neglected to mention that they might have been distracted by a nice-looking redhead."

I said, "That was cheap of you, using your wife for a lure."

"I'm cheap?" His laugh was so tinged with bile it was eerie. "Listen, I had some time to think while I was sitting in Lucasville. Ever wonder how the cops got on to me? I sure did until I found out a curious thing. One of the places I held up was a drugstore—part of a chain that offers a reward for the capture and conviction of anyone who holds them up. Want to guess who collected it? Want to guess who turned me in?"

I searched Orton's eyes for a sign he was lying. I didn't find it. Inside I knew I was hearing the truth.

"So while I was in prison, she was spending the loot I had brought home, plus the reward money. Any wonder that when I got out, I looked her up. By that time it was all spent. At least she allowed me to stay with her until I got a job and found these palatial digs." Orton laughed again, a sound close to a grunt of pain.

"You had plenty of reason to try to get money from her last night."

"Damned right. When Amerine died, I knew she would come into some money. It was about time I was cut in for some of it." Orton's tone of voice left no doubt he considered the money redress for the pain she had caused him. "I had a few drinks last night until I had myself convinced it was time to collect. She slammed the door in my face when she saw I had been drinking, so I went around to the back door. We had some words there, and maybe I got a little rough. Suddenly there was a gun in her hand. I struggled with her over it, it went off, and the next thing I knew I was tumbling asshole over elbows down the stairs."

"That was your gun?"

"The same one I used in the robberies. I didn't know she still had it." Orton plucked another cigarette out of his pack. "I was out for a spell at the bottom of the stairs. When I came to, Elaine was nowhere around, and I was in no condition to climb the stairs to face her. I had all I could do to hobble back to my car and steer it downhill to the emergency room at University Hospital, where I could get patched up. I guess I gotta count myself lucky any time I tangle with Elaine and come out with nothing worse than a broken arm and a sprained ankle to show for it."

"Maybe it's time to cut your losses."

"The idea occurs to me. But then I've got it so grand here. My landlady brings me food and cigarettes, and later on, she's going down to the liquor store to buy me some anesthetic. What more could I ask for?"

"Then I can leave you in good conscience, knowing there's someone to take care of you."

I turned and started for the door.

"Watch yourself," Orton warned. "You might not come away as easy as I did."

21

I parked in the lot behind Moe Glickman's office, but I didn't go inside. The morning was nearly gone by the time I reached downtown, and I would have to hustle to make my noon appointment with Damon Ortega in Tower City. That was five blocks from my parking lot, the outside limit of how far an American will walk in urban congestion.

It was not a bad day for a hike. The high October sky was a clear blue with only a few wispy clouds overhead, the Rust Belt air remarkably pure thanks to the increasing absence of heavy manufacturing. As with most clear autumn days, the temperature had dropped with a breeze blowing off Lake Erie. I was glad to be wearing a sweater under my wool sports coat.

Around the base of the Soldiers and Sailors Monument on Public Square the usual collection of pensioners had gathered. One of them was a frail old-timer who was puffing contentedly on his pipe. I had to look at him twice to make sure Judge Amerine had not been reincarnated. The sight of him forced me to focus on what I was doing and how far I had come in the last week from my original mission. In a few minutes I would be picking up a wad of cash that would allow Megan Latimer to flee justice. If all went well, my share would be over twelve thousand dollars, money I could never report and therefore tax-free. It was not a guilty conscience that troubled me. My standards are elastic enough to cover a windfall like that. Besides, I was morally certain that Megan was innocent of murder and had as legitimate a claim to the money as anyone ever would.

It was the money itself that made me nervous. I have never been any good at making money in large amounts. I don't have the soul of an arbitrageur, the innate belief that I have vast sums coming to me. I have never fantasized about becoming a millionaire. A decent living, sure, but not the limitless wealth of the superrich. I can't even imagine what I would do with all that excess cash, or with all the toys it would buy me. So when I'm faced with the prospect of substantial sums falling into my lap, I'm eaten by the nagging doubt that, because I don't deserve it, the loot will never be there. In that frame of mind, I entered Tower City with the absolute knowledge that something would go wrong. If Underhill had really left fifty grand lying around, why should Ortega turn it over to me? He would be on his way with all of it in his pocket.

I moseyed along the line of shops as I made my way to the RTA station, the same spot where I had arrived following Elaine last Thursday. From my level, the station was down in a pit one floor below me. I stopped and leaned on the rail, looking down into the pit, then up to the balcony above me where there was another level of shops. The noon rush was on as the downtown office workers hurried past. Some were here to buy an item in one of the stores or hurrying through to the food court in The Avenue, the added section to the rear. I searched among the passersby to pick out Ortega. Above me, more people leaned on the balcony looking down.

Natty in a gray double-breasted suit, a lavender shirt, and a hideous hand-painted tie, Damon Ortega appeared on the balcony directly opposite me. Well I'll be damned! He had kept the appointment after all. He approached the rail on his side of the pit, his patent-leather hair a solid unit atop his head, and scanned all directions. At last his eyes settled on me. I nodded to him. He inclined his head toward the end of the balcony, where the elevator travels in a glass tube, and started that way. I strolled along on my side, matching his stride.

We reached the end of the balcony on our respective sides at the same time. He turned and started walking toward me. I turned and started toward him. A few more steps would bring us together in the center, in front of the elevator doors. Ortega was carrying a brown paper bag that might have held his lunch, if he were an overeater. So what had I expected? A white canvas bag with a huge dollar sign painted on it? Ortega's stride brought him abreast of a square marble pillar. His next step took him past it.

WHANG!

A chunk of marble blew away from the pillar as if a snowball had smacked against it. Simultaneously, the sharp *crack!* of a handgun, its sound magnified indoors as if it had been fired inside a metal pail, split my ears.

Ortega threw himself backward, skidding on his rump across the marble floor to the protection of the pillar. He had dropped the sack, spilling bricks of money out of its mouth, a cornucopia of cash. He was already drawing his .32 automatic from under his coat.

More shots were echoing and redoubling within the confined space, merging themselves into one continuous blast. People screamed and ran wildly in diverse directions, stumbling into one another, tripping themselves. My .45 was magically in my hand as I flattened myself against the marble pillar at my end. Bullets continued to hum through the space between Ortega's pillar and mine.

The trajectory came from above. I chanced exposing one eye to peer around my pillar. The gunman was on the balcony above us, a black man wearing a jacket with the colors of the Crips. He had a two-hand grip on a pistol that was spurting flame even as I looked. No time to make sense of that. I wiped off the safety, aimed my pistol, and cranked off two quick rounds at him. Sparks flew when one of my slugs hit the metal of the balcony rail in front of him. He backed off.

I looked around, desperate for a way out of here, and saw the elevator behind me. Ortega now took a turn firing at the shooter above. I lunged for the elevator and pressed the button, helpless for seconds while I waited for the doors to open with maddening slowness. Come on! Come on!

Behind Ortega a young black man, with the bill of a baseball cap down the back of his neck, stepped around the corner of the balcony with a pistol in his hand. He spotted me by the elevator doors and raised his pistol as I brought up mine. A woman pushing a baby stroller chose that moment to rush by. I held my fire, but the gunman didn't. However, the stroller the woman was pushing banged into his leg, and his shot went wild.

The elevator doors opened, and I dived inside. From my peripheral vision I saw Ortega wheel around to pump three quick shots at the gunman in the baseball cap. By that time I was on the floor of the elevator car holding the door open. I was far back from the balcony rail now, out of range of the gunman on the balcony above. I risked looking out to see how Ortega was getting along. The shooter in the baseball cap was down on the floor on his knees, clutching his midsection. At least one of Ortega's bullets had hit home. Ortega was still crouched behind the pillar, pinned down by the gunman on the balcony.

"In here!" I yelled to him.

Ortega looked my way, calculating his chances for the dash. Down on my knees, leaning out of the elevator car, I had a line of sight out under the overhead balcony to the gunman above us. He was crawling along the balcony behind the rail, moving toward a better angle on Ortega. I aimed up at him and touched off three more rounds.

That gave Ortega the cover he needed to move. He dashed for the elevator, stopping en route to scoop up the money bag and most of the spilled bills. Tucking it under his arm like a football, he plunged headlong into the elevator car. I hit the highest button there was and the doors slid shut.

We were not alone in the elevator. A fat man sat in the corner, his knees drawn up, his pudgy fingers covering his face, while he made whimpering sounds. A woman stood with her back to the open door, her nose nearly touching the back wall as she simply refused to look at what was happening. She was screaming. None of this was contributing to a sense of calm and order.

Ortega had landed against the far wall. As the elevator started to move, he stood up and turned to me. Fear and hatred mingled in his eyes. "Double-crossing bastard!"

Apparently he didn't want to get all mushy with gratitude for my saving his life. He covered it well by raising his Browning and pointing it at me. He tried to squeeze the trigger, but the slide was locked open.

Slow as my thought processes were, it finally dawned on me that Ortega was trying to kill me. I lost it then. I lunged for his throat, forgetting the .45 in my hand. "You son of a bitch!"

Ortega clubbed down at me with his pistol, and a great weight thudded onto the top of my head with enough force to leave me an inch shorter than I used to be. It didn't knock me out. It merely rendered me helpless, unable to stand. I fell to my knees and buried my face against Ortega's legs. He kicked me over onto my back. Amid whimpers and screams, the elevator doors opened. We had reached the Huron Road level, a flight above the gunman on the balcony.

Ortega kicked me again. I sensed more than saw that he was crawling over me to get out the door. I struck out, caught his ankle, and spilled him on the floor outside the elevator. Not that it did me any good. I was so groggy that I couldn't catch up with him before he got to his feet. The elevator doors closed on my ankle. I pried them open and lurched out after Ortega. Ahead of me were the glass doors leading out onto Huron Road. He wasn't there. Inches from a getaway, he had not taken it.

There was nothing else here except the entrance alcove built so pedestrians could enter from the higher street. Once inside, they had to choose the elevator or the escalator down to The Avenue. I looked at the escalator. Ortega had done a belly whopper on the steps, lying flat so no one could shoot at him. He was only now reaching the bottom.

I tucked my gun away in its holster and leaped sitting onto the stone banister beside the escalator. I slid down it like a kid on a playground slide. When I hit bottom, Ortega was scrambling away twenty feet ahead of me. I ran after him as he dashed for the stairway down into The Avenue. The stairway forked around the fountain. Ortega took the right fork and then hit the straightaway at the bottom, a wide aisle in the center of a shopping mall with a long fountain the size of a swimming pool down the center.

I stayed with him, maybe gaining a little, which says a lot for a man who has spent a lifetime avoiding jogging. One thing I had was determination. Nobody tries to shoot me and then clobbers me over the head without expecting to pay for it. Ortega had a right to have fear to speed him along, but he was apparently in worse shape than I was.

Vaguely, through arcs of water in the fountain, I noticed a pair of Cleveland policemen on the other side running toward the stairs I had just come down. All that shooting must have attracted some attention. Ignoring the cops, I concentrated on Ortega's back, trying to reach out for it. Soon. A few more steps. I would have him before he reached the food court.

Something hit me in the side, deflecting me up against the side of the fountains. I managed to keep from falling and struggled to forge on, but hands grabbed me. I looked to see what it was—a security guard in a white shirt and Smokey the Bear hat. He looked as if he should have been in high school.

"Hold on, fella. What's happening?"

"Up there!" I pointed, encouraging him to forget me. "They're shooting." I tried to look frightened and desperate, not a difficult acting job.

"What's going on?" the guard asked.

"Must be a dope deal gone bad!" I shuttled my eyes after Ortega. He had reached the food court, where he had stopped to look back at me while he clutched the bag of money to his heaving chest. "Bunch of guys with guns banging away at each other. I got outa there."

The guard's eyes grew round as he contemplated a real gunfight instead of shoplifters. Dope dealers shooting it out. He couldn't believe his luck.

"You're bleeding," he told me.

I touched the damp spot in my hair and looked at the blood on my fingers. A Positive, I had reason to know. "Ricochet," I said. "I'm going for help."

"Do that." The guard let go of me and sprinted off toward the stairs.

"Watch yourself," I warned his back as he hurried toward the action. I ran the other way, after Ortega, who was disappearing into the food court. By the time I was threading my way through the tables, he had reached the escalator down to the rear exit into the parking lot. His head was sinking below my line of sight.

I leaped over an overturned chair, an obstruction Ortega must have left in my path, and rudely stiff-armed a woman who retaliated by striking me with her purse. Now I had a clear shot at the escalator only a couple of yards ahead of me. I was nearly there when a man holding his food tray before him stepped into my path. I avoided him but hit the tray. French fries, Pepsi, and parts of a cheeseburger flew through the air.

I made it to the escalator and ran down the moving steps, crowding past those who stood patiently on their allotted space. I hit the bottom and slammed through the doors out into the parking lot.

Ortega was out a few yards away from the building. Standing still. What luck! Before I could get to him, a dark Lexus swung in front of him and stopped. He opened the passenger door and got in, slamming it shut as I ran up and grabbed hold of the open window.

"Go!" Ortega yelled at the driver. Still holding his empty .32, he used it to beat on my fingers.

I let go with one hand and punched him on the hinge of his jaw. But by that time, the car was already moving, its screeching tires filling the air with a blue haze. I tried to run along beside it, still clinging to the window, but that was a hopeless effort. I let go and sprawled on the unyielding blacktop of the parking lot.

The Lexus roared away from me, fishtailing as it headed for the most remote exit.

It was a temptation simply to lie there and let myself recuperate, but that could not be. By this time the cops inside would be restoring order among the chaos. The security guard who had stopped me was sure to give them a description of the man seen running away. I pushed myself to my feet and walked off, heading for the nearest street where I could lose myself among the throng of pedestrians. The first plate-glass store window I passed gave me an insight to how easy I would be to recognize. My knee showed through my pants leg, and my sports coat was torn at the elbows. Besides the blood in my hair, my palms were skinned from my fall in the parking lot. My head throbbed with every heartbeat, and already my legs were stiffening from the unaccustomed exercise. I was sure more sore spots would make themselves known shortly.

On a street corner, while I was waiting for a red light, I closed my eyes and tried to recall an image that had been no more than a glimpse. The driver of Ortega's getaway car. Ortega's head had blocked me from getting a good look. All that I could recall was a head of ash blond hair, enough of it for a woman. I was sure I knew who that would be.

22

"We interrupt this program to bring you a bulletin from the newsroom.

"A wild shooting melee erupted at noon in Tower City. Police are still trying to sort out what happened. Early sources report the gun battle may have involved as many as six men. At least one was believed to have been wounded, but he escaped in the confusion.

"Adding to the chaos was the near-riot that developed when hundreds of noontime shoppers scrambled to recover money that was spilled during the course of the gun battle. Observers estimate that several thousand dollars were snatched up. None has yet been recovered.

"Police are looking for a suspect who was seen running from the scene. This suspect is a white male, thirty years old, over six feet tall, and thin. He has light hair and a light brown mustache and is bleeding from a head wound. When last seen, he was wearing a blue plaid sports coat and maroon V-neck sweater.

"Anyone with information about this suspect or other details of this incident is requested to call the police.

"Stay tuned for more information on the two o'clock news, or for a bulletin when news breaks. We now return to *The Rush Limbaugh Show*, already in progress."

I heard the report on my car radio while I was driving east toward Murray Hill. After the fracas at noon, I had gone back to my office to use the men's room down the hall, where I washed the blood out of my hair and managed to stop the bleeding. The cut was not so bad, but a nice lump had been raised up there. When I had gulped a couple of Excedrin tablets, I spent a few minutes in my swivel chair with my ankles crossed on the corner of my desk. Better.

The way I doped it out, only one person would have sent the Crips to open up on me. That was the reason I got in my car as soon as I had recuperated a little and drove out to see Cusimano. No one was around the warehouse at the vending machine company, so I climbed the stairs to the office.

"You can't barge in there," Jarman said as I strode into her office.

"Watch me." I passed her and headed for the door to the private office.

Jarman made it from her seat to the office doorway a step ahead of me and spread-eagled herself across it. "That's as far as you go."

I stopped and looked down at her. Her body had lots to recommend it, but it was hardly fit to stop a virile man who bench presses two hundred pounds. Her eyes flashed determination, not enough to frighten me. "Out of my way, little lady." I put my hands on her shoulders to move her aside.

I might as well have touched a power line, for I was hit with a jolt that was nearly electric. One moment I was totally in charge of the situation. The next I was totally helpless. Don't ask me what happened. I was in a poor position to be a witness. All I know is that the ceiling was under my feet, and the floor was over my head. Then the floor came up and hit me in the back, knocking the wind out of me, and Jarman was tugging on my wrist while pressing the spike heel of her shoe into my throat. If I moved, I would end up talking through an amplifier.

From my perspective I was looking up at the office door with PRIVATE showing upside-down. The door opened, and Pockets hove into my frame of view. He looked down at me with an expression of disgust.

"Disbro, you are pathetic," he said.

It was no time for me to make a sarcastic comment. It was no time for me to say anything.

Pockets was wearing one of his too-bold pinstripe suits with a purple display handkerchief in his breast pocket to match his purple tie. "Let him up."

Jarman took her spike heel off my throat and let go of my wrist. My arm dropped to the floor like a rope. I moved gingerly, checking to see how my recently acquired bruises were acting in concert with the mature bruises acquired two hours ago. I was able to squirm my way into a sitting position.

"Big, tough private eye," Pockets said with a derisive sneer. "Can't you handle a hundred-and-twenty-pound woman?"

"I bench press two hundred pounds." It was a mantra to convince myself.

"Beach boy," Jarman said. "One of those jerks who stands around flexing muscles but never picks up anything heavier than an ice cream cone."

I appealed to Pockets. "Call off your Amazon."

That amused him. He looked at Jarman with an appreciative eye. "Would you feel better if she was a big bruiser with a cauliflower ear and a broken nose? She don't look like that, but the effect is the same."

I pulled myself up with the aid of Jarman's desk. I stood for a moment balancing myself, watching her as she stood at the side, arms folded. She regarded me with a bored expression. Last week she had allowed herself to be slapped around by Cusimano when, as I now had reason to know, she could have taken steps to defend herself. It was plain I didn't understand all the dynamics operating here.

"Now why did you come busting in here with your bowels in an uproar?" Pockets asked.

"I get offended when someone tries to kill me."

His face puckered in confusion that would have been hard to fake. It turned into a pout. "Who shot at you?"

"A pair of Crips. Don't play dumb. I know you use Crips for bodyguards on the east side."

"Where did this happen?" Pockets was still skeptical, ready to tell me I was imagining things.

"Tower City at noon."

"Bullshit." Then he looked at Jarman, who gave a small nod. Some understanding passed between them. Pockets turned back to me. "What were you doing there?"

"Meeting someone."

"Damon Ortega?"

The name came out so glibly I knew there would be no use denying it. "So what?"

"Some people," Pockets said, "have such a swelled head they can't imagine they're not the star player in every drama. Even when bullets start flying, these people think the gun has to be aimed at them."

"Ortega was the target?"

Pockets smiled weakly. "Do you expect me to admit something like that?" He glanced around the office as if he were looking for a government agent hiding behind a potted plant. At last he lowered his voice to say, "Never send those Crips on a serious job. They're cowboys who'll fuck it up every time. I tried to tell him that." He jerked his head toward the inner office.

I looked through the open door. Cusimano's desk was vacant. I wondered if Pockets had been in there practicing sitting in the boss's chair. "Why Ortega?" I asked.

Pockets was tempted to tell me, if only to show off. "He was messing with a deal we got going, tonight's fight with Baxter and Grogan."

"Messing how?" I asked as I straightened up.

Jarman made a throat-clearing noise. Pockets glanced at her, shrugged, and turned my way. "A man who's been shot at deserves a little consideration, right? A man who's bright enough to keep his mouth shut?"

I was bright enough to keep my mouth shut at that instant.

"What do you think of the Baxter fight? A nothing fight in a tank town, no championship, no glamour, no big promotion. No one's ever heard of it, right? So goddamned obscure no one anywhere is paying attention." Pockets paused a moment to let me absorb that. "So there's a reason it gets to be important."

"Important because it's obscure."

"Now you got it. Cusimano has friends in cities all across the country. Family, you understand? If he can do them a favor, it's all to his good. Somewhere down the road he's gonna be able to call in his markers. So what he does, he gives them the Baxter-Grogan fight. The way things stand, Baxter is the favorite on accounta all his fights have been fixed before. The smart money knows Grogan will lay down, so if they bet at all, they put their money on Baxter. He's the favorite, odds high in his favor, and that means bets on him don't bring a big return. Like blue chip stocks, safe but small return. Meanwhile, the odds on Grogan are astronomical. No way he's gonna win, so the bookies give long odds on him. You see the opening you got here."

"If Grogan should win, the bookies take a bath."

"There you go. The gift Cusimano gives his friends is the tip to bet on Grogan. No one gives him the word to lay down, he wins. Trouble with all this is, you have to be careful about the bets you put down. Too much heavy betting on Grogan, the odds shift in his favor. Then the profit margin drops. Cusimano's friends don't lose their money, but they don't make near what they been led to believe. They have to put up six dollars to make seven. Instead of being happy, they're gonna be pissed off, and Cusimano's gonna lose face. That means, above all, we gotta keep the bookies from knocking the odds down. Well, we failed."

"What happened?"

Pockets could only lift and drop his shoulders. "Word got out, that's all. Ten minutes ago, the odds on Grogan are only a hair better than even money. Only one place it coulda come from, Baxter's people, which means Ortega. He couldn'ta done it hisself. He needed help from somewhere to manipulate the odds. The person who coulda done that was Slick Underhill, and he was connected to Ortega through Pete Botkin. Well, Botkin's gone, Underhill's dead, and all we got to take it out on is Ortega. Your bad luck you was standing so close to him when our boys opened up."

It struck me that this would be a poor time to confess I was the one who had raised the questions with Koblenz, which could have led to the flurry of betting that had screwed up the odds. "This doesn't concern me. I have to get a message to Megan Latimer."

"Sure. That can be done." Pockets turned his eyes to Jarman. "You'll come with us."

"Who watches the office?" she asked.

"Lock up. I ain't going to the house alone."

Locking up for Jarman meant getting her purse out of the bottom desk drawer and turning a key in the door to Cusimano's private office. She and Pockets led me out of the office and down the stairs, then out the back door of the building and down an alley to one of the residential side streets where tall frame houses stood shoulder to shoulder like a squad of infantry. Yards were so tiny you could nearly have knocked on one of the front doors with your feet still on the sidewalk. Space between houses seldom left room for a driveway. I walked along near the curb, staying out of Jarman's reach so she couldn't harm me further.

Half a block from the vending machine company, we went up a walk to the front porch of a house where Pockets knocked on the front door. A gust of wind blowing off Lake Erie blew down my neck and along my spine. We waited in silence a long time before someone inside approached the door and began turning locks. The woman who opened it as far as the night latch would allow was elderly, short, heavy, with her gray hair pulled back in a bun and a black dress that seemed like perpetual mourning. "What the fuck do you want?" Cusimano's mother snarled.

"Let us in, please, Mama," Pockets urged her.

She looked at him in confusion, at Jarman, at me, and then at the street over my shoulder. Her eyes weren't seeing us. They were looking over decades of time. "Who the hell are you?"

"Georgie."

"No you're not. Georgie delivers my paper. Always he puts it in my door so I don't have to go outside on cold days looking for it."

As she studied Georgie Pockets, a glimmer of recognition entered her eyes. For a second she was reconciled to the passage of time. Then she shook her head in denial. "Can't be."

Behind her Megan Latimer came skipping down a flight of stairs. "Let them in. That's who I was waiting for."

Mrs. Cusimano acted as if she could not figure out where the voice came from. "Where is Augustine? Only he can let strangers into my house."

"No, Mama," Pockets argued. "Gus has told you it's all right for me to come here."

While Mrs. Cusimano was trying to absorb that, Megan closed in and reached around her for the night latch. "For Chrissakes. Let them in." Megan still wore the safari outfit from Banana Republic she'd had on yesterday.

Mama turned on her then, flailing at her while our group on the porch watched helplessly from a few inches away. Stiff-arming her with one hand, Megan managed to slip the night latch out of its slot before she had to give ground. Pockets and Jarman rushed through, and tried to restrain the old woman without hurting her. Megan had backed through a doorway out of Mama's reach.

"What kind of person are you, taking that bitch's side against me?" Mama was asking as she realized her struggles were getting nowhere. "This is my house."

"It's all right," Pockets was assuring her. "Let's go out in the kitchen and see what you have for your guests."

Between them, Pockets and Jarman managed to steer Mama away, leaving me with Megan. She blew out air and turned into the living room. There she found a bottle and a glass and poured herself a quick shot. She gulped it down and let herself drop into a chair. "It's no fun trying to live here with a crazy woman. I'll be glad to get out."

"That might take a while."

Megan half smiled at that, willing to go along with a joke, and then stopped smiling altogether. "Where's the money?"

"I didn't get it."

"You didn't get my money?" Her voice rose to a shrill register. "That bastard Ortega ran off with it?"

"Not the way you mean that. He was about to hand it to me when someone started shooting at us. There was a scramble, and Ortega ran out with your money still in his hand."

"I gotta have that money," Megan said. "It's the only way I can get outa here."

"Sure you do. I'm still working on that end."

"Well, when will I get it?"

"When I can, all right?" She cowered back in her chair as if my words were pushing her. Seeing that, I eased up on her. "You're just going to have to stay here another day or so."

"With that crazy woman?"

"It can't be helped. As soon as I leave here, I'm going to start after the money."

Megan was not satisfied. "It'll never work out. Everything turns to shit for me."

"Be patient," I said. "You'll get the money."

"Sure I will."

She poured herself another drink, and I went in search of Pockets to let him know Megan's stay was going to be extended.

23

From Murray Hill I cut back to Euclid Avenue and followed that east until it brought me to—big coincidence here—the city of Euclid. Pete Botkin, according to the directory in my car, had lived on one of the residential side streets east of 222nd. Presumably his wife, now likely his widow, still lived there. Lynette Botkin had silver-blond hair. If she turned out to own a dark Lexus, my suspicion that she had been the driver of Ortega's getaway car would be confirmed.

Botkin's house proved to be a two-story brick job with faint touches of Tudor design, a solid petit-bourgeois home dead center in the middle class, not the mansion of a wealthy sports promoter. In a neighborhood where lawn care was the state religion, Botkin's front yard was scruffy with the last fall of leaves. The attached garage had a solid door that allowed no view of the inside. I had to detour to a side window to confirm that it held a Lexus.

On the front stoop, I rang the bell while standing off to one side. The answer was slow in coming. Someone had to peer through the peephole first. When that showed nothing, the door had to be opened carefully to see who was there. The instant it moved inward, I threw my weight against it and slipped my foot through the opening.

She recognized me, all right, as soon as I was in her view, and tried to slam the door shut. I leaned into it and forced her to give ground. So that isn't a big deal. After my session with Jarman, I needed a victory to stroke my manhood.

Lynette collided against a grandfather clock, causing it to strike once. Inside now, I kicked the door shut behind me. "Where's Ortega?" I demanded.

"Not here." Between her fear and ragged breathing, it was as close as she could come to coherence. Even at a moment like that, I was aware how stunning her beauty was. It was so distracting I had to force myself to ignore it.

I grasped her arm hard enough to make her wince. "Don't lie to me."

"No lie."

"Show me." Keeping a grip on her arm, my .45 in my other hand, I pushed her ahead of me.

Room by room we went through the house, upstairs and down, until I was satisfied that Ortega was not hiding in any closet or under any bed. It was not that hard a job, for the house was nearly empty except for the master bedroom. When we had completed our circuit, we were back in the living room. Its furnishings were down to a rocking chair, one end table, a floor lamp, and a Sony portable sitting on a TV tray. Different shades on the bare wood floor showed there had once been a carpet. Atop the end table was a photograph of a man in his forties with a strobe light reflected in his bald pate. I had seen the same man posed with fighters in the offices of Botkin & Ortega. I pushed Lynette into the rocking chair and tucked my .45 away.

"So he's not here. Where did you take him?"

"He's hiding out." The first rush of fear past, her wide eyes narrowed and her face hardened. A moment ago that habitual tough-broad expression had cracked to allow the fear to break through the mask. "He's scared."

I nodded. "With good reason. Not only is Cusimano gunning for him, now I'm piqued. I don't like bullets whizzing around my ears."

"That's too bad." She rubbed her forearm where I had been

gripping her. "Listen, Damon was doing what you wanted. Wasn't he bringing you the money? Is it his fault Cusimano's shooters opened up on him at that moment?"

"If the shooters had got me, Ortega would have been free and clear with the money."

"You think Damon was playing that kind of game?"

"It's happened before."

Lynette shook her head. "What kind of life is it where you have to be so suspicious of everyone?"

"Usually I turn out to be right."

"Not this time. Damon thought you decoyed him there so the shooters could get him."

I shook my head. "Maybe that's what he told you."

"Damon was playing square."

"He double-crossed Cusimano. Why not me? Convince me."

Lynette was sensing a weakening of my resolve. "Sure, I'll do that." She got up from the rocking chair and headed for a shelf in the corner. She was putting a lot of extra motion into so simple a maneuver, letting me see the roll of her flesh under her dress. Not very convincingly, I told myself: She's fat. "Drink?"

"I'll drink in your words."

She poured herself a glass of sherry, sat down in the rocker again, and crossed her legs under her short skirt to allow me the scenic view. "It all has to do with tonight's fight. Kid Grogan is going to win."

"There's been some suspicion about that," I agreed.

"And Cusimano, along with his gambler friends, loses out on a chance to clean up. Damon gets the blame for that, though it's not his fault. My husband set it up before he ran out, him and a con man named Slick Underhill. Their idea was to fiddle with the odds and make some money at Cusimano's expense."

"Underhill set it up?"

"He knew bookmakers all over the country, places where he could lay off bets so Cusimano wouldn't get wise about what was going on. After Pete disappeared, Damon needed this big killing bad. These last few months have been tough." She waved her glass at the room. "You can see how hard it's been. I've had to sell off my furniture."

"Slick and Ortega." I considered the pairing, not convinced about all she was telling me. "I heard your husband was hooked up with Slick in the old days. I didn't know Ortega was such a friend he'd hold Slick's fall money."

"Pete held the money, right here in the house, hidden out in the garage. When Pete took off, Slick had to tell Damon about it." She shook her head in regret over missed opportunities. "Jesus! Fifty grand right here in the house! At the same time I'm selling furniture to make ends meet!"

"It was never your money anyway. Now Ortega has it, and it's due to me. So where's Ortega?"

"I can't tell you that."

"You think you can't." I put menace in my voice.

Lynette squirmed under the threat. Fat, I reminded myself as I watched. "Damon's hiding out so he won't be killed. How can I work this out?" She set her glass down and leaned forward in her chair. "I'll go this far: I'll get hold of Damon and set it up for the two of you to get together."

I weighed my choices. I didn't trust her, but she was my only link to Ortega. I let her think I was going along. "When?"

Lynette rubbed her fingertips over her forehead in concentration. "It's gonna take some time to get to his hideout and get back to you. Oh, God! I gotta go to the fight tonight. I'm the only one left to represent the promoters. Look, meet me at the arena after the fight. If Damon says it's all right, I'll take you to him."

"You'll take me to him no matter what he says."

Lynette stared at me in defiance before she relented by dropping her eyes. "Yeah. All right. Too much has been happening to me today. The police were here, you know."

"Because of that little gunfight in Tower City?"

"That's what I thought when I saw them. But all they wanted was to know which dentist Pete went to. That was strange."

I understood. They were trying to identify the body in Amerine's woods. If the police had not told her her husband was probably dead, I was not about to break the news. "I'm trusting you to play square with me."

"I won't cross you."

"See that you don't." I stared meaningfully at her. "It wouldn't be pleasant if you did." Satisfied that I had made the threat strong enough, I walked out.

* * *

The suburbs are the world's worst place to conduct a stakeout, with the possible exception of the Mojave Desert. In the city you have traffic, parking spaces, strangers passing through, doorways to hide in, and—the greatest aid of all—the natural tendency of city dwellers to avert their eyes and ignore everything but what's between them and their objective. In the suburbs it's another world. Block after block of nothing but widely spaced homes without any commercial buildings. Cars that belong there are known, and strange cars are automatically suspect. Lately stay-at-home residents have organized into Block Watch groups ready to report any stranger as a suspected child molester. The hard-working private eye simply has no chance.

When I left Lynette I drove around the block and parked where I had a sight line between two properties to her garage door. How I envy television land where two men in business suits in the front seat of a four-door sedan can park anywhere without arousing suspicion. No such luck for me. I got out my cardboard sunscreen with the smile face on it, unfolded its accordion pleats, and propped it in my windshield. Then I went to my trunk to get out a pair of binoculars and a wide-mouth jar. When I was reasonably sure no one was watching, I got in the back seat and wedged myself into the corner where my head would not show. I aimed my binoculars on the sightline and adjusted the knob until the garage door was in focus.

Wait.

And wait.

Actually, this was not a long job. Ten minutes after I had got into position, the garage door went up and the Lexus backed out and headed out of the housing development. I pried myself out of the back seat, removed the sunscreen, and started my car.

For the first few blocks, I managed to parallel her with occasional glimpses between houses for reassurance. When she hit the main street, I allowed cars to get between us and followed her radio antenna over the intervening roofs. It was daylight. Traffic was abundant but not yet congested. All I had to do was stick with her until she led me to Ortega's hideout.

Lynette was making her way eastward out of Euclid on a path that would take her into even more remote suburbs, or into open country. My guess was that the trip would not be a long one, for she had already passed two opportunities to enter the freeway system. Wherever Ortega might be, she had taken him there and returned to her home in time to be visited by the police and then me. She could not have done all that if Ortega had fled halfway to the Pennsylvania border.

She zigzagged through some suburban streets, always south and then east again. I was three cars behind her when she turned right once more. By the time I rounded the corner, the train whistle was blowing. I saw the Lexus go over the hump of railroad tracks and tried to step on it to catch up to her. Traffic was too heavy to allow that. Another car made it over the tracks before the gates descended. The car ahead of me stopped, and I was stuck.

For the next few minutes I could only sit drumming my fingers on the steering wheel while I watched gondola cars creep by. At long last the tracks cleared, and the gates went up. If luck had been with me, I would have found the Lexus parked in the first block over the tracks. No such thing. I checked the first few blocks and wound my way down some side streets, but she had gone on to parts unknown.

I gave up the search and went home.

24

When I got home, I found Helen in her study talking on the phone. She blew me a kiss and made some gestures at the phone to convey that she was speaking to the grad student who had covered her classes that day. Her desk was awash with books and journals. Stuck at home for the day, she had devoted her time to catching up on her reading. Unless that was all cover for my benefit while she had actually caught up on *General Hospital.*

I busied myself in the kitchen until Helen finished her call and came looking for me to give me a real welcome. "You're finished early," she observed when we broke our clinch.

"I'm not finished for the day. I have to go out again this evening."

"Where?"

"A prize fight. Want to come along?"

She made a face. "I am assuming you have a business reason for going to an exhibition like that. Surely you aren't so atavistic you would enjoy that so-called sport."

"You're right. My thing is Wrestlemania."

She stuck her tongue out at me and then noticed my sports coat with its dirt and torn elbow, and the ripped knee in my pants. "What happened to you?"

"It was only a minor gunfight."

"Right."

"Would you believe a woman karate expert was throwing me around a room?"

"That's a little better."

"How about I fell down in a parking lot."

"Definitely the best of the choices."

I shrugged. "What can I say? How's the patient?"

"Resting—as she's been doing most of the day." Helen's eyes slipped away from mine. "I gave her a dose of the doctor's medicine an hour ago. It puts her into a deep sleep."

"You'll turn her into an addict," I warned, wondering if that could be Helen's secret plan. "Has she had anything to eat?"

"Some soup at noon. I helped her up twice to go to the bathroom."

"No problems?"

"I checked her bandage afterwards. There was no bleeding."

I left Helen downstairs while I went up to our bedroom so I could change clothes. I ditched my blue plaid sports coat and maroon sweater in case any of the police bulletins were still active. While I was at it, I stripped and took a shower, letting the hot water run on my aching muscles. I came out of the bathroom feeling limp but restored and dressed in a clean blue button-down shirt and a pair of flannel trousers.

Before I went downstairs, I opened the door to the guest bedroom and saw Elaine's copper hair spread over the pillow, her face turned away from the door. I was just closing it when Elaine turned toward me and forced her eyes open.

"Is it morning again?" She was groggy from the effects of the sedative.

I went over to the bed and touched her forehead. There didn't seem to be any fever. "Robert is alive. If it's any comfort, you gave him a broken arm and a sprained ankle. He won't be doing much to anyone for a few weeks."

"You saw him?"

"He told me how you ruined his life."

"I suppose I did." Elaine's head sank back on the pillow. For a moment I thought she was asleep again. "We pulled each other down. That was the story of our marriage."

"He says you were his accomplice on the robberies that sent him to prison."

She forced her eyes open and rolled them toward me. "You believed him?"

"He thinks you turned him in for the reward money."

"He must be very bitter over all that happened." She closed her eyes.

"I know he's bitter. I wonder if he's right."

"I'm so tired."

"And evasive."

"It happened so long ago—it was another life. We got desperate for money and did some foolish things." The words seemed to exhaust her, and Elaine let her head roll aside as her eyes closed.

It had not been a direct confession, but it was the most I could wring out of her in her condition. Sure she had drifted off again, I started for the door.

Behind me, Elaine said lazily, "Your nurse has been a big help."

I nodded to her. "Let's get you well again."

"She's in love with you, and she resents me."

"There's that." When I went downstairs, I carried my shoulder harness with me to the den, where I keep my gun-cleaning equipment. I unloaded my .45, field-stripped it, and cleaned out the powder residue and lead shavings left in it by the shots I had fired that noon in Tower City. Finished with that, I put the pistol away. The odds of the police ever tracing me were remote; still, I had left a number of ejected cartridge cases at the scene, which the lab could match with my pistol, and there was no sense toting something that could land me in jail.

Beneath the staircase is a triangle of wall into which I have built another concealed panel. I slid the panel aside and got a view of the underside of the staircase. One of the step risers is hinged to swing down, revealing a shelf inside the hollow step—a concealed space inside a concealed space. I put my Officer's Model on the shelf.

Also on that shelf was a shoebox holding miscellaneous parts for a Government Model .45, parts I have picked up from various sources over the years, mostly military surplus. I selected a receiver, a slide, a spring, a recoil buffer, a barrel bushing, and a slide stop. Enough parts remained in the box to construct two more guns, plus replacement parts. I closed up my hidey holes and carried the parts into the den, where I assembled them into a working pistol in less than two minutes. (If it weren't for being out of practice, it wouldn't have taken me so long.) It was bigger and heavier than what I'm used to, but it had compensations. No two serial numbers matched on any of the parts, and no government agency had any record that would associate it with me.

When I had worked the action a few times to make sure it functioned, I got out three spare stainless-steel magazines with convex followers. I loaded all three with seven rounds and seated one cartridge in the chamber of the pistol. I released the slide, put the safety on, and slammed one magazine into the butt. The other two magazines went into the pouches in my shoulder holster rig.

I washed my hands in the kitchen, where Helen was fixing dinner for us, and a tray to take up to Elaine. We ate together in a silence that had the weight of a bank vault. Helen pushed her salad around with her fork.

"Sorry I had to inconvenience you today," I said between bites.

"I guess you couldn't help it." Her voice made it sound as if I had plotted against her. "Anyway, I caught up on lots of reading today."

"Elaine said you were a good nurse."

"Miss Knoll slept most of the day."

"I'm sorry she isn't cross-eyed and seventy years old with warts and buck teeth."

Helen had trouble not smiling. "You can't help it when your clients are young and attractive. Will you be out late?"

"God knows. Don't worry if I'm gone a long time."

Helen relented from her pique in time to give me a good-bye kiss that made me want to say hello. Dressed in a tie and a tweed sports coat that was nothing like the one the Tower City Fugitive had worn, my shoulder holster under it, I put on my topcoat and headed for the arena out in the Midtown Corridor. It was a blocky building with a roof like a hangar that had a coating of grime dating back to the days of Gene Tunney. Its parking lot was nearly full. I walked around to the front entrance and bought a ticket without having to stand in line at the box office. Big as the crowd was, it wasn't enough to fill the seats. The real interest in this fight was with the bookies. Inside, a ramp led up into the auditorium where the ring was set up on the floor, surrounded by rows of folding chairs.

The first preliminary was already under way when I entered. My ticket was good only for seats up in the bleachers. I climbed to a vacant seat, squinting through the smoky interior, more interested in the audience than the fight. The crowd was a collection of local sports. The most colorful contingent was made up of pimps displaying their finery as if it were the Easter Parade. Most of the others wouldn't have been out of place at the racetrack. Scattered through the crowd were knots of young black men, each bunch huddled together representing one of the gangs, wearing their colors and flashing elaborate hand signals. Folks, Vice Lords, Gangster Disciples, Bloods, Crips, Blackstone Rangers. Those, at least, were some I could identify, along with many others I couldn't distinguish. My eyes sought out the Crips, scanning them to see if I could recognize anyone who had been shooting at me today. It was a hopeless exercise. All of them or none of them could have been the ones. They had the easy nonchalance of soldiers living for the moment, knowing that tomorrow they would be in a suicide charge against a machine gun nest. They could leave here and buy an ice cream cone or be mowed down by a passing car. It was all the same to them. I couldn't think of a better description of urban hell.

I pulled my thoughts away from the gang sideshow. I was here to meet Lynette Botkin. At the end of the round, the house lights came on, and I scanned the ringside seats. Cusimano was there with his mother and Jarman. Georgie Pockets, alone, stood in the aisle by Cusimano's seat, his back to the ring while his eyes sprayed the crowd. They landed on me, held a moment, and moved on. I knew my presence had been noted and memorized.

"Just the man I wanted to see."

The voice came from my right rear. While I was still trying to place it, I turned my head and recognized Mort Koblenz at my elbow. The bookmaker had a harried look about him as he jotted a note to himself on the paper in his palm. His glasses were up on his forehead.

"Something screwy is going on here," Koblenz announced.

"No!"

"Did you hear about a shooting in Tower City at noon today?"

"Not a thing."

"I got witnesses tell me you was there." Koblenz glanced around before leaning closer to me. "Is it true Cusimano's boys were gunning for Damon Ortega?"

"What if it was?"

"It means you was right all along. It means Ortega pulled a double-cross by not passing the word to Grogan to take a dive. It means the fight is on the square and Grogan will win."

"Then I'll lose my ten bucks." Among the people entering the arena was Barry Sprague. He walked in and down the aisle to Cusimano to chat with him.

"Listen, there's still time for you to switch your bet to Grogan," Koblenz said. "After all, I owe you for tipping me to this. If you hadn't started me asking questions, I coulda lost a bundle."

I worked on digesting the facts. No fix. Low odds on Grogan. "What's the line on Baxter?"

"You kidding me? No one is taking that kind of bet. The only question is whether Grogan kills him or only cripples him for life."

There was no sensible reason to bet on Baxter, I agreed. Yet my purpose had been to get rid of the ten Cusimano had forced on me. "Let my bet on Baxter ride. Ten-to-one odds?"

"You shitting me?" Koblenz was astounded. "Use your ten to light a cigar. That way you've got something to show for it."

"Am I on?"

"Hell, yes. I might as well take your money. The odds on Grogan are down to even money."

Koblenz moved on while I found my seat. Lynette Botkin had joined Cusimano's group at ringside, her ermine coat and silver-blond hair as easy to see as a spotlight in the dark. She must have come in while I was busy with Koblenz, for now she sat chatting with Mama Cusimano. Seeing there would be no getting to her now, I turned my attention to the fight.

The preliminary ended in a decision that drew neither cheers nor boos. They were waiting for the Baxter-Grogan match, even if it was only another preliminary. It was still the action that had drawn them here. Then Grogan entered. He jogged down the aisle and vaulted over the ropes. By contrast Baxter entered the ring as if he were the new kid in town sidling into his first class at the new school.

When the ring announcer bellowed Grogan's name, he threw off his robe and held up his arms. He was a squat man, old for his status, with a bald spot on his crown. He had a crushed-in face and cauliflower ears worn like medals for past campaigns. He had a profusion of hair on his back and tattoos on his arms. He was a journeyman pug, he knew it, and he was enthusiastic about tonight's match. He was going to be allowed to inflict pain, maybe the most memorable night of his life.

Baxter barely moved his seat off his stool when his name was announced. It drew laughter from the crowd, which was anticipating Grogan's savagery. Max Gruen stood close to Baxter, patting his shoulders, whispering in his ear. I imagined I could hear the words. Stay away from him. Don't get hurt. I added my wishes to Gruen's, a get-well card.

At the starting bell, Grogan rushed out of his corner, eager to get on with his job. Deliver the mail and go home. Baxter approached flat-footed, keeping a guard up. They circled, feeling each other out. Grogan feinted and Baxter cringed. Hoots and boos began from the audience. Grogan landed a left that staggered Baxter. More boos.

Grogan had all the confidence in the world. This fight was never going beyond the first round. All he had to do was get close to Baxter and introduce him to the canvas. Baxter gave ground without footwork, simply backing toward the exit. Hoots. Boos. Grogan got in a left. Then a right. Baxter relinquished more space. The hell with it. Grogan came on swinging wildly, heedless of his own defense. Land one good punch and finish this off.

And then Baxter uncorked one left jab that whacked into the bridge of Grogan's nose with a sound that carried to the last row.

Grogan stopped as if he had reached the end of the earth.

All booing stopped, too. The arena was graveyard silent.

25

Baxter wasted no time. He followed his left jab with another. A third. A fourth.

Only the ropes kept Grogan out of the laps of the third row. Baxter was after him, pounding fists into Grogan's midriff. When Grogan dropped his gloves, Baxter looped a downward clout to Grogan's jaw that drove him to his knees.

Grogan took the eight count to regroup his senses. The entire audience was now on their feet, yelling instead of booing. If anyone doubted the sudden reversal, that doubt was canceled by Grogan's face. Blood gushing from his nose was smeared over his cheeks. Baxter's first punch had broken his nose again and blackened both his eyes.

Baxter moved in as soon as Grogan was on his feet. The transformation of Battling Baxter could not have been more complete if a different, and better, fighter had come into the ring. Now it was Grogan who gave ground while Baxter danced toward him. Grogan waited his chance and caught Baxter with a jab that earlier would have rocked him. This time he shook it off and hit Grogan in return.

They exchanged punches, with Grogan getting the worst of it, until Baxter found an opening that dropped Grogan as the bell rang. Grogan's attendants half carried him to his stool.

"Ain't that something?" A fight fan in front of me was pounding his nearest neighbor in his enthusiasm. I directed my attention to Cusimano, who was yelling over the crowd noise at Pockets. He nodded and pushed up toward the ring until he could tug the referee's pants leg. The referee nodded at whatever Pockets told him and went over to Baxter's corner to inspect his gloves. Gruen was agreeable. They had nothing to hide. Baxter was only punching the way he always could—except he had never done it before.

Pockets turned from the ring and looked to the crowd, finding me without effort. Suddenly the two of us were alone in the auditorium with his eyes sending me messages that translated as hate mail. I waved back. His eyes said, *We'll settle this later*.

Round Two. Grogan came out of his corner more warily, refreshed by his rest. He and Baxter toyed with one another for the first minute, giving and taking. Now Baxter was circling, deftly dodging punches that would have landed on him last week. At last Grogan maneuvered him into a corner, finally connecting with a punch that put Baxter on one knee.

He bounced up on the count of three and went after Grogan. A cut had been opened over Grogan's left eye. Baxter worked on that when Grogan clinched. They broke, and Baxter knocked him down.

The arena was filled with cheers. Whichever fighter their money was on, whatever their expectations had been, the fans were seeing a real slugfest. Even more, they were seeing something rarer—a fight on the up and up. Grogan pried himself off the canvas and launched a counterattack that lasted until the bell ending the round.

Mort Koblenz found me when the lights came up. Two feet away, he had to yell his accusations. "Baxter's been sandbagging it all these years! He can fight, and you knew it!" Koblenz was so agitated his glasses slid down onto his nose where they belonged.

I shook my head. "I was guessing." Which was true enough. I had known Slick Underhill had been involved. With Slick on the scene, you could only ask for the most unlikely outcome and expect it.

Before Koblenz could say more, he was beset by a gaggle of bettors beseeching him to book another bet.

Round Three. Baxter went to work like a lumberjack felling a tree. Grogan, who had not trained to go the limit, was exhausted. Baxter knocked him down. He got up, and Baxter knocked him down again. One last time Grogan pulled himself up with the aid of the ropes. Baxter was through toying with him now. He maneuvered Grogan into the center of the ring and set him up for an uppercut that rocked him back on his heels and dropped him on his back. The referee picked up the count on three and went slowly to ten. It didn't matter. Grogan was still out when the referee held up Baxter's right hand.

Grogan, supported by his trainers, cleared the ring in time for the main event, now an anticlimax. Followed by the reporters on the scene, Baxter walked up the aisle to the dressing rooms, his gloves aloft. I lost sight of Max Gruen at his side as cheering fans pressed close. Pockets and Cusimano stood helpless at their seats, cut off from the fighter and his manager by the crowd around them. I had no doubt that Gruen and his fighter had doped out an escape exit. No one who had planned as they had would have overlooked the need for a getaway. It wouldn't be worth their while to hang around to collect the purse. The bets they had down would finance a long vacation out of Cusimano's reach.

I decided it was time to speak to Lynette Botkin and stood up to exit my row. A man stood at the end in the aisle, his arms folded across his chest. He was squat with shoulders too thick for the coat he wore. Beneath his coat was a turtleneck sweater. I had trouble placing him until I ignored the clothes to imagine him naked. Baxter's sparring partner, the one called Jake.

I turned to try the other way and saw that end of the row was also blocked. This time it was a woman who stood there, cool and competent. It might have been fun to visualize her naked, too, but all I could conjure up was an image of white pajamas cinched by a black sash. I held up my hands to Jarman. "Don't hit me. Please."

"Georgie wants to talk to you," she announced.

"I wonder what could be on his mind?"

They led me out of the auditorium, down the ramp into the concession area. We went along the hall that would lead eventually to the locker rooms, but before we got there, Jarman opened an unmarked door. "In here."

It was a storeroom for the concession stand, filled with boxes that held candy bars and potato chips, cases of pop and beer. Looking it over, I observed, "This place makes me hungry."

"Don't touch anything," Jake warned me. "That would be stealing." He moved around behind me and ran his hands over my ribs and found my .45. He looked at it contemptuously and then sent it skidding across the concrete floor, where it disappeared among the boxes. My hope skidded away with it.

Jarman sat on a stack of boxes and crossed her legs. The sight was almost enough to make me quit wondering what was going on.

The wait was not a long one. The door opened to admit Pockets, who slammed it behind him. He stood facing me. He and his two assistants formed a triangle, with me in dead center. He put his hands in the side pockets of his suit jacket, the same overly bold pinstripe he had been wearing that afternoon. He glared at me with an expression that was supposed to strike fear in my heart. It worked.

"You had a part in this."

"No."

He hadn't expected that. His eyebrows went up. "Who then?"

"Slick Underhill."

Pockets frowned. "Easy to blame a dead man."

"He put things in motion. After he died, they kept on rolling."

"You know this?"

"It figures. I can't prove it the way you would in court, but it has Slick's hallmark all over it, the way he loved the double twist. The fight was rigged because it turned out to be perfectly honest. The smart boys, who thought they were so clever, got taken." I held Pockets' eyes, trying to judge how he was taking this. "All that was typical of an Underhill scheme."

Pockets thought it out. "All right. But Ortega and Botkin had to be in it from the start."

"Max Gruen, too. They had a good fighter in Baxter, but they had to come up with a way to present him. If they went the usual route, he'd be lost in the crowd. They decided on something else. They'd hide his talent, lay back, and wait for a chance to clean up.

They sold a piece of him to Cusimano and let him be used as a patsy. In public he held back so he would look like a cream puff. That suited Cusimano because he arranged for the opposition to take dives. Baxter built up his record without even having to show his stuff. A nice deal all around."

"This was Ortega and Botkin, maybe Gruen. Where did Underhill come in?"

"Who knows? This much is clear. Underhill was hooked up with Botkin years ago. One way or another Underhill discovered the truth about Baxter and set out to capitalize on it."

Pockets nodded to confirm that much. "Underhill came to us with this plan to turn a big profit on a nothing fight. Trouble is, we would have to bet on Grogan—against our own boy. If that got out, everyone would know something was up. Underhill offered to lay off our bets with bookies all over the country. The damned thing got too elaborate. Big time gamblers on the East Coast and West Coast and everywhere between were suddenly plunging on a fight no one was supposed to care about. Word got out on the betting, and the odds on Grogan dropped."

"Exactly what Slick wanted to happen," I told him. "While the odds on Grogan dropped, they went up on Baxter, but no one was paying attention to that. Slick, Ortega, and Gruen got their money down on Baxter and uncorked their fighter."

"Except Slick ain't here to cash in on the winnings."

"Of course Ortega is still around, only because your gunmen screwed up. But Botkin isn't. That's what's so hard for me to understand. You couldn't have killed Botkin because he was double-crossing you. If you had known that back then, you never would have been taken."

"We didn't kill Botkin," Pockets said firmly.

"You don't have to be coy with me."

"We didn't kill Botkin," Pockets repeated. "Had nothing to do with the fight. Ortega killed him over his wife. He was screwing around with Lynette over a year. Botkin was supposed to have left town. Instead of getting on the plane to Vegas, he came back home. Suspicious, I suppose. Anyway, he caught them together. There was a fight, and Ortega killed him. Simple as that."

Sure it was. Everything is always simple when you slice right down to the basics. Greed and lust, the old dependables. Beneath it all the old verities remain. "Not so simple when you pile on the complications," I pointed out.

"Ortega called me to get rid of the body for him, out to Euclid where Botkin lived."

"That's some service you got there. Dead bodies disposed of. Evidence removed. Twenty-four-hour service. Discounts for large quantities."

Even Pockets had trouble repressing a smile. "Ortega paid enough for it—or should have. We didn't find out until later that Botkin had cleaned out the company accounts before he left. He must have squirreled the money away somewhere figuring he'd start a new life under a different name after he killed his wife and her lover. No one ever figured out where it went. So what were we supposed to do when Ortega couldn't pay? Dig up the body and dump it on Ortega's desk? We figured to collect in other ways, through Baxter."

"You didn't exactly go broke on the deal. You also collected from Amerine."

"Only because I saw how to make Botkin's body pay off for us in another way." Pockets was proud of his business acumen. "We coulda dumped him in some empty lot, no problem, but hey, I got other things on my mind. Like Sprague. He was welching, and he needed to be mussed up. But, hell, that don't pay the bills. So I got this other idea. We could get rid of the body and get Sprague's money at the same time. Took a little effort to get Sprague to think he came up with the idea, but in the end, that's what we did. You don't see Cusimano thinking like that."

"And Underhill?"

Pockets flopped his arms out. "Had nothing to do with us. Musta been some private matter catching up with him."

I accepted that idea on consignment. Much as I would have liked to pin Underhill's death on them, I couldn't see a way they would have gone after Underhill last week. If they had known about the double-cross then, they could have avoided tonight's loss.

"Now what am I going to do with you?" Pockets asked.

"You don't have to do anything with me. My interests don't affect yours."

"Maybe so. Trouble is, you went to Mort Koblenz and put a bug in his ear. And Koblenz started calling around, and that's what drove down the odds." Pockets reached out and patted my cheek. "Not a good thing to do."

I braced myself for something more, but Pockets turned away from me, more saddened than angry. He strode over to the door and opened it. Before he stepped into the hall, he turned back to deliver a last instruction to his henchpersons. "Hurt that sorry son of a bitch." He slammed the door behind him.

I turned to face my opponents. Jake was moving in on me, cracking his knuckles and flexing his fingers. Jarman stood up and started walking toward me, her eyes suddenly dreamy, her hips swaying provocatively. Two more steps would have brought her close enough to give me a kiss. Jake was hanging back to concede the first move to her. She took another step, and I socked her on the jaw as hard as I could.

All right, criticize me. Put me on the NOW hit list. The simple fact is that of my two opponents, Jarman was the more dangerous. Jake was a fighter, something I could deal with if not defeat, but Jarman was the unknown quantity. She was capable of inflicting damage I could not anticipate, and anyway, she was using her sex for a weapon. Besides, it felt good when the shock of impact ran up my arm to my shoulder, when her head snapped, when her eyes rolled back. She crumpled to the floor.

Jake lost a second or two as he stared in horror at what I had done. I put my head down and charged him. The impact of my hundred and eighty pounds jarred him backward, off his feet and onto the floor, with my weight atop him. That was my advantage. On the floor, he was deprived of what he knew best—footwork and fisticuffs. I got in some good blows before he managed to throw me off and scramble to his feet. I moved in on him, throwing punches to inflict damage.

Alas, it was not to be. Jake blocked my punch and drove his fist into my gut. Suddenly there was no oxygen in the universe, and I was sinking to my knees. Jake pounded me down as if he were driving a nail into a board, knocking out what little sense remained in my head. Vaguely I was aware of Jarman stirring in the distance. Then, while I lay on the concrete floor, I sensed my ribs being kicked by shoes with sharp toes and high heels.

After that it was—mercifully—black.

26

They had thrown me in a cage with a bear. Edging toward consciousness, I lay still awhile, dimly aware that the bear was nearby and that any movement would only frighten it. The bear suspiciously eyed this new critter invading its home. The bear stayed in its corner until curiosity overcame its suspicions, and it lumbered over to my inert form and sniffed me out thoroughly. An odd critter but no threat, the bear decided. The bear pawed at me, got no retaliation, pawed some more. Still the new critter did not move. The bear decided the new critter could be easily dominated. It climbed atop me, its weight crushing me.

"Are you all right? Wake up!" the bear said.

I came to with my face mashed into the bear's fur. I tried to wriggle out from under, to turn my head and breathe. The bear's fur was white. A polar bear. I looked up and saw it had the face of Lynette Botkin.

"Wake up! Come on!"

I closed my eyes instead, held them shut tight, then opened them again. Lynette's face was still there on the polar bear's body. Except it wasn't a bear. It was her ermine coat. Still poised in that nether world of half dream, half reality, I rolled my head to the side to look at the cage. This was no cage. It was still the storeroom.

"Can you get up?" she asked.

"I don't think that's a good idea."

"Come on." Ignoring my suggestion, she tugged me to a sitting position. I had been lying close to the cases of Coca-Cola, so that once I was sitting up, I was able to scoot backward until my shoulders touched the cases.

My head rolled around on my shoulders, causing something loose inside to rattle around like shards of broken pottery. "What are you doing here?" I asked her.

"Looking for you. I saw you go out with that man and woman. Then Georgie left, and I followed him. He came in here, and after a while, he came out, but you didn't. So I looked inside and there were those two kicking you. 'Say,' I yelled at them, and they ran out past me. Nearly knocked me down."

"That's all right. They were about finished anyway." I pulled myself up by the cases and found my balance. Or thought I did. Lynette grabbed hold of my arm as I started to topple over. I sat down on the cases and gathered my strength.

"Down there." I pointed to the area where I had seen my pistol scoot away. "Get my gun."

Lynette humored me by searching among the shadows between boxes until she found it. Holding it by the butt pinched between her thumb and forefinger, she handed it back to me. I checked it and shoved it back up into my shoulder holster. Fine lot of good it had done me so far. "Ready to go," I told her.

Lynette guided me down the hallway by keeping me close to the wall, which proved to be a great help in navigation. Although sounds of a fight in progress still came from the auditorium, customers were straggling out. The main event was drawing less interest than the Baxter-Grogan fight had. When we reached the men's room, I turned in, leaving Lynette in the hall. Two dudes were there, one handing over some money, the other passing over a glassine bag. They looked at me, their hands heading quickly for pockets.

"Beat it," I said.

My words were wasted. Their transaction completed, the dudes were already hustling by me for the door. I stumbled over to a sink and leaned on it, slowly raising my head until I could see my face reflected in the mirror. Surprise. My face wasn't damaged beyond recognition. Jake and Jarman had devoted themselves to damaging my midsection. I splashed water on my face and hair and looked for towels. There were none, only a blower. I uncoiled a vast amount of toilet paper in one of the stalls to dry my face and hair and sat on the commode, the only seat around. I lit a cigarette to prove I could still breathe in and out with only minor pain. While I sat and smoked, contemplating the most recent developments in this saga, the door to the men's room opened.

"Hello?" It was Lynette stepping gingerly into forbidden territory. She looked at the urinals as if she were trying to fathom their purpose. Then she saw me in the stall, averted her eyes, and looked back when she realized my pants were up. She stood there studying me. I studied her, a Rubenseque vision in ermine in a filthy men's room.

"I'm here," I said.

"I was beginning to wonder. You look like shit."

"Funny. I don't feel a day over seventy." I took a drag on my cigarette. "Did you see Ortega today?"

"Yeah."

"And?"

"He'll talk to you. I intended to take you to him now, but—"

"I'll make it." I pulled myself up and pitched my cigarette into the toilet bowl. "Let's go."

We made our way down the hall with me walking on foam rubber. Inside the auditorium the ring announcer was speaking into the microphone, trying to make himself heard over a buzz of conversation. His voice was an electronic noise without connection to any known language on the planet. We passed out the door into the chill night air, which was like getting hit by another fist. It made me want to lie down and sleep. With Lynette holding me up, I waded across the now half-empty parking lot to my car and fished my keys out of my pocket.

"Are you sure you can handle it?" Lynette asked.

"Positive."

"We could take my car."

My expression convinced her that was out of the question. "Where do you want me to go?"

"East on Euclid."

I unlocked the driver's-side door and flicked the switch to unlock the other doors, letting Lynette find her own way in. Would you expect a man who pops a woman on the jaw to hold a door for a lady? I had all I could do to get myself in. Once there I started the motor and turned on the defrosters.

When my rear window began looking like a Venetian blind, I set out, taking Euclid Avenue east as she had directed. I hadn't gone more than a few blocks before I realized how shaky I was. The headlights of oncoming traffic blurred my vision, and I had trouble holding the car in my lane. In front of the Cleveland Clinic, I pulled over to the curb and told Lynette to take the wheel. She did, and I got into the passenger seat and tilted it all the way back. For the rest of the ride, I was on my back, much of the time with my eyes closed. Much better.

From that position I could only sense where she was taking me. Like that afternoon, she stayed on surface streets, avoiding the freeway. I recognized the turn onto Monticello Boulevard before I dozed off. I woke when the car lurched to a stop on a potholed driveway.

"Here we are," Lynette announced.

I levered the seat forward to bring me to a sitting position. The car had stopped in a driveway behind a large house, between it and a barn behind it. Wherever we were, we were isolated—only the black night around with no neighbors nearby.

Taking my flashlight with me, I got out of the car to survey the surroundings. Above was the moon with a corner sliced off and only a few scudding clouds to blur its light. In the distance I could see the bright lights of a building and its grounds. As I was about to conclude it was some kind of factory, I saw red and green lights winking and moving toward me. There was a growing roar, and then the lights left the ground and started climbing into the night sky. An airplane. What I had thought was a factory was an airport. It took me longer than it should have to process that piece of information. Cleveland Hopkins was on the other side of town, so this had to be another facility. It came to me this must be the Cuyahoga County Airport.

With that much solved, I made sense of where we stood. Not so long ago this had been farmland until it was cleared for a flight path. The few farmhouses, of which this place must have been one, had been abandoned in the process. I turned my flashlight on the house to find peeling paint, shutters hanging askew, dark broken windows. It was all appropriate to the Halloween season, the kind of place that kids quickly believe is a haunted house. On that cold, windy night, there was one private eye who could have agreed with them. I started toward it.

"This way." Lynette led me over to the barn. Built into the large barn doors was a human-scale walk-in door. She opened that and stepped across the threshold as if she were entering her beauty shop. I followed.

My flashlight beam showed me that considerable work had been done to remodel the place. All the stalls had been ripped out. In their place, a prizefight ring had been constructed in its center by driving posts into the ground and stringing ropes around them. In a corner hung a speed bag, and nearby, a Nautilus machine.

I jumped suddenly, reaching for my pistol. From the corner of my eye I saw someone standing in the dark, ready to pounce. Then my flashlight let me see it was not a person but a heavy punching bag, like a tackling dummy. I took my hand away from my gun butt.

Lynette went on across the floor, circling the ring as she headed toward the back, where a balcony stretched across the far wall. A door opened up there and splashed a rectangle of light across the floor. I was surprised only because there had been no hint of a light when we had been outside.

"Damon!" Lynette rushed to a staircase that ran across the back wall at a forty-five-degree angle. I followed her at a slower pace and reached the balcony near the source of the light.

Ortega stood in the doorway now with Lynette in his arms. They kissed passionately. After a while, Lynette pulled away and rested her head on his shoulder. He looked over her head and saw me. Ortega, his hair combed back so tight it threatened to lift his eyebrows, smiled at me and said, "Hello, Sport."

I said, "You son of a bitch!" and socked him in the jaw.

27

The blow took Ortega by surprise. His chin pointed ceilingward, and he fell backward through the doorway into the room beyond. He landed sitting, propped up on his elbows. Lynette screamed and knelt down beside him. Ortega touched his jaw and moved his chin to make sure it worked. Only then did he chance speaking. "Say! What did I ever do to you?"

"I don't like being shot at," I told him. "I don't enjoy having to shoot back. Other than the idea of getting killed, there's the possibility I could have killed somebody."

"You think any of that appeals to me?" Ortega asked.

"I think you allowed yourself to be set up because an assassination attempt would make your whole scheme more convincing. If everyone believed Cusimano wanted to kill you, they'd be more sure than ever that Grogan was going to win." I stepped over Ortega into the room. The source of light was a Coleman lantern sitting on a table. It showed me a room with a few pieces of junk shop furniture, among them a couch that could fold out into a bed.

Over the windows were heavy curtains, which explained why the light was not visible from outside.

"I'm not that devious." Ortega pulled himself to his feet with Lynette's help. He was wearing a Chesterfield coat and gloves. It couldn't have been colder in here than it was outside, but the sight of our breath vapor made it seem that way.

"Then consider my punch a down payment." I was in no mood to apologize. "Downstairs is where Baxter trained?"

"He needed someplace. When he sparred in public, he had to hold back. Here he could really cut loose and keep himself fit for the day he let the world know it." Ortega took out a cigarette and lit it, his gloved hands operating the lighter.

"You're still holding the money for Megan," I said.

Ortega opened a drawer in the table and removed the paper sack he'd been carrying earlier. He put it on the table within my reach. "All yours."

I dumped out the contents and counted the money under the light of the lantern. Forty-seven thousand dollars, after what had spilled out today. I cut out my share and stuffed that in my pockets. The rest went back into the sack. Ortega watched me with bored, hooded eyes, but Lynette had an expression like a starving survivor seeing food.

"Now that you've taken a poke at me," Ortega said, "and got your money, you must be satisfied."

"Not quite. I'd still like to know who killed Slick Underhill."

Ortega shrugged. "He was alone in his apartment with Megan. Then he was dead, and she was still alive. I'm no gumshoe, but the list of suspects looks short to me."

"When the cops arrived, there was a toe print in the blood, a man's shoe."

Ortega inhaled smoke, a long, careful drag. "Say what you mean."

"Slick wouldn't be the first partner you iced."

Lynette gasped and looked at Ortega. "What does he know?"

"Nothing," Ortega said. "He's bluffing."

I said, "Botkin was going away on a trip, or said he was. Instead of getting on his plane, he slipped back to his house. He caught you and Lynette together. You killed him and called Pockets to dispose of the body."

"It wasn't like that," Lynette protested. "Pete tried to kill us both. Damon was only defending himself."

"Lots of husbands in Botkin's position might have tried to kill a cheating wife and her lover."

"You don't understand how it was," Lynette insisted. "Pete wasn't acting in the heat of passion. He came back to commit murder. He cleaned out the accounts ahead of time, and he brought along gasoline to set the place on fire. He intended to burn down the house and disappear. The police would have found the burned up bodies of a man and woman in bed together. They would never have dreamed of the possibility that the man was anyone but Pete. He would have been declared officially dead, but actually he would have been free to start over somewhere else with a new name. It would have worked except that Damon was too quick for him. That's why I say it was self-defense."

"Shut up, Lynette," Ortega said evenly.

The sound of a crash outside stopped her if Ortega's words didn't. He leaned over the table to turn off the lantern, then went to the window to part the curtains. I came up behind him so I could see over his shoulder. The window looked down onto the back of the house, where moonlight was strong enough to make out the shapes of two men on the back porch. One of them was helping the other pull his foot out of a hole in the floorboards where it had gone through.

"Fuck! Goddamnit!" The stuck man's voice was strong enough to reach us.

"Quiet!" That hoarse whisper came from the vicinity of my car, where a third man had to be crouching.

The two men on the porch stepped down. Now the moonlight allowed me to pick up a few details about the two. They wore baseball caps, one of them turned around with the bill down the wearer's neck. He walked with a limp.

"Know them?" Ortega whispered in my ear.

"The Crips who ambushed us." The streak of pessimism in me when I get too close to money was being activated again. I should have known I wasn't about to leave here rich.

By a tree in the yard, a shadow moved and stepped up to the two Crips. I could tell enough about him to know he wore a turtleneck sweater and carried a pump shotgun. It was Jake, the sparring partner who had been working me over an hour ago, before Lynette interrupted.

Lynette recognized him, too. She whispered, "They followed us here."

"That's the reason they didn't do a number on me. They wanted us to lead them to Ortega."

The fourth man, the one crouched by my car, the only one I hadn't identified yet, now stood up and pointed the others back to the house. He wore a topcoat now, a broad-shouldered, double-breasted number that fit him tightly and reached below his knees. It was a fashion statement that gave me a solid clue to his identity. Then he spoke: "They're inside. Go get them." The voice cinched the identification for me: Georgie Pockets.

While the two Crips went back to the scut work of entering the house, Pockets stationed Jake at the tree at one corner of the house. Pockets went off to take up a position on the corner diagonally opposite Jake. That was standard procedure. It allowed Pockets and Jake each a line of sight covering two sides of the house so one or the other of them would be able to see anyone who ran off.

Ortega dropped the curtain, turning our room pitch dark. "They'll search the house and then come out here. Looks like you're going to be caught in the crossfire again."

"Yeah," I agreed.

Ortega's cigarette tip glowed in the dark, then dropped to the floor to be stepped on. "It's me they're after. You can hide under the table if you want, but they're not gonna be particular once the fireworks starts."

I said, "Best we face them downstairs. Lynette can stay up here and hope we stop them before they get this far."

"Sounds good to me."

I shrugged out of my topcoat and felt my way in the dark to the door. When I opened it, light from moonbeams leaking into the barn let me see Ortega and Lynette dimly. He hugged and kissed her briefly before he joined me on the balcony overlooking the gym on the floor below. He shut the door to his room behind him.

"It's your play," I said.

"High and low. I'm high."

Clutching the flashlight, I stole down the stairs and concealed myself by the Nautilus machine. With Ortega on the staircase and me here on the floor, we had the barn in a crossfire. Helpful as that would be, I had few illusions that we could come out of this whole while being outnumbered four to two.

I drew my .45 and waited. Without my topcoat, I soon felt the cold penetrating me. I forced my muscles to relax while I strained my ears for sounds. I would soon be shaking enough without additional trembling from the cold. The noises were faint from the house now. The gunmen had learned we were not there and would be heading for the barn.

The walk-in door banged open suddenly, the result of a kick. That was wasted energy, for the door had not been locked. They were as jumpy as I was—a thought that gave me a dram of comfort. After a wait outside, the gunmen came through the doorway.

Jake was first, wielding the shotgun. Behind him came the two Crips. Last was Pockets. He shut the door as soon as he was inside and flattened against the wall with a Crip on either side. When they were ready, Jake started forward. He was their point man, ready to spray buckshot at whatever moved first. The others, as far as I could tell, held nothing but handguns. Remembering the pain Jake had inflicted on me, I felt nearly justified about what was going to happen next.

Jake took a step, then another. Three. Four. Suddenly he swung the muzzle of his shotgun to the left and fired, pumped, and fired again.

Stuffing flew out of the heavy punching bag—the same one that had nearly drawn my fire when I first entered. My ears were still ringing from the overwhelming blast of the shotgun when Ortega's pistol cracked four times, and Jake fell. Stabs of muzzle flash answered from the three remaining guns as the killers fired and dived for cover. Ortega shot back from the staircase.

A lull followed. In the dark the gunmen were moving to position themselves. They knew Ortega was on the staircase now, but I still had not revealed my position. Much as I had tried to keep track of them in the dark, the bright flashes of orange light had left my vision blurred by spots of red. Blinded by light and deafened by noise was not a healthy condition in here. I could be sure about only one of them, someone across the ring from me. I zeroed in on the general area, knowing I was aiming within two feet of him.

Focusing in on that point, I held the flashlight out at arm's length and high. Directing the beam from that position, I turned it on. One of the Crips was spotlighted in the beam for only a second, which was long enough for my thumb to wipe off the safety on my .45 and for me to fire his way. His body was jerking under the impact of my third bullet when I snapped the flashlight off.

Bullets were zinging around the vicinity where my flashlight had just been—the aiming point for the other two. That suited me, for their shots were going three feet over my head. Except their aim was not that good, so that stray shots were coming too close. Worse, one of them was using an Uzi or Mac 10 that sprayed lead indiscriminately. One bullet whanged off the Nautilus as I rolled away from my starting position.

The burst of shooting ended in another lull. I listened, sure I could hear the clicks of reloading—if my noise-muffled ears could be trusted. I tried locating the two remaining gunmen. Pockets was somewhere along the wall opposite me. The last of the Crips, who wielded the Uzi, was still over by the door. He immediately became my top priority.

As far as I could tell, Ortega still had a position on the staircase. I made ready to throw my flashlight. In one motion I turned it on and rolled it away from me, under the ropes of the ring. Its wriggling beam brushed over the Crip with the Uzi. He fired at the flashlight, kicking up dirt geysers.

Using the Uzi's muzzle flashes for a target, I fired that way four times, spacing my shots from lower left to upper right. Two more shots aimed at the Crip came from the staircase. Then Pockets opened up—not at me but at the staircase.

Ortega grunted. He fell forward into the banister, which snapped. Ortega's body made a slow turn in the air, landed on the ring ropes, tangled in them, and fell into the ring.

Footsteps beat on the stairs, Pockets running up them for high ground. I fired wildly at him, and my slide locked open. I slammed a loaded magazine into the butt of my .45, released the slide, and fired again. By that time my angle on Pockets was bad, and only wood chips flew. Pockets was now on the balcony. That was not a pleasing development. He now had the advantage of the high ground, and Ortega was out of the fight.

I dived under the ring ropes and grabbed my flashlight, leaving it on the ground but turning its beam on the Crip against the wall. He was sitting there under a smear of his own blood on the wall, trying to bring up his Uzi. I finished him off with one shot and rolled away as Pockets, from the balcony, fired at the spot where I had been.

I was now at the bottom of the stairs. Stepping carefully to avoid noise, I started up the stairs to the balcony, hoping that Pockets' ears were as damaged by the noise as mine. Walking on the balls of my feet, keeping close to the wall, I was halfway up when I heard the shot. It was a flat report from a distance, not from the balcony, where I had expected Pockets to be. Cautiously I raised my head until my eyes were level with the balcony floor. No one there.

The only place Pockets could have gone was into Ortega's room.

I edged my way along the wall to the open door and peered around the frame. After a moment, I began to separate vague shapes from the deeper shadows of the room. A head, attached to a form on the floor, lying on its back. Its hair was too short and too dark for it to be Lynette.

"Are you all right?" I asked.

"Yes." Her voice was pitched two notes below hysteria.

"Don't shoot. I'm coming in." I eased around the door jamb, trying to see her in the dark. Her ermine was a lighter gray than the rest of the room. I holstered my auto and took out my Zippo. I flicked it alight and stooped down to examine the body. Pockets lay on his back, eyes fixed unseeing on a ceiling beam. In the center of his forehead was a bullet hole.

I used my lighter to find my way to the table, where I got the Coleman lantern going again. When its light came up, I saw Lynette standing near Pockets' feet, holding a small revolver that was still smoking. Until she saw Pockets' body in the light, she couldn't let herself relax. When she did, she let her right arm sag to her side and turned her head to my shoulder. "He came in. It wasn't Damon—or you. He had a gun in his hand. I had to—"

"You did the right thing," I assured her. "Where did your gun come from?"

She looked down at the small revolver in her hand as if she were just realizing she held it. "Mine. In my purse." Suddenly she pulled back and looked into my eyes. "Damon! Where's Damon?" Much as I tried to keep my expression neutral, she saw something there. "Oh my God!" She ran out of the room and down the stairs.

By the time I caught up with her, she was in the ring with Ortega's head in her lap, holding his face against her ermine just as she had cradled me earlier. Despite his wounds and the fall, Ortega was still breathing—shakily. I picked up my flashlight and used it to locate his wounds, two hits in the chest that were pumping blood onto his shirt. Each breath produced a whistle. I looked at Lynette and shook my head.

". . . smoke . . ." Ortega said.

Bad as that may have been as a prescription, I was not about to deny a dying man his last request. I lit a cigarette and put it between Ortega's lips. He inhaled gratefully. A lock of hair had fallen across his forehead like a fishhook, the only time I had seen him with mussed hair.

The smoke revived him. ". . . wrong . . . slant . . ." He inhaled again. "Got . . . one . . . thing . . . wrong." Ortega blinked.

"Damon! Damon!" Lynette shook him, but his head only rolled meaninglessly.

"Not . . ." He coughed. The cough turned into a gasp.

"Damon! No!" Lynette threw herself across his chest. "Don't die on me!"

Ortega struggled to get something out, but his lips moved without producing sound. His body tensed, then gave out one long exhale that ended in the guttural noise people call a death rattle. His eyelids lowered without closing, and the cigarette dropped out of his lips to roll across his shoulder onto the floor.

I stamped the cigarette out.

28

Lynette and I spent the night together, though not the way that might sound. We stayed one hour in the barn after I finally convinced her there was no point in cradling Ortega's head any longer. With five dead bodies in the place, the barn was not the most pleasant site in the Midwest. I would have left right away except I couldn't be sure Cusimano hadn't sent more gunmen. When no one else showed up, I slipped outside and scouted the area. The car that had brought the crew, the same Imperial I had seen Pockets drive, was parked at the front of the house, but there was nothing else around.

Once I was sure we weren't walking into a trap, I led Lynette out to my car and settled her into the passenger seat. By this time she was allowing herself to be led, her will gone, her thoughts keeping their own counsel. When I got behind the wheel, my dashboard clock showed it was only a little past midnight. Unbelievable. The way I felt it should have been next week.

I didn't go far. When I found a quiet bar, I turned into the parking lot and steered Lynette to the ladies room. She did all it is that women do inside those places and came out looking presentable, except for the whiteness in her complexion. I prescribed a drink for that. We took a back booth where she put away a scotch while I sipped coffee.

Lynette was working on her second drink when I got up to use the pay phone. I called Helen, catching her asleep on the downstairs couch with the voice of David Letterman in the background. I told her I was fine but wouldn't be home until later, maybe not before dawn.

"What's wrong?"

"Nothing. The job is more complicated than I thought."

"You sound strange."

"Maybe I'm catching a cold." Maybe I had killed two men and watched three others die. "How is our patient?"

"Coming along. I think we can dismiss her tomorrow."

I brought the conversation to an end before Helen could press further to know what was eating at me. I had evaded the explanations I owed her, but I hadn't erased the sights of the recent past from my mind. I returned to the booth and considered the immediate consequences. The chance that the police would discover the bodies soon and trace them to me was not the problem. I had to keep reliving those events in my mind until I could convince myself—make myself really believe it—that I'd had no choice.

"I loved Damon." I wasn't sure where the voice had come from until I realized Lynette was speaking. "It was the real thing for us."

I studied her across the table, aware again of the delicate bone structure of her face and her stunning beauty. That face matched with her full body and ermine coat was not going to be soon forgotten. I decided to play along. "You had that much, at least."

"It wasn't dirty. I wanted to tell Pete we were finished. I wanted to live with Damon, get married if we could."

"It must have been complicated for him, too, his partner's wife and all."

"Something was there from the first day we met." Lynette took a swallow from her drink. "We fought it at first, but it was pulling us together. Pete went East once to scout a fighter in New Jersey. He told Damon to watch out for me for the week he was gone. Neither one of us wanted that. It was like fate was throwing us together. Then Damon took me out for dinner, and afterwards I invited him in for a drink—and it happened."

Somehow I was visualizing all this in black and white with lots of deep shadows—the middle reels of a film noir.

"We didn't know what to do about it. We went on seeing each other when we could. After the Baxter fight, we decided, would be the time to tell Pete. Then he was supposed to fly out to Vegas for a few days. Damon and I had a chance to be together for a while, except Pete showed up." She shrank into a corner of the booth in her expensive fur, with her arms around herself as if they were the tentacles of an octopus gripping her from behind. Seeing her like that, I had a hard time remembering her as the tough cookie who had rescued me from a beating.

"He caught us in bed together and then there was a fight. Pete had a gun. They fought over it, and it went off."

"The same gun in your purse? The one you used on Pockets?"

She nodded. "So there we were with Pete dead. Damon called Cusimano to get rid of the body. It was a perfect setup for us. Pete was supposed to be in Vegas, so there was nothing to explain. Sure, it would cost us to get rid of the body, but we figured to pay for it with money we had. It was only later that we discovered Pete had cleaned out the company accounts. That's when we figured out it was no accident he caught us together. We never did find out what happened to the money."

"He had a ticket in his pocket for Chicago," I pointed out.

"Sure, and where would he go from there? He had someplace in mind, probably somewhere in the Sunbelt on accounta he never liked the cold. Where that is, you can bet he's got the money there under a false name. We'll never know."

I studied the woman across the table from me, my mind scratching out revisions as fast as I could make them. She was a self-indulgent woman who had two-timed her husband, who sold her furniture in hard times but kept her furs and her car. She lusted for money but risked all she had for love. She was a bundle of contradictions, not unlike the rest of us.

Last call was being sounded in the bar. I told Lynette I would take her home.

"No. It's not safe. They might come looking for me there."

She was probably right. It wouldn't be safe for either of us to be out on the streets until I settled some affairs with Cusimano. Taking Lynette home with me was no good, so I compromised by driving downtown to my office. In Moe Glickman's waiting room was a bench where she could stretch out, using her fur for a blanket. When she was comfortable, I went into my office to settle myself in.

First order of business was handling my cut from the money I had collected from Ortega. For a few wild seconds, I considered the possibility of giving it all to Megan. Lord knows enough of my counterparts in fiction would have done that, which might explain why it's fiction. I had killed, but I hadn't killed for money. Now here I sat with nearly twelve thousand dollars in my hand, tax free. I compromised by earmarking it for charity, the Gil Disbro Improvement Fund. I put it in a manila envelope and put that away in my file cabinet—under *M*, of course. The rest of the money, Megan's share, stayed in my topcoat pocket.

That done, I settled into my swivel chair. I tilted it back and crossed my ankles on a corner of my desk. My eyelids closed and I slept—the deep, dreamless sleep that is usually the hallmark of a clear conscience. When I awoke, I had a crick in my neck.

Near dawn, before anyone arrived for the day, I woke Lynette and drove her back to the arena. The parking lot, so crowded last night, was vacant now, with only a few cars still sitting with their windows frosted over. Lynette's Lexus was alone near the building.

"Now where?" she asked. "I still can't go back home."

It was a problem I had mulled over. "Judge Amerine's house is empty. Try that. If it's locked up, go next door to Dr. Mount's. I'll catch up with you there in a couple hours."

When Lynette had started her car and driven off, I lit a cigarette and sat for a moment while I plotted my next move. When my cigarette was finished, I drove out to Mayfield Road and then to the Cusimano house on the side street. I parked at the curb and mounted the porch to ring the bell.

Jarman answered the door. When she recognized me, she stood there a moment, letting cold air into the house. Her hair was up, and she was wearing a sweatshirt and jeans. The edge of her jaw showed a bruise where my fist had caught her. Now her fingertips touched it as she looked me over. "What business could you possibly have here?"

I held up the sack. "Package for Megan Latimer."

"I'll see she gets it."

"Sorry. I have to deliver it in person."

She admitted me, backing away from the door as if she couldn't trust herself as long as I was within reach. "I'll have to wake her. You can wait in the kitchen."

Jarman showed me the way. Cusimano was already there in a robe, his tinted glasses in place, while his mother fussed over the stove, possibly aimlessly, possibly fixing him breakfast. She stopped long enough to see who was entering her domain. "You have to get your own coffee." She turned back to the stove.

I poured a mug and sat down at the table opposite Cusimano, who was scanning the headlines in the *Plain Dealer*. He finished the article he was reading before he put the paper aside and looked up at me. If he was surprised to see me, he hid it well.

"Pockets is dead," I told him.

He stared at me, still the portrait of a Renaissance prince. "You killed him?"

"I could have. There were lots of bullets flying around, but it so happens I was shooting in the other direction."

"Ortega, then?"

"He's dead, too." If Cusimano wanted to take that as an answer to his question, I wasn't about to set him straight.

"Georgie was a smartass kid too goddamned big for his britches," Mama commented. "He wanted your job, Augustine. He thought he would be better at it."

Behind his tinted glasses, Cusimano's eyes were too veiled to tell me anything. He said, "Georgie wanted my job. Who else was killed?"

"I was the only one to walk away from it, except for Botkin's wife. But she was never in any danger, was she?"

"What's that supposed to mean?"

"It was a game you set up. You had me worked over, but not too bad. Then Lynette Botkin came along to rescue me, or so I was supposed to think. She took me to meet Ortega out in the boondocks so your gunmen could follow us and get us both. It went wrong for you, no thanks to anything Lynette did. How much did you pay her?"

"She was cheap."

"Well, she's been hard up for money, so she was willing to lead you to Ortega's hideout. Did she understand that you would kill him when you got to him?"

"She didn't allow herself to think about that end, I guess," Cusimano said. Mama set his breakfast plate before him—eggs sunny-side up, bacon, hashbrowns, all oozing cholesterol.

"If I happened to be a vengeful man, I could take offense at the way you tried to kill me." I met the lenses of Cusimano's glasses when he looked up from his plate. "Being a generous soul, I'll settle at a bargain rate."

"How much?"

"First, you clean up the mess out at the farmhouse. What I did was righteous, but I don't intend to spend the next six months justifying myself to the cops and the courts."

Cusimano thought it over. "I guess I owe you that much." He had plenty of reason of his own for not wanting five dead bodies to lead back to him.

"Do it so they'll never be found. I don't want anything leading back to me."

"You think I do?"

I gave him directions to the farmhouse and then said, "There's another point that needs clearing up."

"Something else? How much do you want?"

"Clear Slick Underhill's murder off the books. You killed him."

"No." It was a straightforward answer without hesitation or rancor. He might have been passing on a second helping.

"Excuse me if I cross-check with Megan Latimer."

"That bitch drinks," Mrs. Cusimano contributed.

"Thank you for sharing that with me."

"The reason I didn't do Underhill," Cusimano said, "was that I thought he was working for me then. If I had known what he was up to, things would have been different."

Footsteps clattered on the stairs. Seconds later, Megan entered the kitchen, followed by Jarman. Megan looked the way someone just awakened from sleep should look. Her eyes were puffy, her hair mussed, her pockmarks now more prominent, her Banana Republic outfit wrinkled. The bruise on her face, Underhill's last gift to her, was starting to fade. She groped her way to an unoccupied chair at the table, where she settled her elbows on the enamel top and braced her forehead in her hands. "Well?" she asked, speaking to the tabletop. Her accent made the word a yard long.

I took the sack of money out of my topcoat pocket and set it in front of her. "I already took my fee out."

Megan looked inside the sack. The sight of money rejuvenated her the way coffee had restored me. "Miami, here I come!"

"Is that such a good idea?" I asked.

"That's the place to go. Lots of sun and warm weather."

"You should square yourself with the police before you leave town," I advised. "You want to start a new life with a clean slate."

"Let them find me in Miami if they want me. I got nothing to hide."

"Who was the man in your apartment when Slick was killed?"

"What man?" Even half awake, she realized the bluff would not work when she saw my face.

"He left a toe print in the blood," I explained, "but later, not at the time of the killing. The blood was hardening by the time he stepped in it. Otherwise, he would have left prints on the carpet walking away."

"Georgie Pockets," she said softly, looking at her money.

Cusimano, who had been eating as if he feared someone would snatch his food away, stopped to look up.

"How did he get there?"

"When I came back, after I'd been to a couple bars, he was out in the hall knocking on the door. He was mad about something to do with the prizefight. I unlocked the door, and he barged in and there was Slick on the floor. Pockets went over and checked on him. I guess that's when he stepped in the blood."

I thought that over. "Pockets looked at the dead body and then brought you to Cusimano's office to hide out."

"He asked me a lot of questions about what had happened and what I'd seen. Then he told me I'd be in a lot of trouble with the police, but he'd hide me out—for a price. I gave him what money was in the apartment, and then I had him call you for Slick's fall money." Cusimano had devoted himself to eating as if he were alone in the kitchen, but he hadn't gone deaf.

Megan grabbed her money. "I gotta get to the airport and catch a plane." She stood up as if she expected someone to restrain her. When no one did, she hurried out of the room.

Cusimano put his fork down to look at me. "I'll be damned. Pockets killed him."

"Pockets only got to Slick's place after he was dead."

"Megan thought she saw him arriving. Truth is, he'd just left, only he heard someone coming, so he made like he was knocking on the door."

"Why would he kill Slick ?"

"Why would he go see him at all? Had to be he found out what was going on and went to take care of it hisself, without telling me." Cusimano was disappointed, a father finding his son had failed to measure up. "The proof will be when the bookies pay off. If Pockets made a pile, we'll know."

"That's hardly what the legal minds call conclusive evidence."

"Sometimes it's the best we can do."

"Pockets might have pulled a double-cross," I told him, "but he didn't kill Slick."

Cusimano looked up from his eggs. "There's the footprint in the blood."

"There was no blood tracked across the carpet, like there would have been if Pockets had stepped in it when it was fresh. By the time Pockets stepped in it, it had started to dry. That means he was in the room some time after the shooting. Call it an hour later. Pockets was telling the truth on that part."

Cusimano was nearly ecstatic that his man was innocent of something. "So his wife killed him after all."

I didn't want to argue with him. Too much had gone my way. There comes a time when you cash in and walk away from the game. I let Jarman show me the way out. After listening to the conversation with Cusimano, she watched me from a corner of her eye. "I'll drive Megan to the airport when she's ready," Jarman told me.

"Whatever." I was on guard for any punch she might throw my way.

"You know, if you hadn't decked me last night, I would have been with the others when they followed you."

The implication dangled like a piece of mistletoe. I would have killed her, or she would have got me. Jarman parted her lips and ran a pink tongue around the circumference of her mouth.

"You're quite a guy, Disbro."

That gerbil scampering down my spine was unmitigated fear. I opened the door and wasted no time heading for the street.

"Keep in touch," Jarman called after me.

29

Home.

Hard to believe I had been there only twelve hours ago. The long night had elasticized time and space so that I seemed to be returning months later after a world cruise. Helen's car was gone. She had already left for her early class. I entered the house through the kitchen and made directly for the coffee pot Helen had left on for me. I poured a cup as much for a handwarmer as for something to drink. Fatigue was making me feel the cold of a chilly morning. In turn, the cold was making me feel more tired than ever.

The morning paper was lying on the table in the dinette. I scooped it up and carried it with me into the living room, where I flipped on the television to the morning news shows. Sitting on the couch, I sipped coffee and scanned the day's news while I listened to the television with half an ear. There was no report of last night's fight, nor was there anything related to a shooting incident near the Cuyahoga County Airport.

"Good morning."

The voice startled me so much I spilled coffee. I looked up to find Elaine Knoll, dressed in the skirt and sweater I had brought for her, standing at the foot of the stairs, one hand braced on the newel post.

"Should you be up?" I asked. It was the only response I could come up with in the circumstances.

"I'm making it. Helen fed me breakfast and helped me get dressed before she had to go to work."

I sprang to my feet and helped her from the staircase to a chair. She held her hand against her side as she walked with slow, short steps. "You're treating me as if I were pregnant," she noted on the way.

When she was settled, I hovered above her as if I were admiring a piece of work I had just finished. Now her hair was combed and her makeup on—that attributable to Helen, I guessed. For all that, the walk down the stairs had taken a toll on her. She spent a moment catching her breath.

"I think I'll survive if I can have a cigarette," she said.

I gave her one and lit it for her. She inhaled the smoke greedily. "You don't have to be on your feet. You could spend the day in bed."

"No, I can get around. I'll recuperate in my own apartment."

"Tomorrow."

"Today," she said firmly.

I sat on the footstool in front of her. "You don't have to go."

"I think I'd better. Your Helen has been swell, but—" She shrugged. "I get the feeling she'd like to poison me."

"She's protecting her turf."

Elaine studied me. "I hope you love her as much as she loves you."

"I love her the best I know how," I said. "Should I call a taxi?"

"Please."

I made the call and set out to help her pack. It turned out that all she needed was her coat from the hall closet. It had bloodstains on its lining but none that had soaked through to attract attention on the outside. I held it for her while she got into it, backing against me.

"Why are all the good men taken?" she asked.

I tried changing subjects. "Dr. Mount will be sending you a bill."

She turned to face me. "Consider this a down payment." Elaine stood on her toes and kissed me.

I held myself stiff, arms at my sides while my fingers bunched into fists to keep them from moving. Her lips brushed over mine until, realizing she was getting no response, she stepped back. We stared at each other in silence for a time.

"Too bad," Elaine said at last. "We could have had something except I spoiled it. I made mistakes, did bad things."

"You blackmailed the man who helped you most. That doesn't sit well, but I could find reasons for excusing you. You saw a chance and tried to grab it. Other people in this world have done the same thing."

"You talked to Robert. He would tell you his version of what happened to make me look bad."

"I'd listen to your side of it, too."

"So it's the other thing." She looked away from me to her fingers toying with her coat. "You have to think—suspect—I killed Judge Amerine."

"You're no killer," I told her. "I know who that is, and you're not the one."

Her eyes widened, and her lips parted in a smile. "I'm free? You don't suspect me?" She leaned against me and put her head on my shoulder. "Oh, Gil! It's all right now. There's nothing standing between us any longer."

Despite myself, my hands came up from my sides and encircled her, pulling her against me. The pounding of my pulse in my head was like the tapping of a blackjack. Her copper hair was tickling my nose, tempting me to bury my face in it.

Beep! The sound of the horn from the taxi at the curb jerked my attention from the woman in my arms. I put my hands on her shoulders and pushed her way. "Time to go."

She tilted her head back to examine me with her green eyes. "I don't have to go right now."

There was no mistaking her meaning. "No."

"What's stopping us?"

"Helen."

Probably there was something in my face that told her she had reached the end. "I guess you do love her as much as she loves you."

"Close to it."

Beep! The horn honked again. I grasped Elaine's arm and steered her through the door, out where the taxi driver could see us coming. I hustled her down the walk to the back door of the cab.

"Gil—" she began, but I was already pushing her inside, more roughly than I intended. I handed the driver a twenty and backed away from the cab, out of her reach.

Elaine was making no move to touch me. Instead, she sat with her head down to study her hands folded in her lap. Her hood, up now, was obscuring her face. The driver hesitated, watching us both suspiciously, wondering if it was time to go yet. Finally, deciding we had no good-byes to say, he started forward, still without a destination.

Back inside, I went upstairs, stripped, and got into the shower. Taking that time was unneeded delay, but for a reason I couldn't explain, I felt a need to be clean. After the shower, I shaved and dressed again, then got in my car and drove a few blocks to Tremont, where I parked opposite Lincoln Park.

Barry Sprague came to the door of his row house wearing a robe and holding an ice bag on his head. "For God's sake, will you stop ringing that infernal gong!" he pleaded.

"I see you're still devastated with grief."

"Oh, please!" Sprague turned away from the door and dashed up the stairs, his Bullwinkle slippers pumping on the steps.

I stayed on the porch only a moment before I decided I was meant to enter. I made my way to the room where Sprague and I had talked yesterday. It was littered with empty bottles, half-filled glasses, and heaped ashtrays. Some of the furniture was knocked over, cushions were pulled out of chairs, a necktie hung from a light fixture, a corner of a window was broken out, and a pair of pantyhose had been tied in a bow around the shaft of a floor lamp.

From upstairs came the sound of retching. Later a toilet flushed, and later still, Sprague came down the stairs, still clamping his ice bag on his head. He looked as if he had taken a worse beating than Grogan. His eyes were bloodshot, with huge bags under them, and his flesh had a funereal gray pallor. Sprague picked up a glass that still held a clear liquid and drank it down. He sighed with satisfaction. "Gin." Sprague dropped onto the couch, where a cushion was missing, leaned his head against its back, and closed his eyes.

"I'm going to need your help," I told him.

"How can I help you if I can't help myself?"

"I want to wrap up a murder case, but I can't do that unless I can get into your uncle's house. Do you have a key?"

"Key?" It was too complex a thought for Sprague to deal with. He got off the couch and started around the room. "Had a little party here last night when some of my most intimate friends dropped by to celebrate my impending fortune." Sprague picked up a large glass and poured the residue of a smaller glass into it. He went to the next small glass and did the same. "Splendid chaps, every one of them. Never saw them before in my life."

"The key," I reminded him.

"You know, someone else mentioned a key."

"I did."

"That's where I heard it." Sprague had amassed two fingers of liquor and melted ice in the large glass. He drank it down and made a face. "Wretched stuff."

I resigned myself to waiting until Sprague had straightened out. "Do you have any coffee?"

"Wouldn't think of touching it."

"I would." I went into the kitchen, where a coffeemaker sat on the counter. After some searching, I found coffee and filters and started a pot. While that was running through, I returned to the living room, where Sprague had fallen asleep sitting up. I found the ice bag on the floor, shook him awake, and slapped the bag atop his head. "That will help."

"It's killing me." Sprague's eyes were closed, but Bullwinkle was watching me.

When the coffee was ready, I poured two cups and forced one down Sprague, sipping the other myself. After more time than I would have liked to see pass, Sprague came around a little.

"The key to your uncle's house," I reminded him.

"Ah, yes." Sprague got up and walked over to the mantel, where he lifted a candlestick to reveal the key that had been lying beneath it. He handed me the key. "There you are." Exhausted, he returned to his seat.

"I'll have it back this afternoon," I promised and started for the door.

"My good man, I simply cannot allow you to enter the place alone. No reflection on you, of course, but I absolutely must accompany you."

Frustrated, I realized I had no grudge against him. I helped him out of the chair and steered him to the staircase and up to his bedroom. There I had to keep after him so his mind wouldn't wander from the job at hand.

After getting into his underwear, Sprague dithered over his choice of clothes. Keeping my fuming inward, I threw a shirt, a pair of twill pants, and a leather jacket at him. Sprague chose his own socks, shoes, and tie. He took his time inspecting himself in the mirror.

"Will this be warm enough?"

"Fine," I assured him, not caring if his ass froze.

Sprague filled his pockets and at last started out of the house. Not yet. From the downstairs closet he took out a tweed cap and settled it on his head. Which required another inspection in the mirror. "Quite dashing, don't you think?"

"Absolutely."

"I, of course, will drive."

"No way."

We went outside and got into my car. Sprague was asleep before I turned onto the freeway ramp.

Morning rush hour had ended, leaving the freeways clear except for the construction crews rolling out their last orange barrels before winter set in. I dodged around everything they could throw in my path until I reached the eastern suburbs. Magically, Sprague awoke when we were on Chagrin River Road a few hundred yards from Amerine's driveway.

I pulled up to the pipe gate, rolled down my window, and reached out to punch the bell to Amerine's house. "If you had let me drive my car, we could have unlocked the gate with my opener," Sprague groused.

I rang Amerine's bell again without getting an answer, so I tried Dr. Mount's. This time my answer came when Mount's voice, strained through the speaker, asked, "Is that you, Disbro?"

"Sure is. Do you have Lynette with you?"

"I expect an explanation of why you sent her here." There was a buzz, and the pipe gate swung open.

I drove on through and took the left fork in the driveway to Mount's home. Although Mount was Amerine's neighbor, this was my first look at his house. It was brick, solid and roomy, somehow reminiscent of a hospital. Seeing the Lexus in the driveway gave me a sense of satisfaction.

Dr. Mount did not wait for us to ring the bell. Fully dressed, eager to leave for the office, he was standing with his front door open before we could get out of my car.

"There you are," he said as we approached. "About time I had an explanation, don't you think? A strange woman shows up on my doorstep and tells me you sent her here. She doesn't have any more idea what she's doing here than I do, except you told her to wait."

"Sorry." But deep down I wasn't. Knowing that for once I had made a doctor wait for me gave me a sense of accomplishment. "Entertaining a young woman can't be that painful."

"When my wife comes down and finds me with a peroxide blonde, it may be quite painful if I have no explanation."

Sprague pushed past us. "I'm chilled to the bone. Do you suppose you would have a drop to warm me up?"

"You know where the liquor is kept," Mount told him.

We went into Mount's living room, which had the ambience of a waiting room. Lynette was there in a wingback chair with her ermine thrown carelessly over the back, her legs crossed provocatively. Relief was plain on her hard-set face when she saw me.

"I thought you might have forgotten me," she said.

"Not much chance of that. I see you found your way here."

"Shouldn't I have? You gave me directions."

"As a matter of fact, I didn't. I just told you to come."

"Patients are waiting at my office," Mount announced. "At the risk of being a poor host, I have to insist—"

Sprague raised the glass he had poured at the liquor cabinet. "We can be on our way as soon as I have the medicine you prescribed." As he finished tossing off his drink, he noticed Lynette for the first time. He smiled appreciatively. "Then again, it might take longer."

"It would be better if we stayed here a few more minutes," I told them all. "Lynette will probably be making some admissions about her involvement in a few crimes. The two of you will make important witnesses at the trial."

Sprague nearly choked on his drink. Mount swiveled his head back and forth between Lynette and me. Lynette opened her mouth as if she wanted to say something, then changed her mind. I addressed Sprague:

"As Judge Amerine's heir, you're the nearest thing I have to a client. You'll want to hear what Lynette has to say." I turned to Mount. "It would be best to have you here for your medical expertise."

"If this is some kind of joke," Lynette said at last, "it isn't funny."

"Worse than that, you could end up in the chair. Of course, there's not much danger of that if you show your charms to the jury. I'd say your best chance is to admit everything. They'll never fry a woman if you've got a half-smart lawyer."

Sprague poured more whiskey in his glass and headed for a seat. "You're making strong accusations. I hope you have some proof."

I pointed to Lynette. "She's here. That's proof enough she killed your uncle. How did she know where he lived? There's only one way she would know. She was here the night he died. She was desperate for money, and her lover, Damon Ortega, was part of the burial party you brought here that night to dispose of her husband's body. She knew the truth about the incident, and she thought Judge Amerine would reward her for telling him the lowdown. Instead, the truth shocked him so badly he died."

Lynette spoke up in her own defense. "That isn't murder. Old people have heart attacks and die all the time. It was my bad luck to be there when it happened."

"That could have been an accident. Moving him wasn't. The strange thing was, you didn't have to move him. It really wouldn't have mattered if Amerine's body was found downstairs. The heart attack could have hit him anywhere. It was your own guilt that made you move him."

"He was in his pajamas, and I knew he'd been in bed when I rang the bell out at the gate. I thought it was best if I put him back the way he was. But what of it? That's still not a crime. All right, it wasn't the best thing for me to do, but I wasn't thinking straight at the time. You can't arrest me for that."

I reluctantly had to agree. "Maybe you're right, and that's a shame because it's the one crime I most wanted to pin on you. That's all right, though. I've still got three chances more."

30

"*Three?*" Dr. Mount asked incredulously. He was looking at the woman he had admitted to his house, trying to imagine her a four-time killer. "You must be exaggerating."

"I'm not even counting the man she shot last night," I said. I took out my cigarettes and shook one out of the pack. "That was pure self-defense."

"Which saved your hide." Lynette sat casually in her chair, back against her ermine coat, foot swinging pendulumlike.

"Excuse me for not thanking you. If that's ingratitude, remember you're the one who put me in that position in the first place."

Lynette appealed to Mount, to Sprague. She was accustomed to using her femininity to get her way. "I must be some kinda dangerous character." While she said that, her hand toyed with her necklace near her breasts, and her eyes fluttered. For all her efforts, the little girl affectations could not hide the hardness in the set of her mouth.

Sprague looked at his drink, but Mount reacted by turning on me. "I know you enjoy playing Sherlock Holmes, the way you reconstruct crimes. Let's hear it, then."

"I hardly know where to begin." With a cigarette in my fingers, I put my pack away. "Let's start in order, which takes us back eight months. Anything she might have done before that is something we haven't begun to investigate yet. Anyway, we'll start in February when she shot her husband."

"Now that's a lie!" Lynette snapped quickly, appealing to the other two men. "Damon Ortega killed Pete, as he very well knows. Not twelve hours ago he heard Damon confess. See if he'll deny it!"

Sprague looked up from his drink to me. "Is that the truth?"

I was lighting my cigarette. "Let her tell it."

Their heads turned back to Lynette. She tried to meet six eyes and dropped hers. "I'm an adulteress. I was having an affair with Damon, and my husband caught us together." Even as she confessed, she managed to convey a mixed message—not so much *I'm a sinner* as informing them *I'm available*. "There was a fight, and Damon killed him."

Two susceptible men looked at me with indignation for making this poor child's pain worse. "Well?" Mount asked.

"Pete Botkin was shot point blank in the forehead. Ask her how that came about in a fight."

This time the two men looked at her with expressions that showed eroding sympathy. Lynette said, "It was dark in the house. They were rolling around on the floor. I didn't see how it happened."

I said, "Time for a medical opinion, Doctor."

Mount shook his head. "Impossible. That kind of wound couldn't be inflicted with two men locked together in a fight. They would have to be arm's length apart."

"That kind of wound," I explained, "is typical of an amateur who isn't familiar with firearms. The killer stood so close the muzzle was almost touching the victim and aimed for the forehead. Someone who knew guns better would have pointed the gun dead center in the victim's chest."

Mount nodded in agreement and offered his conclusion: "That means Ortega deliberately murdered her husband, and she was his accomplice."

"It means," I countered, "she murdered her husband, and Ortega covered up for her, at least until the very end. He knew guns too well to pull the forehead trick, but when Lynette had to shoot a man in the dark last night, she used exactly the same pose. Like she did with her husband. Like she did with Slick Underhill."

"You're accusing me of a lot," Lynette spoke up. "Don't for get Pete broke in on me and Damon. Whatever happened, he started it."

"How do we know that's the way it happened? Because you say so? Not good enough. For all we know, you were alone in the house when Pete came back. You waited in the dark and bushwhacked him. By the time Damon got there, Pete was already dead."

"Damon would back me up."

"But Damon's dead, and I'm not so sure he would have kept on backing you. He was trying to gasp out something to me before he died, something about me having it wrong. You crushed him to you and smothered him before he could get it out."

"That's an awful thing to say." She was speaking for the benefit of the two men she had to convince. "He was shot—dying. All I wanted to do was hold him, comfort him."

"And squeeze the life out of him before he could say too much."

"Do you really think that's what I did?"

"I saw it." I shrugged. "Then comes another question. Your affair with Damon went on a long time. Why did you suddenly get careless? It doesn't sound much like an accident. It sounds more like you deliberately left clues or hints for Pete to find. Nothing conclusive. Just enough to make him suspicious before he was due to go off to Vegas. You expected him to double back and catch you with Damon. The only place it went wrong was with Pete. He cleaned out the accounts because he had plans of his own."

"What sort of plans?" Sprague asked, so caught up in the drama he was sobering faster than he could drink.

"Lynette thinks he was going to burn the house down after he killed her and Ortega. The police would have found the charred bodies of a man and woman in bed together. It would have been so obvious those bodies were Mr. and Mrs. Botkin, they would never have thought to question it. If they started looking for anyone, it would have been Ortega. Meanwhile, Botkin would have settled somewhere else. He had a ticket to Chicago in his pocket, if that means anything. More than likely, it was a jumping-off spot.

Whatever his final destination was, you can bet the money is in a bank there under whatever name he intended to use."

The two-man jury was less impressed with Lynette now. Mount was studying the pattern in his carpet, giving her no more than a sidelong glance. Sprague returned to the liquor cabinet to refill his glass.

"He hasn't proved a thing," Lynette said. "It's all guesswork."

"Sure, I'm guessing," I admitted readily. "Not about Judge Amerine, because you knew where he lived. Not about Ortega, because I saw you smother him. I am guessing about Botkin only because so much time has passed there's not much chance of proving anything. I'm not guessing about the way you sold Damon and me out."

"What do you mean?"

"Two thugs were beating me up. Then you showed up and they ran off." I shook my head. "If I'm going to let myself be worked over by the kind of thugs who could be scared off by a woman, it's time for me to start crocheting doilies. Truth is, they ran off at the sight of you because that's the way it was supposed to happen. Because you cut a deal with Pockets to set up Ortega and me for his gunmen."

"Why should I do that?"

"Money. You were desperate for it. Then you found out fifty grand had been hidden in your house all along when Damon produced Underhill's fall money. That pissed you off at Damon—enough so that you went to Pockets at the arena after the fight. By that time Pockets was plenty happy to pay to find out where Ortega was hiding."

"All right. He paid me. Why shouldn't I get money from Pockets? He wanted me to show him where Damon was hiding, and he wanted to get you away from the arena at the same time. If I was allowed to rescue you from a beating, you wouldn't be suspicious about them following us to Damon. Sure I took money for doing that. It was no big deal."

"Except you were selling out your lover."

"I thought you and Damon could handle Pockets' gunslingers. You did, too. I just didn't count on Damon being hit." Lynette looked up at Mount, then at Sprague. "Can't you see what he's doing?" Sprague took a sip of his drink, and she turned to Mount.

"There have been all these deaths this last week. He's trying to pin everything on me because I'm a defenseless woman alone in the world. You see that, don't you, Dr. Mount?"

"I don't know what to think," Mount confessed. "It sounds plausible."

Lynette appealed to Sprague. "You won't let him do this, will you?"

"He can't do anything until you've had a fair trial."

I put my cigarette out. "There's one place I'm not guessing. Slick Underhill. You went to his apartment Sunday night to demand money. Damon had told you some of the deal around the Baxter fight. You thought you could scare him into giving you some money if you threatened to tip off Cusimano. He laughed, and that's what did it for you. You already had the gun on him. It just went off in your hand."

"You're still guessing," she scoffed.

"Not this time," I said. "Megan was in the bedroom. She heard you, she heard Slick laugh, and then she heard the shot. She opened the bedroom door a crack in time to see you before you left."

"You believe her? A drunk?"

I was not about to press my bluff beyond credibility. "Look at it this way. The law has four chances to prove a case against you. Slick, your husband, Damon, and Judge Amerine. They can strike out three times and still get you on the fourth at-bat. If you luck out and get life in prison, you could be out of there in only ten years."

"Oh, God! Oh, God!" Lynette put her face in her hands and sobbed into them. "There's no hope for me. I can't fight all that power."

Three men stood by helpless as she cried. Mount leaned forward, fighting an instinct to comfort her. Sprague clutched his glass as if it were an anchor holding him in place. I watched her with the objective eye of a drama critic gauging her performance.

After a while, the sobs slowed down. Lynette dropped her hands to show us her face streaked with tears. She sniffled. "I need a handkerchief." She turned to the ermine coat on the back of her chair.

I moved in one stride and grasped her wrist as she tried to bring her hand out of the coat pocket. She struggled, but I held on, yanked her hand out, and pried the gun out of her fingers. It was a small .32, the same one that had stopped Pockets.

Lynette sat holding her wrist, the tears on her face now the result of frustration instead of sorrow. Her lips peeled back, exposing her teeth, as she stared at me with a feral look. She hissed and lunged at me, clawing at my face with her fingernails. I slapped her back-handed. The blow was more vicious than I had intended, a result of my own pent-up frustration. She fell down hard on the floor.

Holding up the revolver, I asked, "Is this the gun that killed Slick and your husband?"

Lynette had no more to say. She sat on the carpet with a trickle of blood running out of the corner of her mouth.

I shrugged. "The police will be able to prove it."

Her facade broke then. This time when she started crying it was no theatrical bid for our sympathy. I let her go as long as I could stand it. Finally I picked her up from the floor and sat her in a chair. I gave her my handkerchief.

Mount said, "I think it's time someone called the police."

31

Late that afternoon we held a meeting in Assistant Prosecutor Ramford's office to sum up all that had happened. Ramford had come to work a junior bureaucrat feeling swamped by his responsibilities. By midafternoon he was clearing homicides off the books faster than he could keep track. Like a mongrel dog who had always chased cars, he had finally caught one but didn't know what to do with it.

"We will charge Mrs. Botkin with murder," he announced. "At least two counts—for her husband and for Felix Underhill. I'm doubtful we can make a case against her for Judge Amerine."

This late in the day I had nearly lost my capacity for caring. My sleepless night was bearing down so heavily I hardly dared blink. "Charge her with all three," I suggested. "Her lawyer will want to strike a deal. Plea bargain Amerine away in exchange for guilty pleas to the others."

"Botkin and Underhill are solid cases. Her gun ties her to both killings." Ramford looked over at Agosta, who was starched and alert enough for us all. "Isn't that right?"

"The lab associated both bullets with the gun," Agosta agreed. He was avoiding looking at me.

Ramford took the pen out of his desk set to examine it. He was weighing his next move for its political implications. If this case went to trial, Ramford would dominate the headlines for months. But would the boss trust him with so sensational a prosecution? More likely the case would be handed over to a senior assistant for the trial, pushing Ramford into the background. In that case he would be better off settling quickly for a plea that would bear his imprint. Ramford wanted more time on the angles.

Agosta said, "Don't be in such a hurry to shut it down. There are angles we haven't cleared up."

"Mrs. Botkin is confessing to both murders, isn't she? What more can we ask?"

"Her statement has a lot more to say. She goes on about a gunfight last night on a farm." Slowly Agosta's head turned to me. "She says you were there."

"That's interesting," I said. "Have you checked out the farm?"

"Yeah." Agosta was reluctant to add more. "There were no dead bodies, no blood. We did find some bullet holes in the walls."

"Beats me. I know there was bad blood between Cusimano and Ortega over last night's fight. I don't pretend to understand it all."

"Like hell. You're covering something."

Ramford cleared his throat. "This is not a productive line to pursue. Perhaps the Strike Force will be interested at an appropriate time."

I smiled at Agosta. "He wants you to shut up."

Agosta turned on Ramford. "What is this? Are you ignoring a killing or two?"

"There are only so many avenues we can follow at one time." Ramford put his pen away.

"He doesn't want you to offend me, Manny," I told him. "He needs my testimony, and he's afraid my memory will go bad if I'm worried about other problems. Right, Les?"

Ramford had to squirm under the blackmail. "The point is well taken. When juries get confused by too many facts, they lose sight of the main issue. Best we concentrate on convicting Mrs. Botkin for the two murders we can prove."

Agosta made a sound that was not part of any known language.

It might have been a curse suppressed to a growl. In spite of everything, I sympathized with him. I knew the frustration of being told to lay off a case.

I asked, "What's left to be tied up?"

Ramford looked at the notes on his desk. "We have a partial confession so far. How is it coming?"

The question was directed at Agosta, who fielded it. "She's admitting what she has to as we trip her up. We're moving slow so we don't give her lawyer an excuse to throw the confession out later."

"Then it seems to be a matter of time."

I pried myself out of the chair, more of an effort than I had expected. "I'm out of here. Call me tomorrow if you need anything."

No one moved to stop me as I walked out of Ramford's office and down the hall. While I was waiting for the elevator to arrive, Agosta caught up with me. He didn't have his handcuffs out, but he was giving serious consideration to reaching for them.

"You're pulling a fast one, Gil. There was a lot more that happened you're not coming clean on."

No one else was around. I said, "There's nothing you have to fret about. I've cleared up a few cases for you. Drop it."

The elevator doors opened, and I took a step forward, only to find Agosta laying a restraining hand on my arm. His face was not the image of suppressed rage I had expected. "Sure. I can live with that. Can you?"

I got on the elevator and rode it down to street level. On the sidewalk I seriously considered the possibility of checking into a downtown hotel to save myself the short trip to Ohio City. On a close call I got my car and started the drive home. Once, while waiting for a red light, I fell asleep until the truck behind me blasted its air horn. It was more than the sleepless night working on me. After a week of tension, the sudden release was pulling me down. I thought what I needed was a bed and a well-deserved rest, but once I got home, I could no more sleep than lift the house.

Helen found me in a chair in the living room when she got home from class. It must have been my posture, or the way I stared at the blank television screen, or the lack of lights on a dull day, that tipped her. She walked around to stand in my line of sight.

"What's wrong?"

I had been waiting for this moment too long to keep it from gushing out of me. "I killed a couple of men last night."

She took too long to frame a reply. "It must have been necessary."

"It was. Just like an Old West gunfight. It could have gone the other way."

"Oh, Gil!" She reached out to touch me. I caught her wrist and steered her to a seat on the footstool. "Are you all right?"

"I wasn't wounded or anything like that."

"You must feel terrible."

"That's just it—I don't. When it was happening, I reacted. Afterwards, it struck me that I had snuffed out two lives with no more feeling than flicking a light switch. I did it and went on."

Helen had adopted her nonjudgmental pose. If I hadn't known her so well, I wouldn't have seen how flustered she was. "The inquiry will exonerate you."

"There won't be any inquiry. The bodies will never be found." When she looked skeptical, I added, "Organized crime was involved."

"Then—" Helen looked confused. "You were morally justified, and there won't be any repercussions. It doesn't sound like a problem."

"There's a problem, all right. How is this going to affect us? I crossed a line. I'm not the man I was six months ago, or even yesterday. Can you handle that?"

"Of course I can." She stood up and tried to put her arms around me, but once more I urged her away, back down on the footstool.

"That's too easy," I told her. "It's an impulsive reaction, and I love you for it. But this is a problem you never dreamed you'd have to face in your wildest nightmare. You've got to think about it and consider it from every angle before we can even think about going on. Be sure you can handle it."

I saw it in her eyes then, the beginning of her grasp of the enormity of the whole thing. She bit her lower lip and looked away. Softly, she said, "You're wrong. I've thought about it."

"You have?"

She nodded. "The kind of life you lead makes me think about these things. Not a day goes by I don't wonder if something's going to happen to you, or if you're going to do something like this.

Don't you think I braced myself long ago for the possibility of a scene like this, or something even worse?"

"I didn't know."

"I didn't tell you."

I got up from my seat and took a few steps away to remove myself from her touch. This was a time that required no prejudice for what she had to decide. "You've got to be honest with me and with yourself. What is this going to do to us? Will we be able to go on?"

"Honestly?" She struggled to come up with an answer and failed. "I don't know. There's a side of me that recoils from the violence you deal with. Maybe that side is so strong I won't be able to accept the killing in the end. Right now I'm so confused I can't make any promises."

It wasn't what I had been hoping to hear. It wasn't as bad as my worst fears. "It might be best if I cleared out. I'll pack a few things and get a room—"

"Gil." She spoke my name softly, cutting me off without harshness. "That isn't what I want."

"All right." It was a mild reply considering all the relief I felt. Still, I was handling her carefully, the way I would have talked to someone threatening to jump off a ledge.

"I know this much," she went on. "No matter what you've done, there's an honesty in you that wouldn't let you hide it from me. That's the part of you I love. It's not a bad basis for going on with our lives."

Then she stood up and took those few steps that brought her into my arms. I still didn't know what would come next, but Helen and I would be together to face it.

Tough, Suspenseful Novels by
Edgar Award-winning Author

LAWRENCE BLOCK

FEATURING MATTHEW SCUDDER

THE DEVIL KNOWS YOU'RE DEAD
72023-X/ $5.99 US/ $6.99 Can

A DANCE AT THE SLAUGHTERHOUSE
71374-8/ $4.99 US/ $5.99 Can

A TICKET TO THE BONEYARD
70994-5/ $4.99 US/ $5.99 Can

OUT ON THE CUTTING EDGE
70993-7/ $4.95 US/ $5.95 Can

THE SINS OF THE FATHERS
76363-X/ $4.99 US/ $5.99 Can

TIME TO MURDER AND CREATE
76365-6/ $4.99 US/ $5.99 Can

A STAB IN THE DARK
71574-0/ $4.99 US/ $5.99 Can

IN THE MIDST OF DEATH
76362-1/ $4.99 US/ $5.99 Can

EIGHT MILLION WAYS TO DIE
71573-2/ $4.99 US/ $5.99 Can

A WALK AMONG THE TOMBSTONES
71375-6/ $4.99 US/ $5.99 Can

Buy these books at your local bookstore or use this coupon for ordering:

Mail to: Avon Books, Dept BP, Box 767, Rte 2, Dresden, TN 38225 D
Please send me the book(s) I have checked above.
❑ My check or money order—no cash or CODs please—for $__________is enclosed (please add $1.50 to cover postage and handling for each book ordered—Canadian residents add 7% GST).
❑ Charge my VISA/MC Acct#____________________Exp Date______________
Minimum credit card order is two books or $7.50 (please add postage and handling charge of $1.50 per book—Canadian residents add 7% GST). For faster service, call 1-800-762-0779. Residents of Tennessee, please call 1-800-633-1607. Prices and numbers are subject to change without notice. Please allow six to eight weeks for delivery.

Name____
Address_______________________________________
City____________________State/Zip____________________
Telephone No._________________ BLK 0595

CAJUN CRIME
FEATURING DAVE ROBICHEAUX
BY EDGAR AWARD-WINNING AUTHOR

JAMES LEE BURKE

IN THE ELECTRIC MIST WITH CONFEDERATE DEAD

72121-X/ $5.99 US/ $6.99 Can

"Awesome"

The Wall Street Journal

A STAINED WHITE RADIANCE

72047-7/ $5.50 US/ $6.50 Can

"No one captures Louisiana culture as well as James Lee Burke. . . it is also possible that no one writes better detective novels."

Washington Post Book World

BLACK CHERRY BLUES

71204-0/ $5.99 US/ $7.99 Can

"Remarkable. . .A terrific story. . . Not to be missed!"

Los Angeles Times Book Review

A MORNING FOR FLAMINGOS

71360-8/ $5.50 US/ $6.50 Can

"Truly astonishing"

Washington Post Book World

Buy these books at your local bookstore or use this coupon for ordering:

Mail to: Avon Books, Dept BP, Box 767, Rte 2, Dresden, TN 38225 D

Please send me the book(s) I have checked above.

❑ My check or money order—no cash or CODs please—for $__________is enclosed (please add $1.50 to cover postage and handling for each book ordered—Canadian residents add 7% GST).

❑ Charge my VISA/MC Acct#____________________Exp Date__________

Minimum credit card order is two books or $7.50 (please add postage and handling charge of $1.50 per book—Canadian residents add 7% GST). For faster service, call 1-800-762-0779. Residents of Tennessee, please call 1-800-633-1607. Prices and numbers are subject to change without notice. Please allow six to eight weeks for delivery.

Name______________________________

Address______________________________

City____________________State/Zip____________________

Telephone No.____________________

BUR 0595

Riveting Mysteries from Shamus Award-Winning Author

EARL EMERSON

Featuring Mac Fontana

MORONS AND MADMEN

72075-2/ $4.99 US/ $5.99 Can

Three firefighters died in a blazing Seattle inferno...the truth died next.

HELP WANTED: ORPHANS PREFERRED

71047-1/ $3.95 US/ $4.95 Can

Something's burning in the fire department, and where there's smoke there's murder.

Featuring Thomas Black

NERVOUS LAUGHTER	89906-X/ $4.99 US/ $6.50 Can
POVERTY BAY	89647-8/ $4.99 US/ $5.99 Can
THE RAINY CITY	89517-X/ $3.95 US/ $4.95 Can

Buy these books at your local bookstore or use this coupon for ordering:

Mail to: Avon Books, Dept BP, Box 767, Rte 2, Dresden, TN 38225 D
Please send me the book(s) I have checked above.
❑ My check or money order—no cash or CODs please—for $__________is enclosed (please add $1.50 to cover postage and handling for each book ordered—Canadian residents add 7% GST).
❑ Charge my VISA/MC Acct#____________________Exp Date______________
Minimum credit card order is two books or $7.50 (please add postage and handling charge of $1.50 per book—Canadian residents add 7% GST). For faster service, call 1-800-762-0779. Residents of Tennessee, please call 1-800-633-1607. Prices and numbers are subject to change without notice. Please allow six to eight weeks for delivery.

Name____
Address______________________________________
City____________________State/Zip____________________
Telephone No.__________________ EE 0695

TAUT, SUSPENSEFUL THRILLERS BY EDGAR AWARD-WINNING AUTHOR

PATRICIA D. CORNWELL

Featuring Kay Scarpetta, M.E.

POSTMORTEM

71021-8/ $6.50 US/ $8.50 Can

"Taut, riveting—whatever your favorite strong adjective, you'll use it about this book!"

Sara Paretsky

ALL THAT REMAINS

71833-2/ $6.50 US/ $8.50 Can

"Riveting...compelling...original..."

Cosmopolitan

BODY OF EVIDENCE

71701-8/ $6.50 US/ $8.50 Can

CRUEL AND UNUSUAL

71834-0/ $6.50 US/ $8.50 Can

Buy these books at your local bookstore or use this coupon for ordering:

Mail to: Avon Books, Dept BP, Box 767, Rte 2, Dresden, TN 38225 D

Please send me the book(s) I have checked above.

❑ My check or money order—no cash or CODs please—for $__________ is enclosed (please add $1.50 to cover postage and handling for each book ordered—Canadian residents add 7% GST).

❑ Charge my VISA/MC Acct#____________________ Exp Date____________

Minimum credit card order is two books or $7.50 (please add postage and handling charge of $1.50 per book—Canadian residents add 7% GST). For faster service, call 1-800-762-0779. Residents of Tennessee, please call 1-800-633-1607. Prices and numbers are subject to change without notice. Please allow six to eight weeks for delivery.

Name______________________________

Address______________________________

City________________ State/Zip________________

Telephone No.________________ PDC 0595